RISE OF THE FIRE QUEEN

Kingdoms of Lore: Underworld Book Two

ALISHA KLAPHEKE

PROLOGUE

In the land of shadow elves and spirits, wyverns and lords of shadow magic, a human witch with the power to wield spirit fire sacrificed her freedom to save the realms from ruin.

To set the Sacred Oak on its path to healing and stop the end of the world, this witch—also called the Awenydd—performed the rites of the Bond and tied herself to the evil King Tiergan, wielder of the great sword Cynnwrf. Their union balanced the magic and the Oak began to heal.

But all was not well...

KING TIERGAN'S
KINGDOM

THE
DARK SEA

Possible locations
of Calon y Dderwen

Pocket of
Dark Magic

Monster
Sighting

HIGH KING KYNAN'S
HOMELANDS

CHAPTER 1
MAREN

Blocking the sun from her eyes, Maren glared at her jailer as he dragged her around a grassy expanse lined in flowered shrubbery. The beauty hurt her eyes after being in the rotting, dark dungeon for so long, and she was far too weak for this little jaunt.

Her knees gave out, and he caught her for the third time.

"I need more food." She loathed begging, but if she didn't get more sustenance, Kynan would arrive to break her out and find only a pile of bones. Plus, she was fairly certain her body was attempting to fight off an ague. She felt that tugging fatigue of approaching illness and was fairly certain she was running a fever.

"If you smiled once in a while, maybe the king would be more merciful."

With a snort, Maren shook her head. "Can I perhaps wait on the attitude adjustment until I'm not a prisoner?"

He marched her back through the side door and returned her to her cell. "You're lucky the king cares enough to allow you a walk in the sun from time to time." Shoving her to the ground, he clamped her manacles back onto her wrists and ankles. Her skin was beginning to rub raw where the metal scraped her.

Scowling, her jailer headed for the desk where the keys to her cell normally were and where her wand had been shoved unceremoniously into a drawer.

Her blood boiled recalling how Tiergan had used shadow magic to travel here to his castle with her in tow. He'd offered her a life with him, a life in which she would be his wife in full. Because he was the lowest creature that had ever crawled the ground, she passed on that offer. He had promptly stolen her wand and, with it, any chance of her using her spirit magic to escape.

She dragged her manacles across the damp stone floor, making a grating sound that she knew well annoyed her jailer. Keeping on for minute upon minute —stones, it could have been hours for all she could tell; she'd quite lost her mind—she finally got him to turn and look at her again.

"Stop," he barked.

"Tell the king I wish to speak with him."

"You do?" He nearly broke his chair standing up so quickly.

"Yes." Maren pulled herself off the floor, the chains and the lack of food in her body making the deed nearly impossible. She raised her chin and looked at the jailer, who'd scrambled over to stare. "Tell him I'm ready to make a deal."

The jailer smiled. It was disgusting.

As he scurried away, his boots clunking up the dungeon steps, Maren wrapped her hands around the bars of her prison. Her manacles clanged against the metal barrier, and the bars were cool against her forehead. Being here in this condition might very well kill her before she found a way out or Kynan and the others found a way in with the Calon y Dderwen in hand.

Her stomach growled furiously, and a wave of nausea swept over her. Not a fun mix. "Eh! King Arse Head!" she shouted at Tiergan. "I thought you wanted to chitchat."

Slow steps preceded Tiergan's appearance in the dungeon. He wore a dark green cloak and the most obnoxiously gilded and gem-encrusted crown ever crafted above or below ground.

He leaned against her cell door and crossed his arms. "You look atrocious."

"You know how when people are married they begin to look like one another?"

"Ha." He eyed the window behind her, the only peek she had at the world outside this dank and horrid place. "Are you finished with the banter yet, or should I come back later?"

She smelled the bread before he pulled it from his cloak pocket. Her stomach clenched.

A grin slicked across his wide mouth. "I thought

perhaps you'd be interested in breaking your fast. But you must do one thing for me first."

"Kiss your boot? I'm good with that. Let's get on with it."

"I am not here for petty flattery or false shows of obedience. I know your heart, my queen."

She was going to vomit. "Then what do you want?"

"For you to live with me as my wife—"

"Old Lackwit has a better chance than you do, darling." She slid her gaze to the jailer who stammered.

Tiergan slammed his hand on the bars, and the metal knocked against Maren's cheekbone, pain flaring hot under her skin. "Shut your mouth, or I will do it for you."

She longed to go on aggravating him, but she knew there were worse treatments than starvation and a cold place to sleep.

Tiergan pulled the bread apart, and the scent of butter wafted across the cell, dulling the odor of the bucket in the corner and the mold growing on the walls. She wanted that bread. She wanted it very, very badly.

"Tell me, Awenydd, what is your plan here? To slowly die and thus end the realms and undo what our union mended?"

She wanted out of this cell, access to her wand, and his head on a platter.

And for Kynan to arrive with the Calon y Dderwen so that the realms would in fact not end in dead iciness when she killed Tiergan, the master of the legendary sword, Cynnwrf. Then Kynan could claim his sword once more. And if Kynan wanted a future with her, she would reign alongside him happy and packed full of bread.

But of course, she couldn't tell Tiergan that. He knew already. Surely, he knew. He had spies, and neither she nor Kynan had been quiet about fighting this situation at the Binding.

What could she say to Tiergan that might benefit her in some way? A tidbit or an action that might sway things in her favor? "I want an hour with my wand every day." He pursed his lips and narrowed his eyes, but she kept on. "In exchange, I'll sit with you and the nobles at your fancy dinners and pretend I don't wish I could stab you repeatedly with a dull and dangerously rusty blade."

"What do you think you can accomplish with your one hour?"

He hadn't said no. Hope lit a spark inside her. "I feel like I'm missing a limb going without it. I'm not stupid enough to think I can attack you or tie you up or some such nonsense. I only want to work some simple spells to feel more like myself again." It was true. She did feel horrible without her wand, and she longed to feel whole again. But the second she had that wand, she would try something. She didn't know what yet, but something.

"I'd have to put you at the point of a sword while you work your spells. To ensure my safety. At least until you earn my trust. I'm sure you understand."

"Completely." Would she be able to do anything?

"I would give my man orders to maim your wand hand if you act out of line."

A lump formed in her throat. The consequence wasn't idiotic. If he simply cut off her hand, she would stay alive—barring any infection—and thus their Binding would remain intact and the realms secure. She still didn't know how long they had to be Bound for the realms to heal themselves fully. Hafwen had guessed years. Maren said a quick, silent prayer to the Source that Kynan would be successful in finding the Calon y Dderwen. Successful and fast.

"I understand. Now, can we seal the deal with that baguette you are manhandling?"

Tiergan's predator eyes studied her face. "Agreed."

Maren snatched the piece of bread from between the bars, and as she shoved it in her mouth, she silently called out for any spirits that might be wandering nearby. Since the near death of the land of the living and the Underworld, the spirits had been painfully quiet. Not a single one had visited her or spoken with her since Tiergan had brought her here to his castle beyond the Dark Sea. Perhaps it was simply this place and not the stress that the spirits had been through before the Binding, when the poison had almost ended everything in existence. There were stories about spirits not being able to travel over water. She'd seen them do just that in the Upperworld, but maybe the Dark Sea was different. Perhaps the salty, cursed body of water that housed the Calon y Dderwen—where Kynan and the others were currently searching—was the source of those old stories and superstitions.

Should she simply ask? She glanced at Tiergan, who was giving orders to the jailer.

"...and have the staff meet me in her chambers. Do

not leave the wand here without supervision. Do you understand me?"

"Yes, my lord," the jailer answered.

Tiergan turned toward Maren. "Soon, you will be escorted to your rooms. Remember the agreement. Behave, and you will be treated as my wife. I will not lay a hand on you as long as you act according to your station."

"Of course, my lord," Maren said snidely.

"Ah, ah. Watch the tone."

The jailer gave her an I-warned-you look, and she flicked an obscene gesture at him at an angle Tiergan couldn't see. It was childish, but it felt good.

"As you command," she said to Tiergan. She attempted a curtsey and a smirk, but her legs gave out, and she landed on her bottom on the gritty floor.

He left her as the jailer picked up the bronze speaking tube and called for Tiergan's orders to be carried out. The tube reached up through the ceiling and most likely terminated in some sort of staff room. She'd seen something like it in the Wylfenden castle.

With Tiergan gone and the jailer busy, Maren began to plot.

It was difficult to know how much time had passed since she'd been in the dungeon. The light coming in from the window was mostly blocked by dirt and dust, and the light in the Underworld was odd anyway.

About an hour or so after Tiergan left, another elven man unlocked and entered her cell. He had a few scars. Three marred his cheek, and they were clearly the mark of someone digging their nails into his face. Well, that led to all sorts of comforting thoughts about this elf. The other scar ran down his neck and under the collar of his black tunic. He certainly had been through some challenging moments. Perhaps those experiences had put the steel in his cold eyes.

Giving her a curt nod, he then handed her a cup of water, which she guzzled. The cool water eased the heat in her throat.

"I am Maddox, the king's Facilitator. I speak and act for King Tiergan. Now, stand."

She did so, legs trembling like a newborn foal's. Swallowing, she fought another wave of lightheadedness. Maddox looked her up and down. What was he examining?

He tilted his head, then mumbled a few elven words as he removed a flat, clear crystal from a small bag tied to his belt. He placed it against her forehead and whispered something as he frowned.

"What is it? What does that do?"

"You have a…" He looked at the ceiling like he was puzzling over a translation. "…a fever."

"It's the least of my worries at the moment. Do you have any food?" She needed more food. Her legs were about to give out on her.

Maddox shook his head. "Sit. It won't be long now."

"Until Tiergan gets me out of here?"

He backhanded her across the face, and pain lashed through her cheek. "King Tiergan."

Maren spat on the ground and glared.

"Say it," Maddox ordered.

She didn't want to. But if it would get her out of here faster... "King Tiergan."

"Very good."

"Are you a healer?" If so, that was troubling seeing as he had just hit her.

"I handle...relations between the king and his prisoners."

Well, that sounded terrifying. Maren nodded. "You'll be the one to lop off an arm if I misbehave?" The fever was making her even more reckless than normal.

His gaze snapped to her face. "Yes."

She swallowed. "Fantastic."

"Remain here," he said. "They will take you up soon."

"I'll clear my schedule."

She refused to ask where she would be taken exactly. Tiergan's chamber? Goddess, she hoped not. A room full of other gals trapped here for Tiergan's pleasure? Shudders raked through her body, and it wasn't because of the fever. The castle beyond this dungeon was a complete mystery. Would it be filled with horror or look nice on the surface but be undercut with darkness?

CHAPTER 2
KYNAN

The forests thinned as Kynan, Hafwen, and their party of Upperworld royals rode hard toward the Dark Sea. Ivar flew overhead; he'd left the rest of the lads at home. Kynan was glad to have his familiar close by because a whirling storm of emotions battered him as he urged Osian onward. The steed's black mane whipped across his cheeks, but he barely noticed.

Maren, the love of his life, was in the hands of the worst man Kynan had ever known.

"He won't hurt her seriously," Hafwen said for the fifth time as she adjusted the wand sheathed at her belt. She turned, and the morning light reflected off of her one golden eye.

"I know. But there are degrees of suffering..." His blood curdled in his veins, and a wave of impotent rage washed over him. "What are our chances?" The question pained him, but he needed to know the truth or as much as his dearest friend—and the only shadow elf witch—knew of the truth. He had to prepare his mind and body. Had to tally the odds.

"You don't want to know what I think."

"Usually when someone asks a question, they want an answer."

"Don't get snippy with me. I understand your anger and fear. I feel it too. But we are on the same side, and you had best control your moods, High King."

Kynan clenched his jaw. She was right, but the feelings he had were overwhelming at times, making it impossible to act rationally. "I apologize."

They rode onward, and he didn't ask about their chances. She was right again. He didn't need to hear that their quest to find the Calon y Dderwen was a wild grasp at a solution to a problem no one had ever experienced. The magical stone had been lost for ages, tossed into the Dark Sea by a long-ago mad king. And the stories of what dangers resided in the sea...well, they would soon learn if those tales held any truth.

The rest of the party rode behind them—Filip and Aury, Rhianne and Werian, Brielle and Dorin. The foreign army had been escorted back to the Upperworld by the spirits. Only this group had demanded to remain in the Underworld despite the spirits' warnings.

Kynan gave Brielle, Maren's close friend, a nod, and the party drew to a stop in a gently sloping area dotted with purple heather and prickly gorse. A wide stream ran between a line of low boulders, its trickling sound disappearing under the noise of the waves crashing at the base of the cliffs one hundred yards or so away.

Ivar landed gracefully on the ground, tucking his

wings against the wind and raising his chin to scent the air.

Kynan slid from Osian's back, then stroked the horse's sweating neck and slipped the reins over his head. "Let's have a drink, shall we?" He knelt beside Osian, and both drank the cool, sweet water.

The others did likewise, and once the horses had been rubbed down and fed, everyone gathered in a rough circle to talk.

The mood was grim.

A memory of Maren's bright eyes and the defiance in their depths stole his breath. His hands fisted, and his blood caught fire. He couldn't wait to lay Tiergan at Maren's feet so she could end him. The way he had spoken to Maren... Kynan's jaw tensed, and his nostrils flared. She was his and his alone. His territorial instincts urged him to shadow his way to Maren's side immediately and claim her, to destroy anyone foolish enough to stand in their way. With his shadows, he would unmake Tiergan's warriors...

"Do you want me to speak?" Hafwen whispered.

"No. Thank you. I am fine."

"You are not, and it would be best if you don't pretend. This lot feels just the same as you, I imagine. Feigning a cool head will only show you to be false. Tell them, show them your pain, and lead them anyway."

Kynan closed his eyes briefly, then took a slow breath. He kissed Hafwen's hand and looked at her. "Thank you. I don't know what I would do without you. Are you holding up?" Tiergan had captured her during the battle and destroyed her home. She had to be suffering quietly just as he was.

She patted his shoulder. "I feel like a pile of dung."

Surprise pulled what was almost a chuckle out of him, and he turned to face the group. "We have arrived at the Dark Sea." Ivar rose into the air, then landed lightly on Kynan's shoulder. Kynan welcomed his presence. "I have a ship on the one dock that sits at the base of the cliffs. I maintain the ship for defense, but rarely have occasion to use it."

He glanced at Hafwen, who nodded.

Continuing, he kept his voice as steady as was possible, rage making it nearly impossible. "This quest will be madness. There is no other way to describe it." He fisted his hands and forced his mind away from thoughts of what Tiergan might be doing to Maren right now. Soon, he could act. But not yet. Not yet. "The old tales say the Dark Sea is home to a host of mysterious creatures, none of which you would enjoy spending great swathes of time with."

Aury snorted a laugh, and Filip grimaced as he flexed his fingers—a movement Kynan sometimes did after riding long hours gripping the reins too tightly.

Werian's hand hung loosely on the hilt of his sword, and his wife, Rhianne, had her arms crossed and her eyes narrowed as if in concentration.

Brielle had one hand held over her womb, her red hair stark against the last trees of the foggy forest. Dorin's wings shielded her partially from the light. He, for one, looked more than ready to fight, but Kynan worried that his focus would be on Brielle and their unborn child rather than on the quest. He would certainly understand that, but it was a factor they would have to consider.

"Who here has sailing experience? Prince Werian and Princess Rhianne, I believe?"

"Let's dispense with the titles, if you please," Rhianne said. "This is a quest that needs speed and efficiency, and none of us needs the placating."

"Agreed," everyone said in near unison.

Werian cleared his throat and tied his hair back, his ebony horns prominent and otherworldly. "We do indeed have much experience on the water."

"I have some," Kynan said, "but I would love for you two to captain the ship as needed. Please feel free to take the lead. Hafwen and I will serve as guides."

Hafwen stepped forward. "I have read of three possible locations of the Calon y Dderwen."

"Good," Kynan said. "We have a direction to take, at the very least."

Dorin shuffled his wings slightly. "I'd like to provide spotting."

From the air, his view would be valuable indeed. "Thank you."

Filip thumped his axe with a thumb. "Aury and I are keen to be the battle masters, checking on weaponry and calling out orders when attacked."

Brielle looked toward the sea. "I'm good with a compass. And I've studied history my whole life. Granted, it was in the Upperworld, but perhaps my knowledge of cultures and traditions might prove useful if we find artifacts or some mysteries surrounding the Calon y Dderwen?"

Rhianne gave Hafwen, her fellow witch, a respectful nod. "I have a keen knowledge of runes as well, being a witch."

Kynan studied the group. "We're as stocked with talent and skill as any assembly could be for such a wild quest. If we can secure the Calon y Dderwen, the stories claim the crystal will balance the Sacred Oak's magic all on its own with no need of a Binding between the master of Cynnwrf and the Awenydd. The crystal may have additional powers as well. We will have to see. It's difficult to know what is fanciful tale and what is truth passed down through the ages. You yourselves witnessed the realms nearly coming to an end. I can only guess that if we don't find the Calon y Dderwen, my lady Maren will be forced to remain with Tiergan for years upon years until the Sacred Oak is fully healed and secure." His blood sizzled in his veins, and he fought the urge to growl like a wolf ready to tear out throats.

"Not acceptable," Aury said, her eyes blazing with loyalty.

"Exactly," Brielle said. Her jaw worked as she seemed to rein in her anger.

Kynan nodded in agreement, his heart aching like his long age was finally rushing up to meet him in a human way.

Brielle pointed toward the sea. "What's that?"

Kynan squinted. A haze of blue-white appeared

along the gorse-choked cliff's edge. "Spirits?" As soon as he said the word, a host of spirits grew visible.

A spirit in the front of the gathering, a fellow with a wide cap and a prominent brow bone, stepped forward. His words were only a hiss on the wind, but his lips moved as if he were speaking.

"Can anyone understand him?" Kynan eyed his fellow royals and Hafwen too.

The hissing rounded out, and suddenly he could understand the spirit's words.

"We can't cross over the Dark Sea," the spirit said. "There is a foul wind there and beyond, in King Tiergan's lands. But we are here to offer a final exit to the Upperworld to those who made the agreement with us and with our Awenydd. Does anyone wish to leave? Though we search for new ways to help you through the veil and found one that is tentatively open at the moment, we can't promise you will be able to leave later on."

Aury made a sound like a growl and lowered her head. "None of us will leave Maren to that beast." Her words were blades.

"What of your kingdoms? Your people?" Kynan wanted to be certain of their devotion to this mad plan.

Dorin traded a look with Brielle. "Our people have rulers that can help them if we are delayed in returning." His Balaur accent was sharp. "Maren has no one but us. She is family."

Brielle touched the knives at her belt. "I would be a dishonorable soul if I turned my back on my chosen sister. I want to live as the person my daughter will look up to. Even if she must live in a place far from our home."

"I will develop spells and potions similar to what I used on Samhain," Hafwen said. "I'm sure I can devise something with the spirits help," she eyed them, and they nodded in unison, "and we will eventually return you home. I can't promise it will be pleasant."

The spirits shimmered and blinked but remained visible. "We will be watching from here to see what aid we may give."

Kynan suddenly wondered if Maren was truly without any sort of friendly contact. His fated mate should never suffer like this. It was against everything in him to allow it. "Can you not visit the Awenydd?" His hearts sang her name. His blood roared for her touch.

The spirits shook their heads. "Sadly, we can't communicate with her where she is."

Cold touched Kynan's chest, and he imagined Maren trying and failing to reach the spirits, to send word to him. He hadn't realized he'd been waiting for such a thing to happen, but now he felt the raw disappointment that he'd never get a message from her during this quest.

The spirits' bodies wavered like an image seen through water, then their glimmering forms faded from view.

Numbly, Kynan answered Werian's questions about the ship and the crew, and then they released the horses and set to climbing down the steep steps carved into the cliffside.

The Dark Sea's presence felt like the intuitive sense

one had when an enemy's gaze pressed down. Kynan curled his shadows around him and partially cloaked himself from view. No one questioned the use of his magic, but their glances said they knew he was afraid.

CHAPTER 3

TIERGAN

Tiergan dipped the quill into the inkwell, then finished the last line of the speech he would give to his new council. This season was going rather well now considering its challenging start. He smiled thinking of Kynan and those Upperworld fools riding about the countryside, trying to rouse a rebel force. A scout was due any moment, and he cherished these entertaining tidbits of information.

A voice vibrated into existence before a man cloaked in shadow magic appeared at the open door. "Lord King."

Tiergan set down the quill and greeted his scout with a nod. Lord Glanusk, a minor noble with remarkable shadow power, had come groveling the moment Kynan rejected his request to overtake lands that should have been his in the first place. Kynan was too interested in avoiding violence and cared far too little for those with noble blood. He used it when it benefitted him though, that was certain. Seeing as he'd claimed his place as High King mostly by impressing the council with his shadow magic. Tiergan should have killed Kynan when he had the chance. He could have done it if he hadn't made that deal with Maren. Normally, he'd simply ignore a foolish deal made during the fatigue after a major battle, but the Bond complicated things...

"Should I come back at a later time?" Glanusk asked.

"No. Tell me what you know."

"The false king and the Upperworlders have boarded a ship on the Dark Sea and are actively seeking something."

"What do they hope to find?"

Glanusk swallowed and looked toward the door. "That isn't clear. I spoke with my spies in Cliffton, by the coast, but no one heard anything specific."

It would make sense that Kynan would try to sail his ragtag force across the water to cause trouble, but why were they spending time and risking their lives to poke about the Dark Sea? "Go to my library and have the master there search out scrolls that speak of the sea. If you find anything of note, anything at all, come to me right away."

"As you say, Lord King." Glanusk bowed and left.

He was such a weasel. And ugly to boot. Not a good fit at the court Tiergan was building. If Glanusk failed in finding any information, Tiergan would kill him off and be glad to see the last of that simpering smile of his. Maybe he'd then take the man's wife as his mistress. She was very beautiful.

There was another knock at the door.

Gods, can I not have a moment's peace? "Come in."

The herbalist, Ceri, entered and curtseyed deeply. Tiergan had never liked her, but he wasn't entirely sure why. Maybe the arrogant way she did her work without ever doubting herself. It was far preferable when elven women knew their place. Perhaps he would find a male herbalist and place him above her in ranking to suppress her pride.

She held a small case of green glass vials, one of which seemed to have spilled a foul substance onto the apron tied over her dress. "Lord King, the Facilitator has informed me your wife has a fever."

Tiergan looked out the window at the rolling hills of deep green grass and the ancient oaks that lined the road leading toward the Dark Sea. She couldn't be dying, or the land would show damage as its Awenydd faded away. But he could sense that the realms were not yet healed. He would have to stay Bonded to her and keep her alive for at least a year, maybe longer, before it was safe to do as he pleased. As soon as he knew the realms were secure and that the Sacred Oak and the Spirit Well were fully healed and balanced, he would make her death a fine show for Kynan. If the fool didn't kill himself first on the Dark Sea.

"I assume that means you are on your way to treat her."

"Exactly so, Lord King. Do you love her?"

He whirled away from the window, and she dropped into another curtsey, remaining there. "What did you say?"

"Nothing."

"I thought so. Be gone."

He gave her his back, and the sounds of her footsteps and the door said she left. It was past time to have a bit of fun. If he couldn't taunt and argue with Maren at the moment, he'd enjoy other pleasures.

Opening the right side of his chamber door, he eyed one of the two guards who stood watch. "Bring me wine and no fewer than three beautiful ladies of the court. Make sure you choose young ones and that their husbands are in attendance." It was important to remind his nobles of their position. If any balked at him taking his pleasure with their wives, he would know the limits of their loyalty. And any with limits would be removed from his court, preferably in a death shroud.

By the time he'd bathed and dressed, his requests had been filled, and the ladies awaited him in his bedchamber. They curtseyed and looked up at him with careful glances.

"Don't worry, ladies. This will be fun, and your obedience will open doors for your husbands."

Surely, Kynan would die on the Dark Sea. Then Tiergan could fully claim the crown.

He smiled.

Life as High King was going to be lovely.

Two elves in dusky white leathers took Maren from the cell. The knights took an arm each and accompanied Maren out of the dungeon and into a long, dark corridor. The man on the right of her had a slight limp and looked like he'd never smiled a day in his life. Lefty was a spry young thing with a head of golden curls.

"You look too happy to be a person who swore fealty to King Tiergan," Maren said to Lefty.

"Shut it," Righty snapped.

"See? That's how you should look. All that scowling is spot on for this place. Take heed of your mentor, Lefty."

Lefty peered over her head at Righty. "Is she mad?"

"Excuse me. I am perfectly sane. I might have a bit of a fever, but aside from that—"

Old Righty kept hold of her upper arm but distanced himself and regarded her like she carried the Third Age plague.

A maid with a blank face and a tight white bun greeted them with a curtsey at the double doors of a chamber. The men practically tossed Maren at the maid, then took up positions at either side of the entrance. Sweat beaded on Maren's forehead, and a shiver chilled its way down her back. She was definitely sick.

The maid dragged her into the chamber and sat her roughly on a firm bed. Maren fell back and tried to will her illness away as the maid shuffled about, gathering what appeared to be bathing items—a sheet, a tub of soaps and vials of only the Source knew what, and an intense-looking scrub brush.

The chamber's ceiling was quite high. Instead of fascinating wyverns like the ones that had decorated her room at Kynan's castle, this room's creature feature was a host of snakes. Maren didn't hate snakes the way some did, but they weren't what she would have picked for a bedroom ceiling. Their sinuous curves tangled and bunched at the room's corners, where the painter had extended the ceiling work all the way to the floorboards. Maren flipped onto her stomach, her head spinning. The floor was a patchwork of very dark wood and slate, and the maid's shoes clicked over the surface as she approached Maren.

"You must bathe. You smell like a goat."

Maren nearly laughed. "I can't argue that. Perhaps if your fine master hadn't thrown me into the pits of his scary snake palace—"

The maid put a hand on Maren's forehead and tsked.

"Ceri will be here soon with a tonic. Let's wash you and get you to bed."

The maid wasn't cruel in the way she helped Maren from the bed and into the tepid bathwater, but she certainly wasn't pleasant.

"What's your name?" Maren asked as she dragged her wet hair over one shoulder and the maid scrubbed her back.

"It doesn't matter."

Maren turned, sloshing the soap-clouded water. The rose scent was too much, and it made her head pound. "Of course it matters."

"I'm a maid. You are to be queen."

"And I was a prisoner about ten seconds ago, so..."

"Bethan is my name. Happy now?"

"Not at all. But it's nice to meet you, Bethan."

After washing all the stubborn dungeon dirt from Maren's body, Bethan dressed her in a plain shift, then escorted her to the bed. A knock sounded at the double doors.

"Come in," Bethan said.

One of the doors swung wide, and a woman wearing a long dark blue tunic and a necklace that showed yet another snake hurried in. She had dark hair and gray eyes like many shadow elves, but she was more muscled than most of the elven women Maren had seen in the Underworld. Hafwen was the nearest to her body type.

She promptly stuck a hand behind Maren's upper back, lifted her slightly, and set a vial against Maren's lips. Maren had little choice but to swallow down the foul-tasting stuff. The herbalist—presumably Ceri—

eased her back down, then turned and left without so much as a sound.

So much for a potential ally. None of these folks seemed even slightly persuadable. Was that a word? "Is that tonic supposed to make me sleep? I don't want to sleep. I have questions."

She tried to say more, but her mouth wasn't working properly, and soon, she was dreaming of Kynan's hands, his mouth on hers, and a ceiling of wyverns instead of snakes.

Maren woke to a dark room lit only by a minuscule lantern on her nightstand and a slice of yellow light slipping under the doors. Blinking, she sat up and took a deep breath. The taste of that awful tonic remained on her tongue. Was there water or wine anywhere?

The nightstand was empty of everything but the lantern and one small set of bound parchment pages.

Had it been there earlier?

She picked it up and lifted the wooden cover. Writing in what she guessed was the shadow elf language covered the first page, the ink sharp and neat. Below the writings, a messily sketched arrow indicated that she should keep reading. Tongue puckering from the tonic's leftover taste, she replaced the bound writings on the small table. She didn't care what Tiergan had set out for her to read.

She had to snort at what Kynan had tried to get her

to study at his castle during her first days in the Underworld. He'd been so lost on how to deal with her.

"Goddess Nix bless him." He'd been an idiot in the beginning, but Kynan was a good man, and he held every single inch of her heart. If she could just send him a message through the spirits... But there were none here to ask.

Shaking off the doom and gloom mood, she climbed out of bed. She was actually feeling better. The tonic must have killed off her fever. She went to the doors. She'd face Lefty and Righty for a chance at a cool drink. Stones, she'd face Tiergan himself. She tugged at the handles only to find the doors locked.

"Eh! I need something to drink. I'm dying."

The left side door flew open, nearly sending her tumbling. Lefty grabbed her hand before she fell and helped her remain standing.

"You are dying?"

"I was being dramatic, but I do need a drink. Fresh water, preferably?"

He spoke to Righty, and before she could think up how to blast past them both and run to her wand, a crockery cup of water was being handed to her.

She drank it greedily. "More?"

Righty leaned through the open doorway and glared. "Now? You'll have Bethan coming to your rooms in less than an hour." He glanced at the candle on the corridor wall across from her room. The silver backing showed black lines that marked the hours. As the candle burned, it measured time.

"We could call for the herbalist if you're still feeling ill?" Lefty asked.

Hmm. It was better than sitting here doing nothing. Maybe she'd get some information from Herbalist Ceri. "Yes, please."

Righty eyed her. "You aren't sick. Get back inside and shut your mouth."

"I'm to be queen, right? Aren't you a touch worried about ordering me around like that?"

"Not really. I've served King Tiergan since he was in nappies. I don't care if my behavior warrants punishment. He'll never off me. Not with what I know."

Interesting.

He shoved her backward and slammed the door tightly shut.

"Trapped doing nothing it is, then." Maren turned on her heel and crawled back into bed. She grabbed the stupid bound writings again because there was little else in this room to snoop around. No armoire. No chests. Not even a proper window—just three long glazed openings that didn't allow her to see anything of note beside some treetops and a glint of moonlight over a stretch of water.

She turned to the next page of writings as the shabby arrow demanded.

To her surprise, the following bit was written in the Lore language, the common tongue.

What you need, the spirits provide. True shadow elves know the path. Find a bird, make it sing.

What in all the realms was that about? It had been

written in the same scrawling hand as the arrow. A wing symbol sat below the writing, almost too tiny to see.

She lifted the lantern and cast buttery light over the chamber. The room held no bird art. Only snakes. She went to the three windows and searched for anything she'd missed. Nothing. Just stone and glass and wood. Unpainted. Unmarked.

The bathing chamber, set off of the main room, had one large snake painted across the far wall. An alcove held a chamber pot seat, and an open chest held folded bathing sheets.

For as long as she could hold her eyes open, she searched both rooms for a bird. Maybe she was being silly and this wasn't some possible ally speaking to her through writings slipped into her chamber? Maybe it was just an old writing and that was it.

But she didn't stop looking. On the cold floor, she maneuvered around the baseboards of the bathing chamber and wondered if that fever had completely annihilated the small amount of sense she'd once had.

Wind cascaded across the choppy surface of the Dark Sea, lashing Kynan's cheeks and lips. He stood at the prow near Hafwen, with Ivar and Dorin flying overhead. Light glittered over Dorin's jade-colored wings. Ivar was a shard of obsidian cutting the pale pink sky.

Last night, exhausted from riding, everyone had needed sleep. Some of the crew had given up their hammocks for Kynan and the other nobles while Hafwen had used a lantern to scour the scrolls she'd brought from his library for information about the Dark Sea. Meanwhile Dorin had attempted to sleep in a hammock—a feat not easily accomplished when one had dragon wings.

A sad smile stretched Kynan's mouth. Maren would have loved that.

"Have they spotted anything at all?" Hafwen turned toward the table they'd nailed to the decking. She untied her bundle of scrolls and the map she was creating of the Dark Sea.

Kynan breathed out through his nose. "No."

Hafwen unrolled a map written on vellum. They'd discussed the map at length on the journey here, reading and weighing ideas during their stops for the night. The map now showed various creatures and landforms hiding under the waves, recorded sightings of the afanc, and three possible locations of the Calon y Dderwen.

Werian loped over, his eyes squinted against the reflection of the sky's light on the sea. "This sea doesn't smell like it should."

"How should a sea smell?" Kynan asked.

"Like salt and fish," the fae prince said. "Not an unpleasant odor to me. But this place has the scent of old magic and of death."

"Old magic?" Hafwen paused in securing the corners of her map with large flat rocks and took a sniff of the air.

Werian glanced at her. "You're most likely used to it? As an Underworld witch?"

Hafwen shrugged. "Perhaps it's so familiar I can't separate it from other scents."

Nodding, Werian leaned on a barrel. "To me, it holds a touch of buried things, of the deep earth, and also a bit of that odd scent you get when you burn pennyroyal."

"We don't have that plant here."

"It smells a little like mint."

"Ah."

Werian pointed at a set of horizontal lines Hafwen had drawn on her map. "What is this?"

Kynan leaned in.

Hafwen pointed to each of the sets of lines. "A few of the old stories mentioned whirlpools and violently strange currents in the places where you see these."

Werian's eyes widened. "And our crew is well versed in this?"

"I have just now created the map," Hafwen said, "but I informed them of the approximate whereabouts of this one here because we will potentially run into it first if it indeed exists."

"So we are headed northwest in an attempt to reach..." Werian's strange fae gaze flicked from the map to Hafwen.

"This location, midway between the coasts and in line with the giant's thumb." She turned and gestured back toward Kynan's homelands where a black rock stood out against the sky, high above the cliffs. "The scrolls say that a light may appear when the crystal is guiding a person to its location, but I'm not sure if the phrase means that a spell can do this or if the light will occur on its own. The translation is incredibly vague."

Werian pursed his lips. "Do I even want to know what those sea creature sketches indicate?"

Kynan swallowed. "The afanc sightings."

"Pretty sure I don't want to know," Werian said, "but I suppose I must face the truth. What in all the gods is an afanc? Perhaps a nice little octopus that hails us from the white-capped waves?"

Hafwen raised an eyebrow. "Definitely not."

"Then maybe a slightly grouchy eel that becomes perturbed when we approach but who is pacified with a lovely serving of freshly caught fish?"

Kynan's jaw tensed. His fated mate was in the hands of his greatest enemy, and the fae wished to jest.

"I wish," Hafwen said.

Maybe a dose of information would encourage Werian to take this more seriously. "The afanc is a legendary sea monster twice the length of this vessel. It has the scales of a dragon, a tail that can upend a ship with little effort," Kynan said, "and talons that ooze a poison to which we have no antidote."

"Discussing my mother-in-law?" Rhianne said, smirking.

Werian barked a laugh. "My fae queen mother has nicer skin than this beast, you must admit."

"I thank her only for your good looks, my love." Rhianne set a kiss on Werian's cheek.

Hafwen looked to Kynan and almost chuckled. Kynan gave her a smile as Werian wrapped Rhianne in his arms in a territorial type of stance. Werian's gaze moved to Kynan, and a flash of aggression showed before the fae blinked it away.

"Thank you for working on the map, Hafwen," Kynan said.

"Of course." She looked back and forth between Werian and him. "I'm on this ship too. I want to know what we're up against."

Still holding Rhianne possessively, Werian filled her in on what Hafwen had told him thus far.

Hafwen tapped a spot that they would sail into very

soon. "These dotted lines indicate the presence of some type of thorny kelp bed."

"Pleasant," Werian whispered.

"Cozy," Rhianne replied.

Hafwen drew her finger to a cloud shape surrounded by swirls. "This is a pocket of unknown dark magic. The scrolls were not overly helpful in describing it."

Rhianne rubbed a hand over Werian's upper arm, her head tilted as she studied the map. "I like your choice of swirls like wind-drawn flames." Her sheathed wand stuck out over her hip. "Helps us visualize the severity of the situation."

"We could literally be lit on fire if we cross into that zone?" Werian asked.

The map appeared properly to scale considering the distance they'd traveled from the coast. He could sense his homeland still, so it wasn't impossible to make a solid guess.

Hafwen unrolled one set of her notes that she'd jotted onto a tiny curl of parchment. "The translation is rough, but there is mention of light and heat and disorientation."

Filip walked over with Aury on his arm. "Sounds like our Samhain celebration."

Kynan looked from Filip to Werian. "Is every one of you an aspiring jester?" He didn't give them time to answer before he continued, "If my estimations are correct, we will hit that bed of thorny kelp very soon."

Everyone turned toward the water as Dorin and Ivar both landed on the deck, shaking out wings and breathing heavily.

"Anything?" Kynan asked.

Dorin tucked his wings and approached, his glance skirting to where Brielle stood at the bow, her red hair a flame in the wind. "A darkness sits just there. Perhaps a mile out."

Werian and Rhianne spoke together quickly and began shouting orders to the crew. Kynan was relieved they had expert sailors on board, for this was only the beginning of this horrendous journey.

"What if the Calon y Dderwen isn't at this indicated point? What if it's at this one? Or the one far to the southeast?" Dorin studied the map, his heavy brow bunching.

The wind tried to snatch the map, and Hafwen set her palms across the vellum. "Then we try again. And again. And again. Until we..."

Kynan lightly touched her back. "Until we succeed."

He pushed his will into those words, but alas, he was no witch, and it was only the dearest longings of his heart that begged the statement to evolve into truth.

CHAPTER 6
KYNAN

At the prow, a crewman called out and pointed to a point somewhere off starboard. The sky had gone flinty and the air cold. A grating sound reverberated from the ship's hull, and the craft jerked, making everyone exclaim.

"That'll be the thorny kelp." Hafwen walked with Kynan toward starboard, where they looked over the side.

Strips of pale green undulated on the sea's surface, small silver fish darting here and there. On each leaf of kelp, a series of bright red thorns reached out like claws. Some were longer than Kynan's arm.

"Though they don't look like something I'd enjoy swimming in," Hafwen said, "I can't believe they've caught the ship up like this."

Werian was calling out for the sails to be trimmed, and Rhianne was talking quickly to one crewman who, despite this situation, couldn't decide between staring at her wand or her chest.

Aury and Filip joined Kynan and Hafwen.

Filip clicked his tongue as if he was thinking. "Can your shadows untangle us?"

"Perhaps, but I was hoping to save my strength for underwater work. I can create a cocoon of air when we decide to dive. It will use a significant amount of my energy."

Filip nodded, the braids above his ears shifting slightly with the movement.

Aury leaned on the boat's side and tapped her foot impatiently. That woman's entire presence oozed violence. Kynan was glad she was on his side.

Rhianne left the sailor, traded a few words with Werian, then approached Kynan. "We are stuck, and I'm going to try to blast us out of here." She unsheathed her wand and wiggled it.

"Carry on as you see fit."

Aury turned and set her back against the side. "But fire and ships don't tend to mix well," she said to Rhianne.

"I don't think it'll be a problem," Rhianne said. "The ship is soaked, and I am pretty good at aiming."

Filip grimaced. "Pretty good."

Aury cracked a smile and winked at Rhianne. "If you do catch the ship on fire, I'm here to put it out."

Rhianne gave her friends a smirk as Werian joined them. "Any advice as I move forward with this plan?"

Kynan was incredibly glad they were here and he and Hafwen weren't alone on this quest. They truly were a remarkable group. "Aury...it still feels off to call you by a nickname."

Aury waved a hand. "Ah, it's fine."

He dipped his head in acknowledgment. "If you feel up to it, perhaps you could drive the water away from where Rhianne aims her witch fire."

"I can do that. I wish I could shift the water enough to move us, but I have no way to do that well."

"Understood." Kynan turned to look for Dorin. He was talking with Brielle and sharing a flask. "Dorin?" The dragon shifter prince hurried over, Brielle at his side. "Would you be willing to aim your dragonfire where Rhianne sets flame to the thorny kelp?" Kynan asked.

"Of course. I'm not as strong here as I am in the Upperworld, as I believe you mentioned being a problem as well, yes, Rhianne?" Dorin looked to Rhianne.

"Yes. This place drains me a bit."

"But as long as you don't believe you'll need my fire to defend us against any attacks, then it should be fine."

"What about that afanc beastie on your map, Hafwen?" Werian asked.

The edge of the scroll under Hafwen's hand flapped in the wind, and she smoothed it down. "The afanc. Yes, maybe we should keep Dorin's full power in reserve in case the creature appears."

Cold sliced across Kynan's chest. He prayed that beast was fictional. But so far, the stories had held true, because here they were, stuck in legendary kelp. "Agreed. Dorin, let's save your strength for our upcoming challenges."

"I'm calling the afanc DC now," Werian said.

Kynan attempted to translate numerous meanings of those letters, but nothing came to mind.

Rhianne frowned. "What does that mean?"

"Dorin's Challenge."

Dorin snorted. "I'll take him on. And I'll fully shift for it."

A sliver of humor lifted Kynan's heart for a moment. Part of him wanted to act brazenly positive, to joke and carry on as they did, but the larger part of him wished everyone would turn a more serious eye to the issues at hand. This was no jaunt into the unknown for glory and pleasure. If they failed, Maren was tied to Tiergan for at least a full year, maybe longer, and would suffer only the Source knew what at his foul hands.

Hafwen glanced down, and he realized he'd been fisting his hands like he was about to explode into a raging fit.

He forced himself to breathe and to remember that everyone had different ways of dealing with terrible situations and that perhaps humor was how Maren's chosen kin dealt with the harsh realities of life.

Ivar flew down from the topmast sail where he'd been perched and landed lightly on Kynan's shoulder. The wyvern nuzzled his ear. Kynan ran a hand over Ivar's tucked head, and the wyvern communicated thoughts of Maren—her features screwed into a fierce grimace and her cheeks blackened with dirt. It was a memory of a moment during the battle on the moors.

"We will get her back, my friend. Have no doubt. Or you and I will die trying."

Ivar cooed and clicked his forked tongue approvingly.

After some discussion, Werian called out, "Come about!" The crew scattered and set to working the lines.

Rhianne and Aury positioned themselves on the starboard side and took aim.

A bright purple and orange shower of crackling sparks lit the air, then fell onto a length of thorny kelp waving along the water's surface. Aury thrust her mage staff outward, and the sea pulled away from Rhianne's chosen target in long silver threads of streaming salt water. Rhianne hit the plant again, this time with a fury of sparks that turned to riotous flame as they ate at the green growth and red thorns. They worked their way through all the visible kelp on starboard, then moved to do the same port side.

The ship lurched, the current dragging it roughly over the growth. A crack sounded, and the deck vibrated.

Werian's gaze met Kynan's, and a question bloomed there. Should they continue? The ship couldn't hold under this stress.

Rhianne and Aury must not have heard the ship's complaints because they kept up their work, sweat beading their foreheads and sticking small tendrils of their hair to their cheeks. Over their heads, Ivar hovered and let out small roars now and again in support.

Still, the ship remained caught. The craft shifted easterly but only managed to partially turn toward the last of the thorny kelp.

Rhianne stopped firing and wiped her brow with her sleeve. "There's a section below the ship that won't budge."

Aury moved her staff to her other hand, then shook out her free fingers as if she'd been gripping the magical weapon with all her might.

They were truly trying their best to complete this quest for Maren. Love for them broke ground in his heart.

"I'll get you below the ship." He removed his cloak, shucking off his shirt and his boots as well. Ivar flew low over his head, buffeting his hair, before landing on the sailor's brew barrel beside the compass box.

"I thought you needed to save your power for later," Hafwen said. "Perhaps I can help? I can draw the kelp toward you both with my witch's will. I would love to be brave and fantastic and say I'll go into the sea with you, but you know how I feel about water." Her gaze skirted to the dark waves.

Kynan recalled the tale...

When she was a girl, she had fallen into the river beside her house and nearly drowned. Her parents had recovered her, and she'd been sick for months afterward. Ever since that event, she'd stayed firmly on land, never once willing to go anywhere near a body of water until now, when Maren needed her.

Kynan nodded. "Unless it is a life-or-death situation, you will remain on the ship."

Hafwen gave him a grateful smile.

"And, Aury," he said, "can you peel the water away if I provide a bubble of air for you under the surface?"

"I'm not sure, but I'll give it a go."

Filip helped her remove her cloak and boots, then murmured something to her and tugged on her tunic.

She elbowed him in the stomach and hissed something back, and then they were both laughing. She did remove all but her small clothes in the same way Rhianne did.

Kynan summoned his power, the soft brush of his shadows gathering like rings around his fingers and gauntlets on his forearms. He imagined the shadows thinning to thread, then braiding themselves into a spinning mass of darkness dotted with sparks of golden light.

"Might be tough to see through that," Aury said to Rhianne.

"The shadows will be like a basket or a cage around you." Kynan cast the storm of dark magic toward the women. The shadows parted and cocooned them. Their men looked pale, so Kynan reassured them with a nod and a shallow bow. "I will keep them safe. I swear to you."

Filip and Werian nodded in thanks and acknowledgement, and then it was time to dive into the cursed waters of the legendary Dark Sea.

The women eyed Kynan through the openings between the threads of shadow magic. The weaving would keep the water out even with the openings because the spell extended slightly past itself. The shadow cages sucked at his energy. Such a draining spell.

Kynan prayed he could keep his promise.

CHAPTER 7
TIERGAN

Courtiers murmured nervously as Tiergan sat on his blackwood throne and Lady Ash stood beside him in a place of honor. He had one arm draped over the side of the throne, and his hand rested on Lady Ash's thigh. In the other hand, he held a goblet of the finest vintage in all the Underworld. Lord Ash stared at his wife, and Tiergan slid his hand higher. Lady Ash had a fine shape, and he had greatly enjoyed her company this afternoon, but she was a weeper, afraid he would do more than chat with her and steal a kiss or two. If he didn't keep a good eye on her, she would dissolve into tears.

"Now, now. No weeping, Lady Ash. You are luckiest in the land. Remember your place."

The council filtered into the great hall and gathered at the foot of the dais.

Tiergan didn't bother to stand. "Welcome. I won't waste your time. Do you or do you not agree to name me High King and give your approval to my proposed tax increases?"

They bowed low, and the eldest of the fine-robed bunch spoke as he lifted his head. "No, King Tiergan. Once a High King is crowned, the crown remains on his head until death. You know this. We do not approve."

Tiergan smiled as he stood and unsheathed Cynnwrf. A vein in his head throbbed uncomfortably as his anger grew. "He'll be dead soon enough. I just want your approval." His boots echoed on the steps as he approached the councilman. "No?"

The eldest of the councilmen, a fool who always wore homespun wool even though he had nearly as much wealth as Tiergan, stared at him. "Alas, no."

Tiergan shrugged and swung the sword.

The man's head toppled to the flagstone floor.

"You," Tiergan said to the next councilman, "clean that up."

"Of course, King Tiergan." The man looked left and right, color rising in his cheeks and sweat beading on his brow. "With what, Lord King?"

"With your tunic." Tiergan used Cynnwrf to point to the man's velvet clothing.

"But..."

"Or would you rather number three here clean up? He would have to mop up your blood as well, of course, seeing as you have disobeyed."

The councilman made a wise choice and disrobed. Dressed only in his small clothes, he wiped up the first councilman's blood.

"Is everyone still a *no* on this topic?" Tiergan lifted

Cynnwrf. It was sullied with blood, so he drew it across the third councilman's cloak and smiled. "I would have thought once I claimed Cynnwrf, I would have been guaranteed the title and the taxes that come with it." He thought no such thing considering this group remained enamored with Kynan.

The fourth councilman ran a hand through his short hair and shifted his weight to his other foot. "It has always been that way."

"Ah," Tiergan said, walking over to the man, "I have found a traditionalist. He speaks the truth, and you know it."

The councilman took a knee and bowed his head. "I will serve you well, King Tiergan."

"I don't know. You didn't speak up for me until now..."

"I promise. My Lord King, please."

"I cannot abide a coward." Tiergan sliced the blade through the air, and Cynnwrf neatly relieved the councilman of his head. "You know, I think I'm finished talking."

He cut them all down, one by one, until the only sound in the room was the drip, drip, drip of blood.

"This is how we will deal with those who made up the former High King's regime," he said to the courtiers watching and shaking in their shoes. "They only want all the gold and crops for themselves. They don't care about us here in the original home of shadow elves. They have forgotten how shadow elves should behave. They have grown weak and lost the steel in their spines. Well, we will forge a joint kingdom with no weakness, no love for the Upperworld, and no unfair divides between the land west of the Dark Sea and the land to the east. We will reign supreme, and I pity those who would try to rise against us. Who would like to be on the new council and work with me toward a joint kingdom built on the glory of our ancient days?"

Hands were raised and shouts went up, and Tiergan couldn't stop smiling.

"Now, let us feast. Fetch my queen!"

CHAPTER 8
MAREN

At a feasting table laden with stewed apples, grilled rabbit, and an abundance of breads braided into elaborate patterns, Maren continued to starve.

Tiergan waved the servants away from her place at the table. "Oh, no, she isn't feeling up to more food. She is quite satisfied, I assure you."

Maren refused to even look at Tiergan. Instead, she faked a smile at the beady-eyed noble beside her and aimed to have some fun, if only for a moment. "Yes, Lord Buddletit—"

"It's Benntiton..." The way the vein in his head throbbed was hilarious.

"Yes, of course it is. Lord Bunion, I do not believe your daughter there is quite keen on the idea of wedding that fair-haired lad. Her skin has gone the shade of spoiled milk."

"Benntiton," he spat out, "and I don't believe I asked you about the coming nuptials, I—"

Tiergan tapped his thick crystal goblet with a pearl-handled knife. "My lady Maren."

The warning in his eyes was difficult to ignore but not impossible. "Yes, sweetling?" she said sarcastically. Perhaps if he'd fed her along with the guests instead of telling them she'd already eaten when she'd only been permitted one hard roll and a glass of water in her chamber, she would have schooled her tone. But the roll had been better than nothing, and though she'd never tell him, she was grateful to have it in her aching belly.

His grin faded. "I thought it would be fascinating for you to entertain us with your magic in the gardens."

Entertain? What did that entail exactly? His grin was recovering, and that only made her feel more ill at ease. She'd heard a rumor that he had butchered the council. When she'd first entered and her guards had left her side, she'd asked the servant handing out the wine about the event. He had ignored her question completely. Tiergan was capable of it. He could use this entertainment scenario to do something terrible as well. But he had her wand, and if he was willing to set it into her hands, she would do almost anything.

She pushed away from the dark wood table, dragging the chair across the stone floor loudly, then she stood. "Ready when you are."

The other nobles blinked and looked to Tiergan, so she must have done something less than noble. She fought the near-overwhelming urge to roll her eyes.

Tiergan led her and the rest of the finely dressed dinner guests out of the side doors and into a walled garden lit in shades of lavender and orange by the

Underworld's version of a sunset. Bushes trimmed into geometric shapes were filled in with low purple-leafed bushes and lines of roses pruned and trained like soldiers. From the steps overlooking the garden, Maren studied the outer two rings of bushes. The rest of the party filtered past her, their pointed ears showing under small tiaras, elaborate braids, and a few seriously ugly wigs. The bushes around the shapes formed letters— words. They were in the shadow elf tongue, so she couldn't decipher them.

Tiergan waved her toward him. Five guards remained within arm's reach of her as she approached.

What was he going to do to keep her from using her wand to call up the dragon goddess Nix? Maren couldn't kill Tiergan because the realms weren't secure yet, but she could restrain him and turn this situation around. What would he use to control her?

He was obviously having a fine time with this new life of his, Kynan out of the picture and her in his proverbial pocket. He wouldn't kill her and shatter the Binding and break the realms. He would die as surely as everyone else. So what would his bargaining chip be?

As she walked toward him, the nobles murmured and eyed her like she was a fascinating creature. She supposed she was. Raising her chin and giving Lord Buddletit's daughter a solidarity wave, she made her way to Tiergan.

He smiled at the crowd. "Enjoy a drink while we prepare."

Servants poured out more wine as Tiergan jerked his chin at an area behind the nearest row of fancy bushes.

"Do you see them?"

"See what?"

She leaned a little further, and four young shadow elves came into view—children. One girl held a stick against her chest like it was her beloved sword, and a boy had an arm around her shoulders, the look in his eyes saying he might be her older brother. He was still little though, no more than eight years old. Twin boys—very young—with chubby cheeks sat on the ground, picking at the pebbles that lined the walled garden. Because of the way the light hit the walls and the shrubbery, no one else could see the children or the armed knights and the Facilitator standing a step behind them.

"If you misbehave, one dies. If you repeat the offense, another is cut down."

Maren swallowed bile. Her humor and bravado slid from her like blood from a deep wound. "You're pathetic."

"Shall I show you I am serious?" He made a movement with his hand, and the Facilitator took hold of the little girl's neck.

Cold shot through Maren's chest, and she grabbed Tiergan's arm. "No. I'll be good. Everything will be lovely." She was going to vomit.

"Control yourself, Wife. The nobles are looking now, and it's time for you to save those children's lives." He handed her the wand as the nobles regarded her warily.

Warm power rushed from the wand into her fingers, up her arm, then into her heart. She took a deep breath and blinked, feeling whole again.

Was there any spell she could work right now to save the children and restrain Tiergan? But what about the Facilitator and the knight, the guard unit at the door, and the exit from the garden? It was complicated and far too risky a situation to just start whipping out magic.

"What do you want me to do, King Tiergan?" Her voice came out flat. She was the Awenydd, the one who spoke for the spirits and the one who could raise the spirit dragon's fire. She gritted her teeth. She would have her revenge on Tiergan. Not now. But it would happen. For now, she'd play it safe for the children.

He was studying her, and she longed to rip his horrible head off. "Give us a lovely display of multicolored sparks, if you can."

"You want a pretty rainbow, my king?"

His lips tightened into a line. "Careful."

A year ago, she wouldn't have been able to summon sparks. Her magic had been unwieldy and particular. Well, it still was particular, but her power had increased vastly, and she could manage this even if it wasn't her specialty. He was trying to humiliate her, using her like this, like mere dinner entertainment.

A whisper came from the children, and she glanced their way. The little girl was pointing at Maren's wand and smiling. She had no idea that her life was in such danger.

And she would never find out.

Maren swallowed a lump in her throat and locked her gaze on Tiergan. "I do sparks for the count of ten, then I escort all the children out of this pit of horror. Deal?"

"Deal. Hurry. They are getting curious." His gaze was on the nobles. Why did he care so much about their opinion?

She roused the magic, and the spot between her brows tingled. As she thrust her wand into the air, sparks of gold, purple, blue, and green showered the garden. The nobles gasped and clapped, and Maren whispered a spell to make the sparks fizzle out before any landed on fine clothing and over-styled hair.

"Queen Maren!" the crowd shouted, all smiles.

Didn't they know Tiergan was a monster? Maybe not. Perhaps he only mistreated those lowborn in his kingdom and kept the nobles happy. Their cheers and grins didn't appear falsely created to avoid Tiergan's wrath. Their happiness seemed genuine.

Maren gave the crowd the fakest smile to ever exist in any realm, tilted her head at Tiergan, and raised her eyebrows expectantly. "Well?"

Tiergan snatched the wand from her hand in a quick but ruthless movement, then flicked one quick finger at the knights. Though she felt like she was leaving a part of her behind—it had been so comforting to hold her wand and work magic again—Maren walked toward the knights and the children as if she were simply leaving for a moment alone.

She didn't look back as the Facilitator and the knights escorted Maren and the children out of the garden's shadowed exit under an arch of purple-leafed vines and black blooms with pistils a sickly green.

The girl wrapped her fingers around Maren's. She mumbled something in their language. Maren smiled down at her, heart cracking.

"Will we walk to their homes to return them safely?" she asked the Facilitator.

"Yes."

The boy who was most likely the girl's older brother bumped Maren's hip accidentally, then righted himself. He looked up at her with eyes that were holding back tears.

"I don't like this," he said in the common tongue. "Will you carry my sister?"

"I don't like it either." Maren lifted the girl, who buried her face in Maren's fur-trimmed dress. "But it's almost over now. We're going to your homes."

"I liked your sparks." The boy's accent was thick.

"Thank you. Which was your favorite color?" Maren kept her eyes on the Facilitator, watching for any villainy.

The young boy wiggled his eyebrows. "The gold."

Maren chuckled. "Bit of a dragon, eh?"

"Like Ivar," he whispered, gaze flicking to the back of the Facilitator and the knight.

A chill swept over Maren. She put a finger to her lips.

The boy scrunched up his face and crossed his arms. "I don't care. I like the tale of High King Kynan. I hear he is nice."

He was going to get himself killed. "Yes. Very nice," she whispered even more quietly, hoping to end the conversation before the Facilitator pulled steel and began swinging.

The road turned westward, and an ancient oak shadowed the cobblestones. A shop with a needle and thread on its lopsided sign sat beside a tavern that was oddly quiet this time of evening. The few elves at the place drank from tankards and ate quietly from trenchers filled with beans. Most of them glanced their way and quickly looked in another direction. Most likely they knew trouble when they saw it. One peek at the Facilitator was all it took to know that fellow was no party.

"Will you go to him?" The boy's voice was hardly audible. Maren's heart beat frantically. He was talking about Kynan.

She slowed her steps a bit to give them distance from the Facilitator and the knight. "Of course not. If I did, it would bring back the ice."

The girl in her arms whimpered again and began trembling. Maren rubbed her back to soothe her. "It's all right, little bean." She didn't know much about children, but she remembered her own mother doing this when she was young. "Shh. All is well," she lied.

The knight glanced over his shoulder at them. Most of his face was covered in a silver helmet. Only his pointed ears and downturned mouth showed. "Quiet."

Maren nodded, and the boy took the cue and nodded as well. Sweat beaded on Maren's upper lip and the back of her neck. One wrong move, and this would be a massacre...

A door opened along the street, and an elven woman about Maren's age peered out, her gaze wary. Meeting Maren's eyes, she set her fist against the right side of her mouth, index finger and thumb extended. She moved them up and down. What was that? Some sort of greeting? It brought to mind a beak, and she fluttered her fingers like a wing...

It was a bird.

Was it related to the symbol and writing in the book that the healer had brought?

"Eh!" The knight broke from the Facilitator and slammed into the woman's partially open door.

Maren's heart rammed into her ribs, and she gripped the little girl tightly.

The woman who'd made the hand signal was knocked back by the force of the door swinging. She called out for someone, the sound twisted by her pain. The knight shouted at her in the shadow elf tongue, and the little girl Maren was holding started to cry. The twins began weeping loudly too, and the boy tried to shush them all, his cheeks going red like his blood was up. The sound of a fist on flesh came from the dark doorway.

The Facilitator simply stood and watched. He was waiting to see what Maren would do.

The flame of rage burned over Maren, and she carefully set the girl down, urging her into her brother's arms. She stalked toward the open doorway slowly, chin held high. She had one card to play to save this woman from further harm or even death. Already her family had come down the steps of their home, their faces pale in the weak light from the doorway. They seemed frozen and lost on what to do as the knight towered over the woman who lay sprawled on the wooden floorboards.

Maren roused her best impression of Brielle and remembered the power she had inside of her. "Step away from my subject, knight."

The man turned and looked her up and down. "Suddenly, you are taking on the role of queen willingly?"

Maren took a step closer and gave him a dead stare.

He held her gaze for a heartbeat, then his shoulders dropped and he bowed his head. "Apologies, my queen."

"Go." She pointed toward the door and stepped back so he could leave. The Facilitator had walked closer to the house.

"Eh, important man," the boy said, glancing once at Maren. "Tell me about King Tiergan and the legend of Cynnwrf!" He pulled at the Facilitator's cloak, and the other children joined in.

With half her heart remaining with the children on

the street, Maren knelt beside the woman. "I'm sorry that Tiergan's men are as awful as he is," she whispered. "What did that sign mean?"

The elven woman sat up and licked blood from her lip. She spoke quickly but in the shadow elf language. Maren set a hand on the woman's knee and looked to the man and two young girls on the stairs.

"Do any of you speak the common tongue?" Maren didn't want to leave the children alone out there for long. "That sign..." Checking once to be sure the children were keeping the knight and the Facilitator busy, Maren mimicked the sign the woman had made as best she could.

The elven man shook his head like he didn't understand, but one of the girls began whispering. "I... no speak...meaning." She pointed to the ceiling and then to Maren. "High King."

Maren's chest ached from the intense beating of her heart. "So it's something to do with me and King Kynan, yes?"

"Yes," the girl said, her gaze slipping to her mother.

The knight had reacted like the sign was not allowed and was in fact some sort of crime to use, and the girl said it had to do with her and with Kynan.

Perhaps the woman was a rebel?

Was there a group discussing what had happened in the battle with Tiergan? Maybe they wished to help her? If the Facilitator or the knight knew of this, Maren had to pretend she was not in cahoots with the rebels, or her escorts would tell Tiergan. He might never let her use her wand again and might hold back even more on food. It certainly wouldn't help her situation if he knew she had been kind to those against him.

She stood. "I must pretend to be angry now." She kept her voice very low, silently praying they would somehow understand. Keeping her hand in front of her and out of view from the knights' line of sight, she pointed toward the knights as best she could, then made an overly dramatic angry face that made the other young girl giggle. The sister clapped a hand over the girl's mouth and nodded to Maren. A sigh left Maren, and then she began to act like the best of maskers at a king's court.

"How dare you suppose I have any desire to sully myself with gossip? There is no way to defeat King Tiergan. He has won, and we all must make the best of it. I suggest you refrain from mimicking anything that could be misconstrued as rebellious. If you refuse, I will find this house and burn it to the ground for your treachery."

Goddess Nix, please let them know I am only doing this to keep us all safe. Please let them understand.

The man's eyes widened, and he softly repeated the word *burn*.

Maren sighed again. Great. That was the one thing he'd understood in all of this. Hopefully, the girl would explain. She looked at Maren with a knowing glint in her eye as she helped her mother up. The mother just stared at Maren, and Maren couldn't read her expression.

Outside, the children made a noise of alarm.

Maren looked around the room, suddenly desperate

and clammy palmed at leaving this place with no clue as to what the maybe rebels had planned.

"Queen!" the boy outside shouted.

Maren bowed her head and left the house. "Fools. They didn't even realize that was a rebel sign," she muttered loudly enough that the Facilitator and the knight would hear. "...giving me false hope." She kept that last to a whisper so if the Facilitator did catch it, the act would come off as sincere. "Come, children," she said at a normal volume. She picked up one of the twin boys who had sat on the ground. The eldest boy, his sister, and the other twin joined her in walking along, the Facilitator leading once more.

They arrived at a home with three broken shutters, damage that Maren guessed was due to a fallen tree. A stump and a pile of firewood stood where the tree had once grown. An elven woman flung herself out of the double doors before the knight had time to knock. She threw herself at the brother and sister and wept quietly. She repeated one word over and over. "Dioloch."

The Facilitator led Maren and the rest away from the scene. She gave the boy and girl a wave over her shoulder. Soon, the group had found the twins' home— a three-story plastered place that had once been a remarkable building. Now, mice ran from a hole near the front windows and the right-side door hung on one working hinge. The Facilitator shoved the twins forward, and the knight knocked at the sad doors. An elven man whose face was devoid of emotion even as his body shook with barely restrained anger met them and took the children in.

Maren tried to give him a hopeful smile, but she failed, her heart too heavy.

The only thing that kept her walking with her eyes dry was the thought of finding more rebel evidence in her room.

She should have hidden that writing.

What if whoever gave it to her had been found out? What if Tiergan was there right now, sitting at the edge of her bed and reading the message? Did he know the significance of the bird—well, the bird wing—that she'd now seen in both the writing and in the mother's hand signal?

The water was deadly cold. Even with Kynan's shadows swirling around them, he knew Aury and Rhianne had to be freezing.

The light from Rhianne's wand blinded him as she blasted the kelp.

The ship shifted and bobbed far above their heads.

Between dark stripes of his magic, Aury glared at the thorny kelp like it was her greatest enemy, while Rhianne's face was smooth, her gaze focused. Rhianne was wearing a vest covered in spirit agate, a stone that enhanced the power of some magic-workers. It had no effect on him, but it did seem to give Rhianne a boost, so he was grateful for it. The spelled flames from her wand seared the kelp exposed when Aury peeled back the water and left pockets of dry air. Such fascinating magic they had.

He worked to keep his shadows firmly around their heads so breathing wouldn't be an issue. He'd only created cocoons of air under water twice in his long life, and the spell's workings were complicated. Truly, it was more like several spells in one, all bred of shadows and will. Shadow magic was a power born for war, with energy spent on attacking. Rarely was it used to shelter or to be so subtle. He had to keep his mind trained on the task to avoid injuring the women.

A sound vibrated through the water behind him. Dread clutched at his heart as he risked a glance into the green-black expanse.

The flash of white teeth showed in the dark.

Kynan tightened his shadows, grabbing both women and launching them toward the surface. He couldn't move them in the way he could above the water; this type of spellwork was slower and unwieldy. They shouted, voices bubbling. The familiar tumbling and falling feeling that always resulted from shadow travel came over him. Something was cutting him though. That wasn't normal. What was... Shards of ice sliced his shadows to bite into his cheeks and arms. He ignored the attack and lifted them toward the ship.

A beast of scale and tooth shot from the dark water. Blood racing, Kynan pressed more energy into his shadows. The afanc's teeth gnashed the water beside his elbow, narrowly missing as Kynan, Aury, and Rhianne broke the surface and Kynan's shadows hurled them onto the ship.

He collapsed on deck. Blood flowed onto the planks from numerous cuts. Ivar swooped low, circled, then landed beside him, the wyvern's throat shaking in a staccato roar for help.

Shouting and footsteps echoed around Kynan.

"Why did you attack him?" Rhianne asked Aury. "The afanc was there!"

She looked at Kynan, and her eyes went wide. "I thought it was an attack from another shadow lord or some shadow magic creature." She knelt beside him, and Werian joined her. "Kynan," Aury said, "I had no idea I was attacking you. I was disoriented down there. I thought—"

"It's fine. I understand." Remaining on his knees, supporting himself with one hand, he pointed to the sea. "The afanc swam right behind us."

Hafwen ran to the ship's side, and the rest followed except for Werian, who set a hand on Kynan and began to heal him. Warm magic sifted through the fae prince's point of contact and across Kynan's flesh, mending cuts and easing pain with a gentle tingling.

"Thank you," Kynan said, getting to his feet with a hand from Werian.

Werian clapped him on the back. "Of course."

The ship rocked hard, its prow nosing the air as everyone found something to grab. A foul stench like rotting fish rode the wind, and a roar sounded as the boat leveled out and moved easterly.

Werian grimaced. "At least we're freed from the kelp?"

Filip whistled from the side where he stood next to Aury. "Look at that thing."

And Kynan did. The afanc's wake showed the beast to be exactly as massive as Hafwen had supposed. Fins of reptilian armor cut the waves. The one in the middle of the afanc's back was roughly the size of the table in his great hall. Kynan held to the side of the rocking ship with one hand and gripped his sword with the other. He wished he still had Cynnwrf.

The afanc swam away, its tail whipping and throwing a wave that, when it reached them, tossed them all onto their arses again.

But at least the afanc was gone for now. The crew resumed their duties as everyone dusted themselves off and had a much-needed swig of sailor's brew. The stuff burned its way over Kynan's mouth. It tasted like he'd taken a mouthful of fire and mint. Disgusting, but the way it relaxed his mind was welcome. He wiped his mouth with the back of his hand and gave his mug to Hafwen. There couldn't be fine manners here. There were far too many people on this ship. Hafwen finished what was left in the mug.

"If that thing decides we don't belong in his sea, what do we do?" Hafwen cleaned the mug with the slack in her long tunic, then tied the small handle to her belt.

"Fight it. I'm not sure what you're really asking."

"The ship will be destroyed even if we manage to kill it before it ends all of us. We would drown out here. We're too far from shore, and you can't shadow the entire party back to the cliffs, nor can Dorin or Ivar fly us. We need a backup plan."

Aury came forward. "What's wrong?"

Kynan and Hafwen switched to using the common tongue.

Hafwen jerked her chin at the skiff tied to port side.

"We need to figure out if we have enough skiffs to hold everyone."

Aury crossed her arms. Her mage staff was secured on her back; the coral in the wooden cage at the top of the staff was a bright orange. "And after seeing that beast, you're wisely worried about ship damage if it decides to hunt us."

"The crew will know about the capacity of the skiffs," Werian said.

"I think we have bigger fish to fry," Aury said.

Werian snorted. "I see what you did there."

Aury gave a half smile. "This whole quest is madness. What's one more problem?"

Brielle rebraided her red hair. "Why do we have so many mad quests? Someday, we need to simply take a group nap."

Dorin chuckled. "You'd be bored in one afternoon, my love."

She smiled and gently tugged the bottom edge of Dorin's wing. "Probably right."

Kynan pinched the bridge of his nose. "I need to lose more of my good sense to put up with this lot," he said to Hafwen, not caring if they all heard. They needed to focus.

"I can help with losing good sense." Werian pulled a small gourd from his cloak pocket. A cork stuck out from the top of the vegetable, and it had been partially covered in leather.

Kynan thanked him and took a swig from the hollowed gourd. The stuff was far better than sailor's brew. It tasted like currants. "Where did you get this? We rode so hard for days…"

"At that last village stop. It's blackcurrant brandy."

Rhianne brightened. "The stuff from the female blacksmith? I loved her."

Werian nodded. "Her cousin had a crock of this." He took the gourd from Kynan and drank a bit. "Delicious. Shadow elves are quickly becoming my favorite elven group."

From across the deck, Filip flicked his fingers at Werian, an obscene gesture the Upperworlders seemed to share with the Underworld shadow elves. Also, Balaur elves seemed as good with hearing as Kynan and his kind were.

A crewman with copper-bright hair leaned over the side of the crow's nest. "Captain!"

Kynan jerked his head at Werian, who seemed careful about claiming the role of captain even though Kynan had encouraged it. Kynan certainly had no sailing experience. Regardless, he did appreciate the fae prince's respect for Kynan's position here in the Underworld.

Werian gave him a head nod, then looked up at the sailor. "What is it?"

Kynan was glad most of his people knew the common tongue. It made him proud they were so well educated.

The crewman gestured to the east. "There's a disturbance in the water. Rough currents, I'm guessing. Might want to avoid."

Werian shouted a variety of orders about trimming

this sail and that and using the wheel to pull the ship against the water.

Kynan saw the churning waves. "It almost looks as though they are breaking on a reef," he said to Hafwen, Aury, and Filip. Rhianne had joined Werian in running about the ship to be certain all commands were understood.

Hafwen removed her wand from her belt and whispered a spell. Golden light danced from the wand and traveled over the surface of the water. Ivar took flight and followed, his head cocking as he studied the magic. The light swirled around the tumultuous current, then flew back toward the ship along with Ivar, whose black belly was illuminated by Hafwen's magic.

Beneath the golden light and Ivar, small iridescent fins edged in sea foam broke the sea's surface.

"What are you up to, my friend?" Kynan asked Hafwen.

"Have you ever read about water sprites?"

"No, and I don't think I like that look on your face."

Hafwen's laugh was low and dangerous.

Kynan was truly surrounded by wild folk. Not a one of them was fully sane.

Tiergan wrapped his shadows around himself tightly and focused on a mental image of the Spirit Well. With the sensation of flying, falling, and having the breath stolen from his lungs, he arrived, boots firmly planted on the soft moss beside the well.

This place reminded him of Kynan's arrogance and of how Kynan had looked at Maren before she Bonded with Tiergan instead. The well should have felt like his stomping grounds now, but it still held the scent of Kynan and a ghost of his presence. Tiergan stepped on a cluster of blue poppies and ground them into the earth with his heel. If this place wouldn't willingly accept him as its new master, then he would force it into submission.

He closed his eyes and entered the Between. When he opened them, white mist surrounded his spirit body, cooling his chin and cheeks. It smelled like nothing here. He gripped his sword hilt, seeking comfort from the worn bone and leather there, but that too held the idea of Kynan. With a grunt, he strode forward, hating that he wanted comfort at all.

"I come to offer sacrifice." He slid his dagger from his belt—a dagger that was thankfully his and his alone—and sliced open his palm. Holding his hand up, he squeezed his fingers into a fist and dropped the blood into the Between. The spirits kept their distance, whispering and looking. "Stop acting like frightened children. I bring you noble shadow lord blood as is my duty. Come, and be blessed."

But the spirits didn't draw near. They had gone quiet and merely stared at him.

"Fools." He took the strip of cloth he'd prepared in advance from the pouch at his belt, wrapped his hand, and willed himself out of the Between and back to the Underworld.

Running his other hand through his hair, he swore. The spirits wanted a blood sacrifice from the one who wore the High King crown. Cynnwrf was a good start toward the proper level of blood power, but the crown would make him that much stronger and more capable of feeding the spirits and keeping them satiated. He hated that he had to worry about the spirits and their needs. What had they ever done for him? Not a thing.

He loomed over the well, staring into its swirling depths. The Sacred Oak's roots divided the flow into fingers of current that spun and combined in silvery patterns. Shaking his head, he blew out a frustrated breath.

"Once Kynan is dead, I'll return with the High

King's crown. When I do, prepare to beg forgiveness for your reluctance today."

He smiled, wrapped his shadows around himself, and used his power to travel as quickly as possible back to his kingdom, where all was well in hand.

Maren returned to her chambers and thankfully didn't see Tiergan anywhere. The nobles had returned to their homes, and the castle was quiet again with just the usual sounds of servants padding about lighting fires and cleaning while Bethan went over the list of Tiergan's cronies so Maren could learn to say their names correctly in company. The kitchen was a far-off din of clattering spoons and the bang of pots. She longed to be there. But there was no time for befriending the kitchen staff and baking cinnamon rolls. She had to find out more about this rebellion and the bird symbol and how it might help her find some power over Tiergan and this impossible situation.

Bethan shook her head. "That's not how you pronounce it. Try again. My lord king says you did a horrible job of speaking with the nobles at the feasting. Say it again. Lord Rhydderch."

Maren's eyes longed to glance at the bound writings that remained on her bedside table, but she kept her gaze on Bethan. She couldn't draw attention to the potential secrets of the rebels who might wish to support her and Kynan. "Rhydderish."

"My lady. You aren't trying hard enough."

"Lord Rhydderch."

"Yes!" Bethan looked ready to get up and dance. "Let's give this one a go. Lord Angharad."

"I need more wine if I am working on that one."

"I truly don't believe wine will improve your language capabilities."

"You haven't known me for long. How could you know?"

"Call it a good guess. Now try it, my lady. Please. I will be evaluated by the Facilitator based on your progress."

"Eegared." Maren squeezed her eyes shut. "No, I already know that one is way off. Angerhead. Ack. Why can't they have simpler names? That should be a new law. Everyone must have a name that those from beyond this realm can pronounce."

"That's disrespectful."

"You're right. I apologize. Angereed. Angharad."

"Yes!" Bethan's elbow knocked over the tray that had held a loaf of warmed and honeyed bread earlier. Said tray and crumbs scattered across the thick rug. "Oh, stones and stars." She began fussing about and cleaning the mess.

Maren bent to help her. "I'm sorry I'm the worst

student. If it makes you feel any better, every tutor I've had has said I'm a waste of time."

Bethan stopped cleaning and touched Maren's sleeve before quickly pulling away. "They should not have said such things to a young lady. You are not a waste of time."

A smile pulled at Maren's lips as they finished tidying and sat once more to study. Bethan wasn't all bad. Maren would have to watch out for her during the coming days of strife.

After a few more names, Bethan tucked her list into the pocket of her apron and went to the doors. "I'll bring up a tray shortly."

The second she was gone, Maren grabbed the writings and leafed through the rest of the pages, the material soft and worn from years of use. All of it was written in the shadow elf tongue, save that one message, and there weren't any more symbols or anything that stuck out.

Eyeing the door and listening for Bethan, she quickly tore the rebel message from the binding. She picked at every shred left in the woven threads so that it would be tough to realize a page had been removed. Then she set it back on the table and began to search the chamber again for any type of symbol that might indicate the rebel's bird.

Her wand hand ached like it had a broken heart, and she pressed it against her stomach to soothe herself. The symbol might not be here, and even if it was here somewhere, it might not lead to any sort of solution or benefit. But she didn't have any other leads on gaining the upper hand with Tiergan, so the bird hunt was on.

After going over the baseboards under the bed, she ran a hand over the cold stones beneath the leaded glass windows.

"Is there something wrong?" Bethan's voice made Maren jump.

Heart blasting blood into her veins, Maren whirled and forced a placid smile. "Nothing at all. I was merely admiring the handiwork. My...father was a mason."

That was a lie. She hoped it wouldn't be a big deal in the grand scheme of things. One never knew when a fib would take one down. Smaller mistakes had toppled kingdoms if Brielle's stories were anything to learn from. She'd told Maren about a noble who had forgotten to wear a pin awarded to him by a rural community's guild to court and how support for his claim to the throne had dropped away after one comment from that area of the kingdom.

"A mason?" Bethan set a tray on the nightstand. Steam curled away from the crockery mug, and the scent of chamomile tea wafted through the air.

Normally, Maren would have enjoyed a nice tea, but she was still starving, so the tea felt like mockery from Tiergan.

"Is there a tray of food coming? I did as the king ordered." Maren swallowed a bitter taste on her tongue. Obeying that arsehead made her sick to her stomach.

Bethan frowned and looked Maren up and down as if she were the ugliest thing she'd ever seen. "Not yet. Perhaps later if High King Tiergan orders it so."

"High King?" Kynan was High King, supported by the population because of his prowess in battle and his highborn blood, not Tiergan. The council had crowned Kynan, and as far as Maren knew, there hadn't been another meeting. The council lived in Kynan's lands. Plus, she was almost certain the magical High King crown remained on the head of one person until that person's death. But perhaps Tiergan was High King in name only, lacking the crown but holding the reins of the entire kingdom.

"Oh, yes. The council announced the decision about an hour ago."

"How did that happen?" She'd heard rumors but knew nothing concrete.

"The former council members have all...stepped down," Bethan said. "New members were chosen."

Maren gave Bethan a glare. "So King Tiergan threatened the former council members with what... death? Torturing their loved ones? How exactly did that occur?" She knew she needed to shut her mouth, but she couldn't quite manage it.

"You should watch what you say."

"Maybe I would if I had some food in my belly."

Bethan stared, eyes narrowing, and Maren held her gaze.

"I'm not afraid." More lies. "There's little else he can do that he hasn't already. I doubt he'd trouble himself to wrangle and horrify more of his subjects' children just because I gave him some lip."

Bethan's throat moved in a swallow. "You have no idea what he is capable of."

"I think I do, but if I don't eat more, I won't even be around to suffer the consequences."

Bethan's face remained unreadable. Would she leave and report this to Tiergan? Would Maren be sent back to the dungeon?

"I will see what I can do," Bethan finally said.

Maren exhaled and tried to hide her relief by keeping a good dollop of anger in her gaze as the maid left through the double doors, her sharp voice echoing in the corridor as she spoke with Lefty and Righty.

The bed called to Maren. She could hardly keep her eyes open. But she had no idea when she'd be left alone again, so she took up her search once more.

After going back over the walls with her hands, trying to feel for anything out of the ordinary, she folded back the tapestry to examine the stone behind. Still nothing. It was difficult to see, so she might have missed it.

Hands on hips, she exhaled. Where was it? Or was she being stupid and it didn't exist?

She set the lantern back on her nightstand. Maybe the wing symbol meant something else entirely. Wiping her face with both hands, she fell into bed. This was impossible. She pulled her hands away from her face and looked up.

And there it was.

Her heart slammed against her chest, and she sat up. Two wings, a simple triangle for a beak, and two dots for eyes had been painted on one of the rough-hewn ceiling beams. It blended in with the runes that decorated the rest of the beam.

All right, so she'd found it. Now what?

She stood on the bed and tried to touch it, but she was far too short. Gritting her teeth, she rolled ideas around in her head. What would the rebels be marking, and why would they tell her about it? Did the symbol lead to information about Tiergan that might be helpful in cutting back his control of her? She couldn't imagine what information could do that. Perhaps the bird indicated a secret store of weapons. But they had to know she couldn't physically strike out at Tiergan. It would threaten the Bond and break the balance, harm the Sacred Oak and the Spirit Well, and bring the realms into ruin again.

Could the symbol signify a secret way out? If that was its meaning, the ceiling would be a bizarre place for a tunnel. It would have to be through the walls or the floor.

Holing up somewhere in the walls while she shivered in fear wasn't her plan—she was the Awenydd, by the gods—but finding a backup plan for putting a slight distance between her and Tiergan sounded wonderful. The Bond surely wouldn't permit for much meandering, but still... Even a secret hideout might come in handy in the near future.

She leapt out of bed, grabbed the lantern, and

wiggled her way under the bed to the spot that sat directly beneath the symbol on the ceiling. Positioning the lantern near the area, she ran a hand over the timber floor. There weren't any painted markings or even a scratched surface here. Fatigue drew her eyelids down, but she blinked, forcing herself to stay awake.

Her fingers caught on a raised edge. She gasped, and hope drove away her fatigue. The board didn't fit as neatly as it should have... Taking hold of the edge, she yanked on the board as best as she could while lying on her stomach with her arm unable to fully bend due to the ropes and mattress above her.

The board came loose. Her heart tapped excitedly, and she plunged her hand into the empty space only to ram her fingers into a solid surface. She set the lantern closer and peered into the rectangular space. A black iron handle was attached to another plank.

Well, now she was getting somewhere.

She tugged on a board next to the one she'd already removed, and it too came away easily. More of the hatch door showed now. With three more planks out of the way, the secret door was fully exposed. Now all she had to do was lift the hatch. She curled her fingers around the handle and tugged. It didn't budge. Swallowing her nervousness and fear that the door would open at any moment, showing a furious Tiergan or a spiteful Bethan, she yanked on the handle again. Her muscles strained, and she set her jaw, pulling, pulling. The hatch shifted, and she slid it slowly out of place. A cool wind blew across her cheeks as she peered into complete darkness. The space smelled like wet stone and mildew, but she didn't care a bit. She turned so that she could go in feet first.

But was this completely foolish? Bethan might be on her way back with food. Her stomach growled, and her head swam with the thought of it. If she waited until Bethan came and went, maybe that would be a better idea. But she couldn't haul the door's cover back into place. She definitely didn't have the strength to do that and then do this again once Bethan was gone.

But if she left the passageway open, Bethan would surely see the cover sitting there with all the loosened planks.

She had to explore now or risk losing the chance entirely.

With a quick prayer to the Source and Goddess Nix, she slid into the darkness.

CHAPTER 14
KYNAN

Most everyone on the ship was distracted by the ever nearer whirlpool, so no one but Brielle and Dorin was paying any attention to Hafwen's spell and the small fins glistening and breaking the water.

Dorin leaned on the ship's side. "Did you say water sprites?"

One side of Hafwen's mouth lifted in a mischievous smirk. "Watch this."

The fins grew larger, not by much, but inch by inch until they were free from the water. Small bodies made from water appeared attached to said fins, and the fins began to work like wings, flapping and helping the sprites rise from the waves. They were beautiful. Each sprite had long, flowing hair—also made of water—and lithe little bodies cloaked in watery gowns that extended past where feet or flippers might have been. They looked like elves with pointed ears and all the basic features of elves.

The sprites hovered before Hafwen, and her magic sparkled around them like a cloud of gold. Their mouths opened in unison, and they began making a sound like wind chimes.

Kynan could hardly believe his eyes. How many wonders would they see on this journey? "They're speaking to you?"

"I believe so, but I have no idea what they're saying." Hafwen tilted her head and drew a circle in the air with the wand. A paler gold light sprang from the end and joined the cloud of gold.

The chiming sounds grew lower and turned into words in the Underworld tongue. "Gold Eye, you have summoned us." Somehow, Hafwen had spelled their language to be understandable to modern elves. "What do you wish to learn?"

Kynan traded a look with Hafwen, who seemed as surprised as he was.

"I had no idea that spell would work," she said.

He grinned. "You're quite pleased with yourself, aren't you?"

"I really am."

"What are they saying?" Brielle asked in the common tongue.

"They want to know what we wish to learn," Hafwen answered in kind.

Dorin's eyes moved quickly like he was assessing this new kind of creature. He seemed the type who was very interested in such things. Kynan had heard his study of dragons was what had ignited the dragon shifter magic sleeping in his blood. "What will you ask?"

Hafwen faced the sprites. "I'm not sure...I'm going to let my witch's intuition lead me." She cleared her throat and continued on. "We are on a mission to find the Calon y Dderwen in order to balance the world's magic and save the Awenydd from foul King Tiergan. To do so, we must have safe passage, and we worry about this stretch of water. What strategy can we use to avoid disaster here?"

"We honor your quest," the sprites replied in a dozen melodic, tinkling voices. "It is a good quest. We have heard fine things of the new Awenydd, even in this dim place where spirits do not travel. The waters speak of you. To avoid ruin in this twist of the sea, you must let the ship do as it will."

Kynan held his breath, trying to understand. "Forgive my doubt, but you truly want to sail into that whirlpool?"

The sprites nodded.

How in the names of all the gods were they to survive this?

Aury walked over, her eyes wide. "What did they tell you?"

Filip joined them as well, his gaze full of wonder as he stared at the water creatures.

"To let the ship go where it may," Kynan said. "Hafwen, are you certain they are on our side in this? Do they stand to gain anything they'd care about if we died here?"

Hafwen kept her eyes trained on the sprites. "They feel good." She said the word like it had another meaning, a layered version of someone who acts with goodwill.

Aury crossed her arms. "They feel good? What kind of evaluation is that?"

Rhianne came over and had apparently caught some of the conversation. "A witch's evaluation, and you should listen to it."

Aury held up her hands in surrender. "Fine. I am not going to argue against two people who could turn me into a goat."

Filip chuckled and raised his eyebrows. "Me neither."

Kynan opened his mouth to respond, but nothing would come out.

"What?" Aury scowled at him. "You're interested in being turned into a goat? Or is there a shadow elf goat shifter from your history scrolls and I've somehow insulted him?"

Filip snorted a laugh and clapped his hands together. "Goat shifter."

Shaking his head, Kynan turned back to the sprites and Hafwen. "Will you ask the sprites if they know what happens when a ship goes into the whirlpool because there must be some magic there we aren't aware of?"

Hafwen did as he suggested, and the sprites just grinned and laughed, a sound like a thousand tiny bells. They dropped back into the water. Everyone leaned over the side, but the sprites were gone. Just like that.

"I didn't like that laugh," Kynan said.

Aury glared at the waves where the creatures had disappeared. "Nor did I."

Hafwen sheathed her wand and greeted Werian as he walked up.

"We might be able to go around it," Werian said to Kynan. "But it'll be a close one."

Kynan glanced at Hafwen, who shrugged and smiled in that all-knowing way of hers. "Werian, please have our crew bring the sails down, tie them up, all the duties you do when you want the boat to do as the sea says," Kynan said.

Werian's eyes flashed with alarm. "With respect, that would be the end of us."

Aury had her mage staff out and was raising up drops of water where the sprites had disappeared like she was trying to find them. She looked at Werian. "Oh, they spoke to water sprites who said to go with the current." The sour note in her voice said she was truly holding back on her arguments against this plan.

"Water sprites? Here?" Werian looked over the side.

Filip leaned against a stack of tied crates. "They're gone now."

Werian pointed a thumb at the whirlpool. "You are certain you want to sail into that thing?"

Kynan wasn't. "Yes. Hafwen," he said. "I pray to all the gods that this isn't our last conversation."

"I feel great about it actually," Hafwen said.

Brielle snorted. "At least someone does."

Dorin rubbed his chin with a knuckle and paced behind Brielle.

"Do you have anything to add? I'm listening," Kynan said to the dragon shifter.

Shaking his head, Dorin stretched his wings wide, then tucked them again. "You are our leader on this quest, and Werian and Rhianne are our captains. If all three of you are in agreement, then I am as well."

"Aye," Rhianne said.

Filip and Aury nodded and said, "Agreed," in unison.

"Well, here goes madness." Werian whirled and shouted orders. Soon they were drifting toward the whirlpool, and with every tip and turn of the ship, Kynan grew more and more certain they were all going to perish in this cursed body of water.

Maren hit hard-packed earth and rolled, remembering her early days of horseback riding and the instructions her mother had given her so many years ago. Tuck your shoulder and your chin. It worked. She lived through the fall from the secret opening under the bed at Tiergan's castle and was now in a corridor of sorts, lit only by the scant glow of the lantern back in her room and a distant circle of pale blue at what she guessed was the end of the tunnel. Starting toward the circle of light, she really hoped this wasn't the dumbest idea she'd ever had.

"Exactly how were you planning on getting back to your room?" she said aloud, scolding herself. "Shut it, me."

"I knew you were special," a voice said from the darkness, "but I didn't realize you were completely mad."

Maren grabbed for a wand that wasn't there. "Who are you? Oh. I remember you."

The herbalist, Ceri, walked closer, and the dim light showed the powerful muscles in her upper arms and the strong set of her jaw. She curtseyed. "Got my message, Awenydd?"

"I did. What is this place? Where does it lead?" Had Maren read this all wrong? Was Ceri about to attack her? Between the frown and the unreadable eyes, Ceri didn't seem pleased to see her, but maybe she was just anxious about the rebellion.

Ceri waved a hand. "I'll show you."

The corridor snaked along unevenly, the edges of the path lined in glowing mushrooms. "How did you get down here? Do you have a way for me to slip back into my room before Bethan returns and without Tiergan knowing?"

Ceri spat at the sound of Tiergan's name and uttered a quick tangle of sounds that might have been a curse in the shadow elf language.

Maren cracked her knuckles and wished for her wand. "My sentiments exactly."

"As for keeping this adventure quiet, I have a spy in place watching your rooms. They'll keep Bethan busy for a while." Ceri glanced at her over her big shoulder. "You aren't what we expected."

"I know. You thought I'd be taller. Sorry to disappoint."

Letting out a huff of a laugh, Ceri led her around a bend. The shuffle and click of mice scattering sounded through the corridor. "We thought you had fallen for Tiergan and would follow him in every word and deed."

"Why in the name of the Source would you have believed that?"

"Because that is what Tiergan told everyone. He crafted stories and had them repeated in taverns and by town criers. We knew he lied about many things, but we were surprised by how much you fought him when he first brought you here."

"You didn't know that I fought at High King Kynan's side against him?"

"No. We were told that you had been captured by the High King and had begged for help. Once we learned that you were in the dungeons, we sent rebel spies to find out the truth."

"How did they discover the story? You can't cross the Dark Sea easily, I would guess."

"There is one way to go across avoiding the water. You are currently on that path."

"What? How?"

Ceri gestured ahead of them, and Maren squinted. The light had gone...liquid. As they got closer, the entire corridor seemed to shimmer and flicker with a blue glow. It looked like a doorway made of magic and water.

"It's a doorway set here before recorded history. Most assume it was magically created by early witches and bolstered by the spirits, though they themselves cannot use it."

"Why can't they pass through?"

"The Dark Sea holds foul magic that, if I understand correctly, hurts the spirits."

"Where does this lead?"

"You'll see." Ceri smiled and walked through the strange doorway.

"Wait. What about the Bond and keeping the realms intact? If this leads too far from Tiergan, the distance might unravel the Bond that is healing the realms. And what if we are gone too long and Bethan finds the passageway?"

But Ceri was gone. Even though the other side of the corridor was vaguely visible beyond the watery passage, the herbalist was nowhere to be seen.

"Well, here goes nothing." Maren trailed her through, trying not to worry about what would happen if Bethan found the passageway while she was gone.

As she passed through the barrier, her skin went cold. It felt like jumping into an icy stream. She shivered, and the pale blue fire—the same that she'd raised with her wand and with dragon goddess Nix— flickered around her fingers and face.

A gasp went up from somewhere ahead, though all she could see was watery light and that magical spirit flame. The magic inside Maren chased the chill away, the heat rising in her chest, her palms, and in the spot between her eyes. And then she was through.

Kynan's homelands spread out before her, and the Spirit Well glowed at the base of the Sacred Oak's magical roots. Her heart was so light she thought she might be able to take flight.

"Welcome." Ceri stood beside two others—one was the woman from town, the one who had made the bird signal. The other was a man in a long dusty cloak who looked like he'd been traveling hard for his entire life. "This is Mags and this is Neddy."

Mags smiled but didn't say anything.

"Mags doesn't speak the common tongue," Ceri added. "Neddy here still isn't so sure about you."

Mags set a hand over her hearts, and Maren returned the gesture.

Neddy swept his cloak to the side and strode past the high grasses around the well until he was right in front of Maren. He looked her dead in the eye. "What do you want more than anything?"

"I mean, a handshake would have been nice for starters."

"You know what I'm asking."

So much for deescalating with humor... "I want my wand back. I want the realms to be secure enough that I can kill Tiergan with said wand."

A smile broke over his dirt-stained, wrinkled face. "Correct answer."

Mags and Ceri traded a few words in the shadow elf tongue, then Ceri snorted. "Neddy, do you think she would risk falling into a dark pit to who knew where if she were happy in Tiergan's castle?"

"I know nothing of humans," Neddy said. "They are a strange sort."

"We are," Maren agreed, "but I don't think humans and shadow elves are all that different. Not from what I've seen."

Ceri's grin was soft and genuine, her eyes shining. "I'm glad you're here. Now, let's talk strategy."

"First, let me speak with the spirits." Maren had

missed their presence and felt disconnected without being able to speak with them and for them.

The three rebels made way for her near the more open side of the well where fewer roots stretched toward the glistening pool. Maren was more than ready to have another good moment in this holy place to wipe out the last experience she'd had here when she'd had to Bond with Tiergan. She knelt at the well and focused her warm and tingling magic into her palms. Fingers hovering over the water, she simply followed her witch's intuition.

The well's water cooled Maren's palms even though she hadn't touched the surface. "I'm here if you want to talk. Is Tiergan caring for you properly? Is there anything I can do to help even if I don't have my wand?"

Light gathered into a circle below her hands, then a spirit rose from the water.

The scent of Kynan remained here, a scent like incense. Suddenly, tears made her vision blurry. She blinked them back and focused again, pushing away thoughts of his strong arms around her.

The spirit was a slender man with a beard that brushed the bottom of his long tunic. He had a mage staff similar to Aury's.

"Greetings, Awenydd."

From the way Ceri, Mags, and Neddy looked around, she could tell they couldn't hear or see the spirit.

Maren regarded the spirit and took a slow breath,

trying to think about what she should say. She might not be able to return anytime soon. "I'm so sorry that I haven't been accessible to you."

"The Dark Sea wasn't always impassable to us. The mad king twisted the magic there by throwing shadows into the sea too often and by casting the Calon y Dderwen into its depths. Your chosen mate is there now."

Maren swallowed. "Is he all right? What about the others with him?"

"I don't know what they face at the moment, but when we last saw them, they were boarding a ship."

"You can't watch over them at all?"

"Sadly, no."

"What can I do to help you continue to heal from the poison's damage?"

"We need High King Kynan's blood as it used to be. King Tiergan gave his blood, but it is not nearly as strong, and he gives it grudgingly. He has a foul aura, and his blood doesn't hold the power of the last master of the sword."

This was bad. Very bad. The realms appeared healthy, but the magic here felt thin, like it could break if not tended correctly. "I'll try to talk to him. Maybe I can say something that will urge him to come humbly to your well."

Maren wasn't sure how, but she had to figure it out. Tiergan had to keep these spirits satiated, or they'd grow hungry again and possibly deplete the well.

A memory surfaced.

Kynan had said that his High King crown—an ancient artifact made of metal and magic—made it so that his blood sacrifice once a year was proper. Tiergan didn't have that crown, of course. If it ever showed up on Tiergan's head, she would know that Kynan was dead.

The spirit shifted and began to fade away.

"May I offer a sacrifice?" she asked.

The spirit nodded, his beard catching on the buttons of his odd tunic. "Of course, Awenydd, but you know it will not have the same power."

"I do, but I can at least give what I have." She turned to face the rebels. "Can we gather some of those blue poppies? I'd like to give respect. Tiergan's blood gift was given with a prideful heart."

Ceri's mouth pulled into a tight line, and she set her hands on her hips. "I can't wait until it's safe to wring his skinny neck."

Maren snorted. "You and me both."

They set to gathering the poppies from a thick patch near the edge of the woods. Once they each had a bundle cradled in a fold of their clothing, they piled them beside the well. Maren knelt again and took up the entire collection of velvet-soft petals and sturdy stems and set them into the well, making sure her hands didn't touch the water.

"I give this as a symbol of my respect and gratitude." The poppies disappeared beneath the water, and the gauzy light rising from the well grew brighter for a moment. "I humbly request to speak with a god or goddess. Maybe Goddess Nix?"

A light shot from the well, swirled above the water, then coalesced into the form of a dragon.

"I hear you are having a difficult time, Awenydd."

Maren had to smile. Nix was not what she had expected in a goddess. "Do you have any idea where the Calon y Dderwen is in the Dark Sea?"

"I have the vague sense that something powerful lies in those cursed waters, but I don't know more than that."

Hopefully, Kynan and Hafwen had learned something of the crystal's whereabouts and they weren't simply searching blindly. "Thank you anyway. Do you know of a way I could restrain Tiergan's power over me?"

Nix's eyes sparkled as she stared at Maren. "Take Cynnwrf."

"But I'm not of royal shadow elf blood or even a shadow elf."

"I am fully aware, but you do hold something of Kynan in your blood. Your heart claimed him on Samhain. Though not nearly as strong as the Bond with Tiergan, your sacred night claiming of him as your choice has a power of its own."

"So I should try to claim Cynnwrf?" Maren swallowed and smoothed her sweating palms on her clothing.

"There is risk," Nix said. "A good amount of it. I'd only attempt to claim it if it is your last resort."

Maren pressed her wand hand against her thigh to pop her knuckles. "I will try to wait a while longer for Kynan to find the Calon y Dderwen, but already Tiergan is spreading his tyranny over his kingdom."

"He is doing the same here on Kynan's lands," Nix said. "I sense the fear in the people here, and their minds shout his name in terror."

Maren turned to face Ceri. "What has Tiergan been doing here?"

Ceri crossed her arms, her jaw working as if she was trying to control her anger. "At home, he raised taxes to an unmanageable degree. I assume he will do the same here since he has killed the old council and named an entirely new one."

Maren had heard the rumors, and Bethan had hinted at foul play, but no one had wanted to talk about it with her at the feast. Now she knew why. Tiergan had proved to be a ruler who was not afraid to kill outright for whatever reason he chose. The nobles at the feast must have been his supporters or at least those too afraid to speak against Tiergan.

Well, now was no time to become the coward she once had been. She was the Awenydd, and she was ready to fight. "Any tips for talking the most dangerous sword in history into playing along?"

Nix chuckled and flew in a tight circle, her glowing throat moving and her spirit scales shimmering beautifully. "Be yourself."

"Umm. That's not as helpful as you might think."

Nix just laughed. "Do you know I can sometimes control the world of dreams now that I am a spirit?"

"Did you live as I do before you became this?"

"I did. Long, long ago. The reason I mention the

dream skill is that I saw King Kynan in his dream once. I could possibly bring you together in one dream if that would be helpful."

Maren's mouth wouldn't work.

"You are overcome. Very well, I will see what I can do. Think on your true mate when you lie down tonight." She blinked out of view, and the well dimmed.

Swallowing, Maren tried to harness her thoughts into something manageable. She could visit Kynan in his dream? Is that what Nix had said?

"What did you learn?" Ceri asked.

"Goddess Nix says I should try to claim Cynnwrf."

"You'll die trying."

Maren shrugged, feigning nonchalance even though her head pounded with thoughts of what a sentient blade would do to her if she did something that displeased it. "That was my first thought, but if the goddess is suggesting it…"

"But won't that disturb the Bond and threaten the healing?"

"I guess not." Maren eyed the well's gently swirling waters and the sparkling light within its depths. "I wish she would have told me more, but she did say that I hold some of Kynan in my blood because my heart chose him on Samhain."

For the thousandth time, Maren mentally kicked herself for not Bonding with Kynan when he first asked. Fat lot of good holding off had been for her freedom. Now she was trapped with a vicious king who killed so many people that only some of the murders spread through gossip.

Hands on hips, Ceri tapped her fingers on her belt.

"Interesting. But even if you somehow managed to claim the sword, Tiergan would come after it and you, and most likely he would claim it again and punish you for your efforts."

"I need a plan that doesn't pull me too far physically away from Tiergan. The Bond is stretching now, with me being this far away." The link between them made her want to vomit. "I think the only reason I can be here without hurting the Bond is because of the well."

"Then maybe once you get Cynnwrf, you can come here."

"He'll use children or other innocents against me," Maren said. "He's done that twice already."

Neddy paled and looked away like he recalled a terrible memory. Mags asked him something in their language.

Ceri glanced at Neddy and Mags. "This is a war, or it will be anyway. There will be losses. We can't avoid all the horror. It will happen. The only thing we can do is try to win quickly and minimize the loss."

"Can we smuggle all the children in the castle keep through the secret passage to these lands? How can we protect the rest of the innocents who wish to leave or who are too unhealthy or old to fight?"

Neddy blew out a heavy breath. "It takes months to travel around the Dark Sea, and you have to scale the Bleak Mountains."

"The seasons are different in the Underworld, as you may have noticed," Ceri said to Maren.

"These flowers bloom continually," Maren said, pointing to the blue poppies, "and though we should be moving into winter, the air isn't nearly as cold as it is in the Upperworld."

"Every place holds its true season, varying only slightly when the seasons change. This area will never fully embrace winter or summer. It is what the old scrolls call the Spring Court. The Bleak Mountains are in the Winter Court."

"I had no idea." She knew so little of the Underworld even though she was supposedly their queen. "I have so much to learn."

Ceri patted her shoulder. "We will help you."

Neddy stuck his staff into the straps on his back. "If we all live long enough."

"Good point." Maren rubbed her hands on her dress and breathed deeply of air in this land that she was quickly growing to love.

Sniffing and taking a seat on a boulder a few steps from the well, Neddy looked at Maren expectantly. "The rebel force has gathered a store of weaponry. We started long before the trouble you've experienced with King Tiergan. We have swords, battle axes, bows. All are stored in a secret basement below the Blind Pig, a tavern in the castle town. We will smuggle those who cannot fight out of a passageway under the tavern. It has three branches. One goes under the outer bailey walls, another snakes into the wild areas beyond the farms, and the third sits under the Blind Pig's foundation. Once those folks are safely away and you give us a signal, we will arm ourselves and rise up against Tiergan's men."

"How can I signal you?" Maren asked. "I assume it

will involve a form of the bird or the wing that you have been using."

Ceri lifted a finger. "I'll see to that. I'll make a red banner with the bird symbol and hide it outside your window. We have one in our crew who is quite the climber. Your window looks out on the inner bailey, and there is always a rebel watching your room."

"I can open the window, or break it, and unfurl the banner when I'm ready."

"Exactly so," Neddy said.

"Now," Ceri started, narrowing her eyes in thought, "how are we going to get to the nobles' children?"

"Not sure. Maybe I'll tell Tiergan I need to get the people to like me by telling stories to the children and showing that I care. He won't see the need, but perhaps he'll grant the request if I pretend to respect him at his next get-together. Or, and this might be better, we can slip the children out of their rooms at night. I just need the names of those I can trust in the castle and the locations of all the children. Can you handle that for me?"

"I can," Ceri said.

"I truly don't like this idea with the children," Neddy said.

Ceri clicked her tongue and looked skyward. "I don't either, but it's a queenly proposition." She eyed Maren. "You truly do have a queen's heart."

Maren's cheeks heated. "If Tiergan notices a goodly number leaving, he's going to know something is up. We do need to have a plan for that."

"They can leave hidden in barrels and under skeins

of wool in market carts. Some can slip out through the Blind Pig's tunnels. I know a lovely gal who is quite good at getting the gate guards drunk as well. We can do it in small groups so it isn't immediately noticeable." Ceri spoke to Mags—presumably interpreting.

"I'll wait three days, then I'll attempt to get my wand, claim Cynnwrf, and meet you at the well. That way, when King Kynan and the others arrive, hopefully with Calon y Dderwen, we will be in a good position to defeat Tiergan."

Neddy scratched at a stain on his trousers' knee patch, his eyebrows lifted. "What if they don't find the crystal?"

"Then I'll go back to Tiergan for the time being and try to stay sane until the realms are fully recovered. I hope there will be a kingdom to reign after all is said and done."

Ceri's pointed ears twitched. Maren hadn't realized they did that. "Many are already starving to death under the weight of his taxes."

Neddy let out a loud breath. "And we are sending those starving children to the Bleak Mountains." He said something to Mags; Maren assumed it was another interpretation.

Mags answered and picked at her cloak.

Looking then at Maren and Neddy, Ceri said, "They may not have to travel that far. If we can gain control of the inner bailey and the keep quickly, they will be fine to hide out in the wilds beyond the farms. If they do end up traveling farther, Mags has a contact that can supply additional heavy clothing and shoes for those leaving, and there is a stash of salted meat and hard tack at the abandoned slate mine near the crossroads outside town."

"That is good news," Neddy said.

Ceri looked at Mags and Neddy. "Who can meet the children here when we find a way to gather them and lower them into the corridor?"

"I'll do that," Neddy said.

"You?" Maren could imagine more than one child running from his rough appearance. He looked more likely to knife a person than rescue them.

"What?" He dusted off his sleeve and tried to smooth his hair. "I'll tidy myself up."

"Smiling wouldn't be a bad move either," Maren said.

Neddy flicked his fingers at her.

Maren's mouth fell open. "That's the same obscene gesture we use in the Upperworld."

Ceri snorted and crossed her large arms. "I guess there are some similarities between humans and elves."

"We are united in our crass behavior."

"Indeed. I'll be in the corridor as well, Neddy. Now, let's get back to the castle before we're found out." Ceri led the way back to the magical doorway and showed Maren two other exits—non-magical ones—off the tunnel under Tiergan's home. She also gave Maren a ladder they had stashed down there, and soon Maren was back in her chamber, sliding the heavy hatch door back into place under the bed.

"Lady Maren?"

Her heart stopped and started again violently. It was a man's voice, but not one she recognized. Hands shaking terribly, she placed the floorboards back into place. The last one didn't want to sit right, its edge sticking up too far.

Whoever it was knocked loudly.

She glared at the stupid floorboard. It would have to do. On her stomach, she scrambled across the floor and crawled into bed. "Come in!"

Her panting breath was a dead giveaway that she certainly hadn't been sleeping.

An elven man with one arm and a wide smile entered with a tray. Rolls steamed beside slices of meat on a pewter plate. "I heard you were hungry." His accent twisted the words, but she understood him well enough. He set the tray beside her on the bed as he glanced over his shoulder. "I should hurry. Eat quickly." With quick fingers, he formed the beak and wing hand symbol.

A rebel. A smile tore the worried frown off her face. "Thank you." She stuffed a roll into her mouth and chewed faster than she had ever chewed in her entire life. She ate so quickly that the taste was missed entirely. The food could have been made of sand for all she cared. She hadn't eaten this much in days.

The elf's light gray eyes widened. "Eh, how about you save some for later?" He took two of the rolls, opened the nightstand drawer, and tucked them inside.

"Thank you." She chewed the last of the fowl and licked her lips. "It was delicious."

"It was plain, and you were starving."

"Thank you all the same."

"I will come again if you leave a handkerchief by the servants' stairs near the walkway to the back garden."

He was gone before she could think of anything to ask him.

She decided the uneven floorboard was even enough. As she crawled into bed, Nix's words came back to her.

Think on your true mate…

With no clue how this bit of goddess magic might work, she closed her eyes and envisioned Kynan. It wasn't difficult to recall the exact feel of his wide shoulders and the scar on his hand. Her body remembered the feel of his, the warmth, the allure of his powerful presence…

And then she was dreaming.

In a field of blue poppies under a star-bright sky, Kynan walked toward her. A hood covered his head and shadowed his face, but she knew his gait and the outline of his large form. Wind tossed the ends of his heavy woolen cloak as he looked up and pushed his hood back. His lips parted, then formed one word. *Maren.*

She ran to him and wrapped her arms around his neck, but she couldn't feel his skin or his grip on her waist. He was there, and yet he wasn't.

His voice echoed as if through deep water even though his face was inches from hers. "Maren? Is that you?"

He looked just as he always did, a scowl bunching his eyebrows and a ferocious glint in his black eyes. They glowed ruby red for a moment, then dimmed again.

"It is. The goddess sewed our dreams together."

Those weren't the right words for it, but it felt close enough to the truth.

"Are you well enough?" He pressed his lips against her forehead, but only the faintest warmth touched her there. She could almost feel the heat of his stomach against her chest, but it was subtle, frustratingly so.

"I am, considering the situation."

He tapped his pointed ear. "I can't hear you."

"At all?"

Shaking his head, he curled his lip as if he too was frustrated. She dragged a hand through his hair, and a growl emanated from his chest. He thrust his hands over her thighs and lifted her roughly, burying his face in her neck. His chest expanded against hers as the distant sound of his inhalation echoed in her ears. Then he threw back his head and shouted, the tendons and veins in his neck standing out as his roar of anger reverberated through her, only a fraction of its vibration making its way into her body.

She gripped the sides of his face, her flesh longing to feel his, and she forced him to look into her eyes again. Using her witch's will, she urged him to hear her words.

"I will take the sword from Tiergan. Somehow. I will do it."

He smiled and kissed her quickly, his fingers accomplishing only a ghost of a grip. "I know you will, my amazing mate. You are the most capable person I've ever met."

She blinked, realizing he had heard her words.

The dream shattered, and Maren sat up in bed, sweat beading on her upper lip. She slammed down a fist and exhaled roughly. She should have told him more. Asked him at least one question. That had been a true connection, not merely a dream. Nix had worked the impossible, and she had all but wasted the opportunity in her desperation to feel Kynan's skin on hers. She dropped her head, covering her face with her hands. Rubbing her cheeks and forehead, she tried to wake up fully. The way he'd shouted, wrath pouring from him in waves of heat she could only partially feel...

He'd called her capable. Some women might not have found that endearing, but she did. It thrilled her that he trusted her to do what had to be done. His faith in her set fire to her blood and renewed her courage like she'd downed a potion from Hafwen.

"Kynan." His name dropped like a stone in the silence of the room. Golden light spilled from the windows and painted the floor. Morning had come, and she had work to do. She swung her legs out of bed, stood, and set a fist against her heart. "I will see this through, Kynan," she whispered. "We will be together again. I refuse to let him win."

CHAPTER 18
KYNAN

Kynan held tight to the side of the ship as they spun slowly around the whirlpool. How were they going to live through this?

Filip looked at Kynan, Aury at his side. "Should we lash ourselves to the masts?"

"I suppose. Is there anything you feel you could do to ease our...to help us survive this, Aurora?"

"Aury. And no. This is madness." She grinned like a demon from the old stories.

"I'm sorry, Maren," Kynan whispered. "You might be on your own after today. I hope you kill Tiergan with your beautiful, calloused bare hands."

Rhianne joined him. "That was lovely." She'd been chatting with Hafwen about witch things. "Do you talk to Maren like that often?"

"We are about to die. I'll fill you in if we in fact don't."

"Grouchy, isn't he?" Aury said. "Dorin, you should

spend your last moments with Kynan. I think you two are soulmates."

"Soulmates? What are you..." Kynan waved his own question away before he could finish. Madness. All of it. All of them.

Brielle was laughing with Rhianne now, and Dorin was muttering something in another language—the Balaur tongue.

"Ivar!" Ivar had been circling the ship for over an hour by Kynan's measuring. "Come down. You might need your strength soon." Maybe he could at least fly to land and live to see another day.

Ivar did as requested and landed lightly on Kynan's shoulder. The wyvern communicated the vague sense of curiosity and passed on the idea that there was magic inside the whirlpool.

"What kind of magic?" Kynan smoothed a hand down Ivar's snout. The warmth of his familiar soothed his nerves a fraction. A sense of discovery and bright colors moved into Kynan's mind. But what did Ivar mean by that? "Can you try to explain in my words?"

Ivar didn't communicate with words usually, but sometimes one or two would find their way into Kynan's mind.

Possibility. Sweet.

Teeth of the gods, what did that mean? Maybe Ivar needed sleep. He'd lost his mind along with everyone else.

Werian leapt onto the railing near the helm. The fae had remarkable balance. No wonder he made a fine sailor. "Grab something sturdy or tie yourself down, folks! It's about to get interesting!"

Ivar and Kynan traded a disgruntled snort.

"My sentiments exactly," Dorin said as he walked past, rope in hand.

Once Kynan ensured that every soul was either lashed down or had a nice hold on a stationary ship part, he knotted a rope around his wrist and attached the other end to a bronze hitch where they sometimes tied down certain lines. Hafwen was arranged likewise beside him, and Ivar perched on his shoulder.

"You've been awfully quiet, Lady Hafwen," Kynan said.

"My king, I am nervous."

His stomach turned. "Please don't say that. I'm leaning on your confidence in your intuition."

She grimaced and shrugged as she looked out over the choppy waves. "Well, we will see if I was right very soon now."

The ship listed and turned a slow circle, and Kynan groaned. The eye of the whirlpool was as black as Osian's hooves, the water around it a dark gray-green. A flash of silver showed at the eye.

"Did you see that?" He pointed toward the spot in the center.

"I didn't. What was it?"

"Probably my mind losing its grip on reality."

"No, really. What did you see, my king?"

"A light maybe? It looked silver in the center there for a moment. It's gone now."

The water roared, and cold mist wet Kynan's face

and hair as he tried to stay focused on the spot where he'd seen the light.

"Hold on!" Werian's voice carried magically over the din of the creaking ship and the growling sea.

The whirlpool sucked them in quickly, and then the world blurred and went sideways. The weight of Ivar left Kynan's shoulder, and he tried to look up and see where the wyvern flew. Water spray made it difficult to see, though Kynan wiped his face over and over. Falling against the side of the ship, he slipped to the decking. He slid forward and banged his head and knee on a rolling barrel that had come unlashed. Shouts went up from Dorin and Brielle.

Kynan twisted and got to his feet as a wave crashed across the deck, leaving a school of flapping black fish. He glimpsed Ivar for a moment before the ship leaned harshly, and Ivar shrieked. Another wave punched the deck, and Ivar disappeared from sight.

"Hafwen!" Kynan's throat was raw from the salt water. "Ivar!"

"I'm here!" Hafwen remained tied to the ship. She was soaked but alive.

Branches of silver and green cracked the sky in two, and Kynan's two hearts shivered in his chest. He stood and shouted for Ivar as the sea crawled right over the side and swamped the entire deck. The world went dark.

Silver light exploded across the sky, and the ship seemed to shift upward. The water on deck drained away, and Kynan hurried to the side to look. "Ivar!"

The ship lurched hard, and then the waters grew calm. The whirlpool was behind them.

Werian untied himself and Rhianne. "I do not understand what just happened." He fisted his hand as if he could squeeze the truth from the air.

"Does anyone see Ivar?" Kynan's stomach turned as he searched the flinty sky. He would know if Ivar died, wouldn't he? They were bonded. But he'd only ever had one familiar, so he didn't know for certain.

Dorin accepted an offered wine skin from one of the crew, drank two long swallows, then stretched his wings wide. "I'll fly and take a look around."

Brielle grabbed him and kissed him soundly, and Dorin's arm snaked around her waist. They broke apart, and Dorin launched into the sky as the crew began setting the sails to continue on.

Hafwen threw off the rope that had been holding her to the ship, then set a hand on Kynan's shoulder. "I'm glad to see you alive. I thought that last wave had taken you."

"Would I feel it if my familiar died?"

Hafwen's gaze slid to the sea's glassy surface. "I don't know."

Werian was suddenly beside Kynan, though Kynan hadn't noticed the fae approaching. "We have reached the first possible site of the Calon y Dderwen."

Kynan shut his eyes and said a silent prayer to the Source that Ivar was safe somehow, somewhere, then he opened his eyes. "Time to dive."

· · ·

Kynan spun shadows around himself as well as Rhianne, Werian, Filip, and Aury as they all swam toward the bottom of the Dark Sea.

The water was murky and dark, and if the afanc returned, they'd be in his great belly before they knew what was happening. The shadows allowed Aury room to work her water spells, and the cages of magic kept a good pocket of air around each one of them so they could all breathe.

Pale rocks jutted from the bottom of the sea, their jagged surfaces lit by the spelled light coming from Rhianne's wand. The light bounced around as Rhianne swam alongside them, the shadows blocking the illumination partially as well. As her lips moved in a spell, bubbles holding the sounds of her words rose from her shadowed cage. They'd decided to try a seeking spell of some sort, and Kynan prayed it would work.

So far, there was nothing but rocks and dark sand stretching into the dim.

They stopped swimming, and Kynan wove his magic carefully to keep them hovering over the sand. Rhianne whispered her spell again. A spark flew from her wand and shot into the water. Everyone turned to watch the tiny speck of light zip through the darkness. The water chilled Kynan's body, and he shivered, both the cold and the use of such powerful magic pulling energy from his body.

The spark spun back to Rhianne, then her wand arm extended roughly as if the spark were tugging her onward. She looked to Werian with wide eyes and jerked her head as if to say *let's go*. Kynan worked the shadow magic as they swam in the direction Rhianne and her spark led. The bones of a long-forgotten ship spread out below their kicking feet—broken planks of petrified wood, the remains of a hull, and glimmering coins like eyes staring into nothingness.

Werian was looking behind them, most likely watching their backs for the afanc.

The surface far, far above was a flickering shade of greenish gray. How far could Kynan take them with his power before his energy gave out? Would they be able to get back to the surface and the ship? Was Dorin able to see their shapes under the water from where he flew just above the waves?

Kynan's hearts quaked. Maren was in the hands of the enemy. Ivar was missing. Shaking off panic, he focused more power into his magic, and his shadows grew sharp as blades.

A school of fish with spiked fins and glowing fangs swam between the group and the surface. They turned toward Rhianne, perhaps thinking humans might serve as food. Aury pushed them gently away with a curling wave of water lit with a silvery glow.

The spark they were following suddenly went dark, and Kynan's hearts fell. Did that mean the crystal wasn't here, or had Rhianne's spell fizzled?

Rhianne shook her head and pointed toward the surface.

He'd have to wait on an answer. Drawing his shadows more tightly around the group, he pushed out and drove them upward. The water seeped through his magical barrier, and he coughed as they broke through the waves and into the bracing air.

Gasping, he turned to see everyone's heads bobbing. "I'm glad to see everyone made it. Rhianne, did your spell falter, or is the crystal not nearby?"

"I don't think it's here. Even though my spell struggles down here in the Underworld, I think it was working."

Aury smoothed her hair away from her face. "What caused the spell to believe it was traveling toward the crystal at first if it's not here?"

Signaling the ship with a wave, Filip said, "Perhaps it's in that direction." He dropped back under the water and came up with a fish in hand.

"Nicely done," Werian said. "Can that fish tell us where the Calon y Dderwen is?"

"No, but it'll make a fine addition to lunch." Filip shoved the fish into the straps across his chest and began to swim toward the ship.

Kynan also swam, not wanting to use more magic. He'd use a portion to dry them off when they were back onboard, but he needed to save every bit he could for a possible afanc attack and for seeking the crystal. The cold water made swimming incredibly difficult, and by the time they reached the plank that the crew was using to raise them from the water and back up onto the ship, his hands and feet were numb.

Hafwen whispered a spell over those who had gone out searching, and a quick wind dried their clothing and hair. She then handed Kynan a crockery mug of something hot.

"Thank you for the drink and the drying." The heat sifted from the mug into his fingers, and he took a cinnamon-tasting sip. "What is this?"

Brielle tucked a strand of her red hair behind her human ear and looked at him sadly. "Maren's favorite tea. I found the ingredients in the galley, and this fellow," she said, jabbing a thumb toward one of the crew, "helped me brew."

"You look so much like a good friend of mine," Filip said to the crewman.

He did indeed have the same look as Sir Costel, a knight in Filip's retinue. The elven warrior and scholar had remained at Calon Dywyll with Aeron, Kynan's best military mind.

He wondered how Ninian, Nia, Saffir, Eefa, Deron, and the rest were holding up there. Certainly, there would be trouble as Tiergan took hold of his assumed role. He would demand higher taxes and perhaps draft young ones into his fighting force.

"What did that mug do to you?" Hafwen eyed his white-knuckled grip on the steaming tea.

He made himself relax. "I wish I had put more safety precautions into place at home. I can imagine Tiergan has his hands full with the council at the moment, but..."

Hafwen nodded and took a deep breath as she looked out over the ocean. Aury was at the helm giving everyone the details of what had happened under the water.

"Maybe," Hafwen said, "I can ask the water sprites to check on everyone back home."

"They can travel from this body of water to another? I've never seen them in our well or rivers. I thought perhaps they could only live in this sea due to the salt content."

"I have no idea, but it's worth an ask."

"Thank you. I'd like to know if Aeron is having any challenges."

"But what will you do if he is?"

Kynan gazed at the group around Magelord Aury. Most faces were set with determination and courage. "You're right. Unless the sprites can rally help for our lands, there is no point in suffering through terrible knowledge. But if the news is good, it might hearten the crew."

"It would hearten you as well, and that is worth it." Hafwen set a hand on his forearm and gave him an encouraging smile. Her golden eye shifted slightly, and he wondered for the thousandth time if that eye could see more than her elven one. "I'll take care of it."

He lifted his arm and kissed her knuckles chastely. "Thanks, my friend. I hate that you are risking your life here, but I am quite glad to have you at my side."

She bowed her head and turned to go, leaving Kynan with tumultuous thoughts filled with blood and vicious, unrelenting revenge against those who might dare to threaten his people.

But that night after a hearty meal and a game of dice with Dorin, Kynan's anger slipped away, and he dreamed of Maren.

He woke, groggy and mad as a caged bull. Tearing out of his hammock below decks, he grabbed his tunic from the nail where he hung it nightly. He tugged it over his head and bent to take up his weapons belt. A crewman shuffled past in the dim light of near dawn, and Kynan all but growled at the sailor instead of greeting him. The sailor bowed and wisely hurried away. Kynan stormed to the upper deck and looked out over port side, his fingers digging into the wood and his shadows licking the air around his face and shoulders dangerously.

"My king." Hafwen approached slowly. "What has happened?"

He forced himself to take a breath and tried to settle his anger so he could speak to her like an elven lord instead of a wild beast. His shadows flared out once, and the spark of power in the crown that would be with him until he died heated his brow momentarily.

"I dreamed of Maren."

Hafwen simply watched the sea. He tried to take in a measure of her patient aura, as she would call it, but his shadows whipped out in a high arc above his head as he fought for control.

Another breath. He swallowed. "It was no ordinary dream. This was a magic due to, well, I know not, but it was magic. I could hold her but not feel her." He inhaled sharply as the desire to tear the ship apart whipped through him. "At first, I couldn't hear her, but then she said something at the end of the dream and I heard her perfectly."

As Hafwen turned, her golden eye caught the morning light. "What did she say?"

"That she will take Cynnwrf."

"But—"

"I know. It would mean her death if she tries."

"Surely she knows that. She is clever. I would bet there is a plan in place."

Kynan's shadows whirled and finally eased their way back into his body, settling into a tentative peace. "Of course. She is the Awenydd. I trust her judgment."

"As do I. But I can't lie. I fear for her."

His magic unspooled again, and he pulled the power back. "I'm going to rip Tiergan limb from limb and set the pieces at her feet."

"She might want that job."

Kynan chuckled darkly. "And I will provide her that opportunity with great joy."

Hafwen set a careful hand on his forearm. "It's good to know your powers remain strong." Her gaze flitted to the space above his head where his shadow crown flickered. "I am proud to be at your side, my king." She bowed her head, and he put his hand over hers.

"I am grateful for you, Lady Hafwen. Always."

She left him there to stare into the Dark Sea. Tonight, he would try to dream of Maren again, and this time, he would bend that magic to suit them fully.

Shoving her tangled mess of fears aside, Maren crept out of her chamber as her guards slept on in their poisoned state. The herbs Ceri had mixed into their watered wine wouldn't cause permanent damage. They'd simply sleep for a few more hours. But Maren a little bit wished it would turn their minds to mush. Dumb guards would have been nice.

In her wool-stockinged feet, she padded down the corridor and up the servants' winding stairs. The rebel spy who had brought her a tray of food not so long ago was waiting right where they had planned.

"Quick," the rebel said in strongly accented common tongue.

It was madness to sneak into Tiergan's office to retrieve her wand, but it had to be done to secure tomorrow night's mission—to slip all the nobles' children out of the castle and beyond Tiergan's reach.

Ceri and the other rebels inside the castle had left notes with each noble family, telling them that their children were safe, but that if they spoke a word about the children missing, they would never see them again. It was a terrible thing to do, but the children truly were safer away from here. If worse came to worst during the children's escape, Maren would do something to restrain Tiergan and his men.

"I wish you were here, Goddess Nix," she whispered to the air. "I'd love to see you set his hair on fire at the least. I realize he and I are Bonded and that might hurt me a little, but it would be thoroughly worth it." Besides, she felt only pure hatred toward him, so the Bond wouldn't hurt her through him too badly—if the scrolls she'd read about it were accurate.

Please let them be right.

She wasn't quite ready to think about what would happen in the future if she could feel serious wounds inflicted on him.

Inside his office, she glared at the desk where he now kept her wand. The desk was a beast of a creation with bronze handles, knobs galore, and enough dark wood to build a seaworthy ship.

Of course this was his desk. "Overkill, Tiergan. Compensating for something, are you?"

Ceri had found out where he had hidden the wand. The herbalist was proving to be a cracking good rebel leader. As the best healer, she had relationships with everyone in the castle and in town. She knew all the gossip. Loads of folks were indebted to her for saving loved ones, so when she sought information on how to locate every noble's child for the escape plan, she had the answers straightaway.

The night air blew in from the small sky window, and the salt of the Dark Sea touched Maren's nose.

Kynan was out there right now with Brielle and the rest.

Stay alive, she whispered to them in her mind, knowing it was foolish.

Were they on the right track for finding the crystal, or were they already dead at the bottom of the sea? She swallowed and tried to calm her frantic heart. They were all ridiculously capable. Surely they'd figure out how to survive. How long would they try to find the Calon y Dderwen? Would Brielle and all the Upperworlders find a way to return to their kingdoms? She blew out a breath. Now wasn't the time to dredge up all the fears that were hiding inside her mind. She had to get her wand and get out of here as quickly as possible.

The worst part of the beastly desk was, of course, the lock.

After giving her knuckles a good popping, she removed the lock picking kit—which she'd bought off a servant—out of the small velvet bag tied to her belt, and with another silent prayer, she went to work.

Her hands were slick with nervous sweat, so turning and fiddling with the metal pin and loop was far more difficult than it had been when she'd used such a kit long ago on the streets near her home. A click sounded, and she held her breath. She curled her fingers around the handle to open the front, which would then allow her access to the ten smaller drawers. She pulled. Then looked skyward. Still locked.

Letting out a whispered string of curses, she tried again. Again. Again.

"Wand, don't you want to help me out here? You're my sidekick still, right? You haven't decided you like the villain in this scenario, have you?" As if the wand could communicate... She was losing her mind, but maybe there was a way to use her magic here. She was the Awenydd, and she'd done things she would have bet in full against before her evolution to this person she was now.

Closing her eyes, she mentally imagined Tiergan's office empty of everything except the lock and the wand. All else went white in her mind. Using only feel to work, she slid the pin and loop back into the lock while she willed the wand's power to reach toward the lock and her tools. She envisioned magic sifting from her fingers through the tools then swirling toward the wand in a stream of power. The magic appeared in her mind's eye, and she gasped. It was so clear. So real. The unspoken spell glittered gold, purple, and a sunset red, but it began to fade.

Forcing her thoughts to focus on her request from the wand and from her magic, she poured every bit of her desire into the lock. The magic in her mind glowed bright, flashing as the scent of sun-warmed acorns and wet leaves rose and chills spread over her forearms. Magic heated her palms, chest, and her forehead. Her temples pounded once painfully.

The lock clicked loudly.

She blinked her eyes, and, grinning like a fiend, she yanked the desk open.

A long, thin drawer in the middle of the desk's back wall hummed.

"Hello, lovely." She slid the drawer open and gazed at her wand.

The moment it was in her hand, she stood straighter and breathed easier. She wouldn't risk using the wand for fear of Tiergan somehow sensing the magical weapon, but she was very glad to have the wand just in case.

Moving carefully, she closed up the desk. She didn't know where the key was, so she couldn't lock it back up again, not without more magic, and really she wanted to leave five minutes ago. Hurrying out of the office, she headed for her chamber, where hopefully her guards would still be snoring peacefully.

Was she truly mad trying to accomplish this feat?

Children were absolutely everywhere in her chamber. One enterprising young lad climbed the curtains in an effort to grab the disgruntled cat that had somehow been thrown into this mix. Another child and her friend ran circles around Ceri, their braids a blur. Three boys wrestled on the ground, one rolling under the bed. Heart stopping, Maren snatched the back of his tunic and pulled him upright before he could discover the secret hatch through which they would all shortly be escaping Tiergan's castle.

First, she had to calm them down and get them to listen to her.

"All right, you lot." She tried not to worry that some of them might not speak the common tongue. They were nobles' children, after all, and had more tutors than good sense most likely. "Sit on your bums, and we'll have a story."

"I hate stories!" Curtain climber snagged the cat's tail. The cat yowled and scratched his cheek, drawing a line of blood. The boy fell from the curtain, and Ceri caught him.

"Serves you right," Ceri said before plopping the miscreant onto the floor where a few had actually deigned to follow Maren's directions.

It had been a massive task secreting the nobles' children from their nannies one at a time in the middle of the night. The whole story-time idea had seemed foolish in the light of day. Tiergan would have known she was up to something, so Maren and the rebels decided to quickly snatch them while the castle was sleeping and leave vague notes for their parents. They hadn't managed to get one older boy from where he slept between two large hounds, but other than that, the mission had been accomplished.

Maren stood on the bed and extended her arms. "This is a tale of blood and monsters."

The room went quiet, and someone began to cry.

"It'll be all right. It's just a story."

One of the girls who had been running around Ceri smacked the crying child. "Shut it." She kept on in their language, waving her arms like she was berating him. It certainly didn't stop the weeping.

"Ceri? Maybe take him into the bath chamber and have a sweeter story time?"

Ceri nodded and scooped him up. Once she'd disappeared behind the bath chamber door, Maren began a tale that she was completely making up on the spot. As she went on, she realized she was telling the story of Dorin and Brielle but with some dramatic twists and fill-ins for the spots she didn't know.

"And the dragon prince ate her?" Curtain boy grinned.

Maren snorted. "No, but it was a close thing." She wiggled her eyebrows. The story went on until Brielle and Dorin were dancing at Balaur Castle and all was happy ever after. "Now, would you like to meet the princess?"

A tall girl raised her hand. "I want to meet the dragon prince!"

Maren jumped off the bed and knelt on the floor. "Under this bed is a secret passage to meet them. Will you go with me if I promise to give you a treat and Herbalist Ceri keeps us safe?"

Ceri must have heard her because she opened the bath chamber door, weeping boy in hand. She smiled at the group, spoke a few sentences in their language, and handed the boy off to the tall girl. Maren crawled under the bed to begin removing the boards. She'd practiced a few times, so she was faster at the chore now. Ceri joined her, and together they had the hatch open fairly quickly. The rope ladder they'd set up remained nailed to a board Ceri had secured just under the opening's far side.

Then they began the arduous task of getting twenty-three children down the ladder without having anyone scream or fall and break a leg. The guards outside the door were planted rebels, but if Tiergan or any of his loyal staff heard, this would end horribly. Maren was sweating like a drunken rich man in a den of thieves.

It was a very long hour.

"That's the last of them," she called down to Ceri as curtain boy took his leave. She shifted on the floor of her chamber and squinted through the secret hatch into the dim passageway below.

The soft voice of Mags and the gritty mumble of Neddy echoed over the whispering of the children. They had gone quieter, a sure sign they were frightened.

Ceri looked up from the bottom of the rope ladder, her wide cheeks pale. "I nearly forgot..." She rummaged in the pocket of her belted dress, then held up some cloth. "This will fit under your clothing and hold your wand safe."

Maren accepted the cloth with a thanks and proceeded to unfold it. The homespun linen was a sheath of sorts set with a leather tie that could fit around her arm under her sleeve or even around her thigh. She could imagine her wand hidden under her dress. "Thank you, Ceri. This is perfect. I truly appreciate it."

"Of course, Awenydd." Ceri peered up at Maren again and gave a small wave. "We have it from here. I'll try to send word, but it might prove difficult."

Maren nodded, placing the new wand sheath down

the front of her dress. Then she began the hard work of closing up and hiding the hatch door.

Lifting the final board, she sneezed.

The board slid from her grip and dragged across her knee. Blood poured from the jagged cut. Growling in frustration and pain, she maneuvered out from under the bed and hurried to the bath chamber.

What could she use to tie this cut up so she didn't cover the entire chamber in blood? For the thousandth time in her life, she wished she could use magic to heal, but only fae had that ability, and she didn't have even the slightest bit of fae blood. If she didn't get this fixed up, there would be no end of questions—especially if a load of blood was soaking a mysterious spot under her bed.

She cursed and searched the cabinet by the tub, but only found large bathing sheets. She could tear one, but that too would make Bethan ask too many questions. Well, she would have to clean up the blood she was dripping everywhere anyway. And her dress was ruined. A slender stain of blood spread down her skirts all the way to the hem, and her stockings were destroyed as well.

"Fat lot of good you did for my knee," she muttered at them as she pulled them free.

She removed the dress and shift, straining about ten muscles as she worked the laces in the back herself, and then she ripped off a strip of the skirts and knotted it around her cut knee. She hissed in pain and set to wiping up the blood dripped all through the chamber as best she could with her dress. Once that was done, she threw the dress and the stockings into the fireplace and watched them burn. Satisfied that evidence was as good as gone, she made for the armoire and prayed there would be clothing enough for her in there. If not, she'd be stark naked when Tiergan called for her in the morning. And that was definitely not a strategy she was willing to use.

The water appeared quiet, with no reports of thorny kelp or otherwise on the horizon. Brielle, Rhianne, and Aury stood with Hafwen, who was calling up the water sprites, her spell's light bouncing off the waves. Dorin circled overhead in his half-dragon, half-elf form, his green wings catching the day's final glow. With his golden hair, the dragon prince looked almost as though he could be related to Maren. Kynan knew they were not kin; she was human and he was a Balaur elf. Perhaps it was only love making him see Maren in everyone and everything. His chest ached.

"Be strong, Awenydd," he whispered. "We will come for you."

The water sprites appeared before Hafwen, their silvery bodies of liquid held aloft on foamy wings. Hafwen's mouth moved quickly as she spoke to them, requesting what he'd spoken to her about. Hopefully, the sprites had the capability to move within other bodies of water and could glean information about the status at home.

A memory of Maren in the chamber he'd chosen for her washed through his mind. In his head, he saw her seated at the desk penning letters. In his imagination, he walked up to her, lifted her, then sat with her on his lap. He told her a joke, and she laughed in that delightfully raspy way she had. He nuzzled his way through her thick golden hair to her neck, where he planted soft kisses. She pinched his arm gently and demanded he answer a question about his language. None of that had happened, of course. But it might if they lived through this and broke her free from Tiergan.

He wished she could magically feel the power in his promise. The longing to comfort her, the pain of being held apart from her... Shadow magic flickering wildly around him, he fisted his hands tightly and pressed them into the ship's side. The sea's wind cooled his flushed cheeks.

If Tiergan so much as touched her...

Werian and Rhianne burst from belowdecks holding mugs and singing.

"It's a damn tough life full of toil and strife,
We sailor folk undergo,
And we don't give a damn when the gale is done,
How hard the winds do blow,
We're homeward bound from the Dragon Sound,
With a good ship taut and free,
And we don't give a damn when we drink our rum,
With the girls of Old Talaynee!" Rhianne had changed the word girls to boys and tripped Werian as

she did so. He laughed, and they started back at the beginning.

With one more round of singing, the crew caught on to the words and joined in. Soon the entire ship was awash with happy singing, several different accents blending into one sound. He had to smile. It was good to see his people losing their prejudice against Upperworlders as he finally had. They needed to work as a cohesive unit to complete this mission. More camaraderie meant a better chance of success in finding the crystal and of survival for them all.

And although he couldn't bring himself to sing, he knew this hour could be their last on this dangerous sea. Perhaps Maren's chosen kin weren't simply mad. Perhaps it was a wise way to live—enjoying life while one had the chance.

Werian and Rhianne hooked arms and began a reel of sorts, dragging Dorin, who had just landed on deck, and Brielle into the dancing. Most of the crew began lifting their feet in time with the singing. Kynan took a seat on a sack of what might have been grain and watched, wishing he had the hearts to join in as Filip and Aury did.

After the dancing, Dorin and Filip decided to spar, and Rhianne began telling ribald jokes that had the crew in fits. She seemed rather drunk and kept mentioning goats...

Kynan shook his head and let them celebrate without his mood interfering.

"Take a turn, Kynan!" Filip waved at him as Dorin took him down. They rolled laughing and punching one another with more vigor than one normally saw in casual sparring matches. But at least they seemed to be enjoying themselves.

It made Kynan wish he'd had a brother. "Not tonight, but thank you for the invitation." He was still incredibly fatigued from the shadow magic he'd used while seeking the crystal underwater.

Peering into the night sky, he mentally called for Ivar.

Please know that I am watching for you, friend.

If he lost Ivar, it would be very difficult indeed to keep on. But he refused to give up. Ivar was a powerful wyvern, and he'd been through scrapes before.

Stay strong like our Lady Maren. One day, we will be together as a family.

That night, Kynan once more dreamed of Maren.

The dream began just as the other had, with a white space like the Between, even though this place was warm and had no spirits. It was just him and her.

He stood and watched her walk to him, her eyes narrowing and her lips perking into a grin. She wore a loose shift, most likely what she had worn to bed. No bruises or dirt marred her body or clothing. But was that only because this was a dream?

When she reached him, he tried to remember what he had wanted to tell her, information that was key to victory against Tiergan. But nothing would come to mind. This place pulled all the practicality out of him and left only raw emotion. He swept her into his arms, and this time he could feel her, as if this were happening outside of a dream.

"Maren." His lips found her earlobe, and he nipped the soft flesh. His voice was clear now, not echoing and distant as it had been in the first dream they'd shared.

She drew his face to hers, and she kissed him. The tip of her tongue dragged over his top lip as she pulled away slightly. Desire lashed through his body, and he held her more tightly.

"I have my wand now," she said. "The rebels helped me steal it back from Tiergan." Her gaze traveled from his eyes to his mouth then higher to look at his crown. She seemed to be struggling to keep her thoughts clear and purposeful too.

"Good. Light Tiergan's world on fire, my vicious queen."

His hands encircled her small waist. The feel of her body flush against his made his shadows expand into great black wings that sheltered them from the hazy light. Her golden hair draped down her back to dust his fingers.

"Knowing you are working your way to me keeps me going," she said her gaze finding his. A blend of stubborn courage and rage flickered through her features.

His shadows flared as anger whipped through his blood. "If I succeed in this quest, I will set Tiergan at your feet and savor his pain as you do as you see fit. Be rage incarnate. Give mercy. It will be your choice, and I will defend it with every ounce of magic in my shadow elf heart."

She gripped his shoulders and set her head against his chest. He put a hand over her cheek and ear, doing his best to comfort her. When she lifted her head, he drew a slow line across her jaw with his nose. He breathed her in, basking in her sweet scent. Desire gathered in him, and he drew her to the ground. Ferns the colors of pearls and ivory moss blanketed this dream space, and the fresh scent of the plant life rose into the air as he lowered himself on top of her.

And the dream faded away, leaving him cold.

In his hammock below decks, he squeezed his eyes shut. Had she truly been there in his dream? Had she felt what he had?

They should have spoken of strategy, but it had been impossible there in that space. It was as if nothing but love demonstrated through their bodies was permitted. He had heard tell of the goddess Nix and her admiration of lovers, and this magic would certainly fit. Catching his breath, he did his best to fall right back into that dream. Sadly, a black sleep came over him that was certainly restful but not nearly as enjoyable.

THE NEXT EVENING, KYNAN MET WITH WERIAN AND Rhianne in the captain's quarters.

Ivar was still missing. Concentrating on the task at hand was growing more and more difficult with every passing hour.

The flickering lantern hanging above the table cast yellow light over Werian's purple and black hair and ebony horns as the fae scratched his chin and frowned at Hafwen's map. He smelled like rum. Where had he found rum? Kynan shook his head. Only Dorin seemed to understand the irritation the fae set under his skin. Werian was just so lackadaisical about all things unless death was staring him directly in the face, sword tip at the throat.

Last night, he had tied a blindfold around Dorin's face while he slept so when the dragon prince awoke, he panicked for a moment before realizing the prank. Kynan smiled thinking of how Dorin had used a bit of dragonfire to scorch Werian's boots in revenge.

Apparently oblivious or uncaring about his alcoholic odor, Werian focused on the map. He set one hand on the stone holding the nearest corner and then pointed at the cloud-like sketches Hafwen had drawn in the southeast region of the sea.

"I can't remember what you said about this bunch of fun we're headed into."

Kynan glanced at the water's surface. There was a strange buzz to the air here. "I didn't say much, but Hafwen only found scant details in the scrolls. All of them mentioned a disturbance of sorts. An area with a mysterious magical element."

Werian scratched his chin. "Did the scrolls have black *X*s over the area? In my experience with sea maps, that can mean here lies what everyone is searching for."

"No, sadly. But there were multiple vague warnings."

"Why must the ancients keep their secrets?" Rhianne said, scowling at the pile of scrolls Hafwen had set on the desk near the one long leaded window at the end of the room. "Perhaps I can make them talk for us?"

Werian rubbed his hands together and grinned. "Ooh, yes. Do some fancy magic, my witchy woman."

She winked at him, unsheathed her wand, and began speaking very quickly and quietly into the air. A whiff of perfumed air hit Kynan's nose—a scent like roses—then a slim thread of bright red light formed a glowing knot over the scrolls on the desk. The thread burst into miniature swirling fog banks, still blood red as they dropped low over the scrolls and spread out.

Kynan crossed his arms. He hoped she wouldn't set the place on fire. Despite her being the wife of the slightly mad fae prince, she did have a good head on her shoulders. A very practical sort.

The magic slithered over the scrolls, then shot back into the air and reformed the complicated knot of light. A whispering filled the cabin, voices bouncing off the walls.

"What language is that?" Werian lifted his horned head to look at the last of the knot untangling above the scrolls.

Kynan could understand it. Though his tutors had rebuked him for his quick temper and lack of patience in learning, he had passed his examinations easily. "It's Elder Shadowtongue, the language of the First Age."

The words came at him so quickly that it was difficult to pull them apart to discern complete thoughts and sentences. After all, Elder Shadowtongue didn't use phrasing like the version of the language they spoke in the Underworld today.

He shut his eyes to focus. "One voice speaks of a storm made of scale and fire. Another...it's difficult to pick them apart."

"Let me try this," Rhianne said, her voice even and

calm. A sound like a fire starting had Kynan opening his eyes.

The spell's flickering light shuddered, a shot of deep purple threaded through the blood-red magic, and the voices moved to separate spots in the room. Kynan and Werian twisted toward a very loud female voice speaking near the door.

"What's she saying?" Werian asked, all traces of arrogance having fled from his features.

Kynan appreciated his curiosity and how he didn't pretend to understand the language. Some men never knew when to admit their ignorance. Kynan listened to the voice near the door, the words clearer but still in an archaic language. "She mentions an experience of watching a second ship sail into a chaotic...I'm not sure about that word...a chaotic something of wings? That can't be right."

Werian winced and leaned against the map table. "Scales. Fire. Wings. The ancients might not have a name for what their fellow saw, but if you ask me, we're about to sail into a thunder of dragons."

Cold frosted Kynan's spine. He gripped his sword's pommel, missing the power of Cynnwrf. "Source save us."

Rhianne moved her wand up and down, and the magic spun back into its tip. The voices went silent. "Perhaps Dorin will have some ideas. He could maybe shift into his full dragon form and serve as a deterrent to keep them away from us as we sail toward the next place the crystal was spotted, or he might be able to apply some form of diplomacy on our behalf."

Werian unhitched himself from the map table. "Smart. I'll call him down here. Is that in line with what you're thinking, Kynan?"

Kynan bowed his head. "Yes, thank you." He had to admit that perhaps the fae prince was growing on him. Possibly, he would be tolerable if he could simply act his age.

A few moments later, Werian returned with Dorin, Filip, Brielle, and Aurora—Aury—in tow.

"What I want to know is why we can't simply chart a course around this storm of dragons," Dorin said as he crossed the cabin and went to the window.

Brielle had been trailing him, but her gaze was drawn to the scrolls. She bent to study them, holding the fallen strands of her hair away from her face. "These are amazing." She touched one corner and gasped. "This is the Lapis mark!"

Werian glanced at her. "As in Lapis Dragon?"

"Please tell me what in the name of the gods you two are going on about." Kynan's tone was sharper than he'd intended.

Filip spun his axe in a tight circle above his head, his moves graceful and exact. "During the time of the gods and goddesses, the Upperworld held two dragon clans. Lapis and Jade. The Lapis were known for their studies and strategy."

Aury was eating a dark apple she must have snatched from the galley. Her gaze went to Filip's back, a pleased gleam in her eyes. "The Jade were praised for their ferocity in battle and their ruthlessness." She grinned with one side of her mouth.

Filip smiled and angled himself toward Aury. "I can see which clan you would've fought beside."

Aury nodded, the look of war in her light eyes. Filip grasped her roughly and kissed her.

Rhianne held up the scroll with the Lapis mark so that the lantern's light glowed over its age-darkened surface. She squinted and gently brushed her finger over a circle of blue ink, then she brought it to Kynan to look. The marking was made up of two dragon wings and an eye in the center.

Werian sidled in close and raised an eyebrow at Brielle, who was completely enraptured with the scroll. "You're stroking that mark like it's Dorin's—"

Quick as a snake, Brielle elbowed him in the stomach, stopping his words and eliciting a proud nod from Dorin, who had turned away from the window.

"She'll teach you manners, fae," Dorin said, his words touched with humor.

Kynan found himself smiling along. "To answer your question, Dorin, we do intend to sail around the... disturbance, but from what the voices said—"

"The ones you heard when Rhianne did her spell?" Filip asked.

"Yes."

Filip fisted his hand and raised it in Rhianne's direction. "That must have been a neat trick."

"Remember, she's the most talented witch in the Upperworld," Aury said proudly.

"I often forget that we have such distinguished friends."

Rhianne laughed. "It's easy to forget when I'm in my cups singing along with the crew."

Kynan eyed them indulgently, then cleared his throat. "As I was saying, the voices of the scrolls indicated a drawing power the disturbance possesses. It is nigh on impossible to avoid, they claimed."

"But they lived to write down the experience."

"They did, but they reported heavy losses, most of the scribes in question being the sole survivors to record the event."

Filip snatched a leather-cloaked flask from Werian's belt and held it high. "Well, here's hoping we are the sole survivors!"

Aury bent laughing. "You are such a dolt. Sole means only."

Filip uncorked the drink and took a swig before handing it back to Werian, who swallowed down a bit as well. "Watch that tongue, Princess. The common tongue is my third language."

"Watch it or what?" Aury faced him.

Kynan exhaled. "All right, everyone on deck. We need eyes on this." He shooed the lot from the cabin. As Dorin passed, Kynan touched his arm. "Are you willing to shift fully and attempt to scout the situation?"

Dorin glanced at Brielle, who remained at the desk —Kynan hadn't realized she was still there. "If my wife agrees, I will try it. It's still very difficult to shift here in the Underworld, especially when Maren isn't around. The Awenydd gives power to us somehow."

Brielle raised her head, still squinting from trying to see the tiny ancient writing. "What? Oh, you are going full dragon to scout? Can you shift?" She swallowed, and the color in her cheeks faded.

"I think so. I've grown...not accustomed, exactly, but used to the struggle of shifting here. I will do it if you agree to the risk. It's considerable."

"What does Filip say?"

"What do you think?"

The corner of her mouth lifted. "Well, I'm not going to keep you tethered for the sake of my heart. We agreed to fight for Maren and for the shadow elves, and this is part of that commitment."

Kynan bowed. "Spoken like a true queen."

Dorin bowed likewise, then set his gaze on Brielle. The fire between them woke Kynan's banked desire for Maren. Gods, he missed her. He recalled their Samhain celebration. Dancing. Her fingers in his hair. A smile on her face. Moonlight. Laughter all around. She had dragged him into the frivolity, but once he'd been there, it had been the happiest of nights. Though he'd only known Maren for a short time, she had such a powerful hold on his soul. But perhaps his soul had known hers since he first saw her in the Between all those years ago...

All three left the cabin together and climbed to the upper deck to begin preparations.

Everyone else stood at the port side, staring at a massive churning cloud in the near distance while Filip explained about the potential for dragons and strange magic.

Kynan joined Hafwen where she stood beside Filip. "I truly do not like the look of that."

Hafwen gripped her wand as if ready to fight. "It's horrifying. But we do have an amazing crew."

Filip whispered something quick to Aury, then turned toward Kynan. "I'm giving us a solid fifty-fifty chance of surviving."

Hafwen raised her eyebrows but kept her gaze on the storm cloud. "Such an optimist. How did you form this percentage?"

Aury leaned over. "Filip doesn't bother himself with actual information. He goes with his gut."

"She is right, but my gut is almost always right too." Filip rubbed his hands and eyed the crew. "It's time we get this small army prepped."

"Agreed."

After a discussion of strategy with all the royals and Hafwen, Kynan ordered the crew to lower to the sea and fetch buckets of sea water, which they used to soak the boat. Dorin informed him that dragonfire was not dulled by water to the degree that regular fire was, but it would be better than nothing.

Hopefully, Dorin would find some positive information when he flew into the misty area, but if not, they would be as ready as possible.

Werian and Rhianne decided on a tack that might possibly help them slip past the disaster while Filip and Aury chose a defensive strategy involving her water magic, Kynan's shadows, Rhianne's magic, Dorin's dragonfire, and the general fighting capabilities of the archers and swordsmen on board. If the dragons attacked, Aury would use her magic to block dragonfire as best she could while Dorin flew around the dragons and struck from behind. Kynan would use his shadows to blind the dragons. It wasn't a simple use of his power, but it wouldn't be as strenuous as traveling by shadow and working with the magic under the water.

Kynan watched Dorin kiss Brielle, then take off into the sky, slowly working his large, jade-hued wings. "I commend his courage," Kynan said to Brielle.

Filip crossed his arms and smiled in Dorin's direction. "He's making up for all the adventuring he missed while having to babysit me during our childhood." He looked at Brielle. "Because of the whole half-dragon thing and that dragon bond between you two, do you think you will be able to track him somewhat?"

"I had a vague sense of where he was during the battle with Tiergan." Brielle set a hand on her abdomen. Her body didn't yet show that she was with child, but Kynan could almost scent the creation on her. It was common in shadow elf culture to be sure to watch out for mothers. "But I'm not sure about the distance and how that might affect my sensitivity to him."

"This will be a true test of that, then," Hafwen said.

Filip put a hand on Brielle's shoulder and gave her a brotherly smile. "I will aid you as you wish in his stead, Sister."

Brielle squeezed his hand, and Aury gave them both a grin of approval.

The bonds between these chosen kin of Maren's were admirable. Kynan found his gaze drawn to Hafwen, and they traded a friendly nod, as if she were thinking along the same lines.

The magical storm that truly was still a mystery appeared to grow larger as they sailed ever closer.

Werian walked over, making a clicking noise with his tongue like he was thinking and not best pleased. "I suppose you can already tell that our best efforts at a tack that avoids it is failing."

"Seems so."

"Rhianne is going to attempt a clearing spell so we might glimpse the inside of that odd chaos before Dorin reaches it."

"Good." Kynan looked to where Rhianne was extending her wand over the prow.

The ship had indeed turned so that its nose pointed directly at the churning clouds. Magic exploded from Rhianne's wand in a flurry of yellow the same bright hue as the leaves on the Awenydd's tree, and a crackling noise combined with the drum of the sea against the ship's progress.

"That sound is coming from the spell, yes?" Kynan tugged at his collar.

Werian's eyebrows lifted. "I certainly hope so."

The yellow light of the spell shot toward the magical storm, and a sensation like the air being sucked from the world pulled at Kynan's lips and nose. He gasped, as did everyone on board, then the sensation evaporated, and the spell spun into another knot similar to the one Rhianne had worked into being in the captain's quarters. This knot had a large loop at the top and three concentric circles below. The loop shimmered and blinked brightly, so much so that Kynan shielded his eyes partially, wincing at the discomfort. Again the sucking sensation arose, and he gripped the ship's side, trusting the feeling of not being able to breathe would pass shortly.

"Hold!" Rhianne called out, her wand hand moving in darting patterns and the wand spitting red sparks.

Black spots danced in front of Kynan's eyes, and he fought to stay calm even as two crewmen dropped to the deck, gasping for a breath that wouldn't come.

"One more moment." Rhianne cast a worried look over her shoulder at the two who had fallen.

It seemed only she could speak and breathe. Perhaps she didn't realize the effect...

Brielle stood beside Rhianne, one hand on Rhianne's arm and her knuckles white. The redheaded princess stared unblinkingly at her mate flying toward only the Source knew what.

Kynan squinted toward the flying spell and Dorin's silhouette against the churning milk-white clouds. The yellow knot soared over Dorin's head and plunged into the mysterious storm, then the air returned to Kynan's lungs in a rush that had him bracing himself against the side and inhaling deeply.

The clouds erupted in a shattering display of yellow sparks.

The mist disappeared completely.

Kynan's hearts shuddered as prayers and curses rang out from the crew. Dorin jerked in the sky, drawing his wings into a motion that allowed him to hover.

Seven dragons flew in a tangled pattern above the wreckage of a long-forgotten ship. They didn't fly at Dorin, but as Kynan's ship sailed closer, he could see that their heads had turned toward Dorin.

"I am not often at a loss for words, but..." Werian whistled and shook his head at the dragons.

"Do you think Dorin will attempt to communicate?" Kynan asked Werian.

Werian waved a hand at Filip, who hurried over, his face ashen. "Filip, do you think Dorin will be able to communicate with them as you do with Jewel?"

"I seriously doubt it. Our familiar bond allows that communication."

Kynan nodded his agreement, his hearts aching for Ivar.

Filip continued. "Dorin knows much of dragons though. He lived among them for a long time studying their habits. Of course, these are quite obviously cursed, so..."

"We have no way to know what to expect," Kynan said, finishing Filip's thought.

Dorin's wings fluttered erratically. He turned and shouted, his words somewhat cloaked by the crash of the sea on the ship and the crackling of the spell. The dragons behind him roared, one after the other, the sound cascading across the water in punches of frightening noise.

"The curse is drawing him in!" Brielle leaned on the ship's side, looking like she was about to leap overboard in some mad effort to save him.

Kynan ran to her and held her fast. "You can't help if you drown." *Or if the afanc finds you.*

She struggled, but he kept her trapped. "Rhianne!"

Forehead bunched in concentration, Rhianne whispered something he couldn't hear. Then she raised her head. "I'm working on it. This is definitely a curse, and it feels like air magic. Kynan, do you think your shadows could do something? What does your intuition tell you?"

He gritted his teeth as Brielle began swearing and her tears hit his clasped forearms. "I am no witch. I don't know," he said.

Rhianne scowled as she moved her wand. "Yes, you do. Just act on impulse. Don't think."

"Brielle, you won't do anything foolish if I let you go, will you?"

"If she does, I'll go in after her," Filip said, coming up beside Rhianne with Werian on his heels.

"And I'll draw you both back up." Aury spun her mage staff and glared at the dragons and Dorin, who was fighting the pull of the curse, his face twisted in agony and his wings working hard against the invisible force.

"What can you do to help him?" Brielle studied Rhianne's face with a desperation that Kynan felt in his pounding hearts.

"I, maybe…I can give him strength." She whirled her wand in the air, and a black and blue wave of power blasted toward Dorin.

Kynan let Brielle go and summoned his shadows. "I can give him a shield." The magic warmed his hands and his shadow heart, then poured from him in a rush. Coiling gray and black slips of darkness swam through the sky toward Dorin. When they reached him, they wove around him in a way similar to the magic he'd created under the water. "It will deflect blows and some of the dragonfire should they attack. The shadows will also hinder any foul magic set on him."

"But not the strength Rhianne sent?" Brielle asked.

"No." Kynan whispered a prayer for Dorin as he was drawn fully into the thunder of dragons. He shifted into his full dragon form and dropped. Brielle hissed a word in a language Kynan didn't know. Dorin plummeted toward the water's surface and the jagged point of the shipwreck's broken main mast. Then a blue wave of power shimmered over his dark green scales and leaf-hued crystalline spikes, and he shot back into the air. He flew with the other dragons, seemingly trapped with them in a never-ending circling pattern above the shipwreck.

In a few moments, their ship would be right on that wreck.

CHAPTER 22
MAREN

Maren followed Bethan down the corridor toward Tiergan's rooms on the western wing of the castle.

"I could have helped you dress. You are to be High Queen. You shouldn't be dressing yourself. It makes the king look as though he can't care for his woman."

Maren was about to sprain her face from so much teeth grinding, but her goal at the moment didn't involve arguments with an elf who would never change her mind. Her aim this morning was to avoid any questions about the blood-stained dress from last night and its whereabouts, to make sure none of the nobles mentioned their missing children and the notes Ceri and the other rebels had left, and also to come up with a plan to steal Cynnwrf from Tiergan so Kynan could have a solid chance at claiming it if—*Source, please make it happen*—Kynan returned with the Calon y Dderwen in hand.

She touched her thick skirts, pressing down for a

moment to feel the wand in its hidden sheath, tied to her thigh. If she could help it, she'd never be separated from her weapon again. How long would it be before Tiergan offered the wand as a reward in exchange for some entertainment for his court again? She just had to act quickly and hope everything would somehow work out.

"Apologies," she said to Bethan belatedly. Best to keep her happy and do as she was told to keep the plans going smoothly. "I'm not accustomed to having a lady-in-waiting. I grew up rather poor."

Bethan turned and smiled a true smile. "That, I understand."

Maybe Bethan could at some point become an ally. Maren returned the friendly look as they continued through the great hall, under the high hand-hewn beams and the hanging banners showing Tiergan's coat of arms—a field of white with a black cliff, a green-striped feather, and a sea monster with a long snout.

A clutch of courtiers whispered as Maren went by. They wore elaborate headpieces shaped like cones. Lacy emerald green veils fell from the headpieces and draped gracefully over their shoulders and backs. They were dressed beautifully, but their glares ruined the whole look.

Ignoring them and gathering her black skirts very carefully, Maren caught up to Bethan.

"I can order a headpiece made for you, my lady."

"Thank you." She had never been one to care much about fashion, but she was just trying to get along with

Bethan. The courtiers' scowls had been what drew her attention.

Beyond the great hall, a corridor narrowed and split, one side showing stairs and the other a set of double doors with gold and silver sea monsters serving as door knockers. Bethan lifted and dropped one of the gilded monsters three times. A voice sounded behind the door, saying something in the shadow elf tongue, and Bethan pushed the doors open.

A shirtless Tiergan lounged on a long couch that was overflowing with pillows and scantily clad shadow elf women. The raven-haired one standing behind Tiergan massaged his temples while two others sat on his lap. The slender ladies on his lap grinned like they were perfectly content, but the one working on his temples and the three sitting stiffly on the couch on either side of Tiergan were definitely uncomfortable. Their elven-gray eyes were flat with what Maren guessed might be reserved rage or fear, and they held themselves too straight, as if afraid to move the wrong way. Every shadow elf in the room, even the servant who served wine from a gilded tray, had purple or yellow marks on their throats, wrists, or faces.

And then there was the gold.

Piles of gold, silver, and copper coins filled every corner of the room. Circlets in tooled iron set with sparkling rubies and sunny amber, cloaks of deep green velvet, rings in every shape and size, and an array of glittering trinkets mixed with the coins. If she didn't know Tiergan was a shadow lord, she'd have thought he was a dragon. He must have reaped this glittering harvest from the people of his lands and maybe Kynan's too, and now he was sitting on it, just enjoying the look of the wealth as children starved in the streets. Soon, the children outside his homelands would always be without enough food; their parents were probably getting news of the raised taxes today.

A bitter taste touched the back of Maren's tongue as she curtseyed to Tiergan and finally met his gaze. He wore low-slung trousers, and his feet were bare. His blond hair was mussed, and his cheeks held the flush of exertion. She didn't want to know what he had been up to before she and Bethan had arrived.

"Lovely to see you this morning, my queen." His voice was a knife at her throat.

She couldn't bring herself to be polite, to greet him or wish him a good morning. She just could not do it. Her lips and tongue flat-out refused, so she stood there before him, waiting, sweating, and praying.

Her wand warmed her skin. Her fingers longed to take it from its sheath and wreak havoc.

"Our coronation will take place quite soon. Do you have a preference on your crown or dress? I want you to look the way you wish to look, darling wife."

"Black suits me."

Tiergan cocked his head and traded a look with the woman at the end of the couch. She gripped the curved armrest, and her bottom lip shook as her gaze darted from Maren to Tiergan, then back again. Peeling the women on him away, Tiergan rose. He stalked around Maren, clasping his hands behind his back.

Maren swallowed as the acid of fear and the heat of anger bubbled under her calm surface.

"Black is the color of mourning in the human world," Tiergan said.

Bethan gasped, and the ladies who seemed to adore Tiergan whispered as they drew their heads together.

Swallowing a retort, Maren stood very still while Tiergan continued pacing a tight circle around her.

Could he sense the wand under her clothing?

He sniffed as if displeased. "You could attempt to enjoy your place beside me, Awenydd. We did, after all, save the realms. We are heroes. We should be celebrating together. This tension could be easily diffused if you would simply come around to my thinking."

"What is that exactly?" Maren silently berated herself. There was no room here for a sharp tongue. She had bigger issues than giving Tiergan some lip even if it did feel amazing to lash out.

Tiergan stopped pacing, crossed his arms, and tilted his head, a lock of his golden hair slipping over one cheekbone. The muscles in his forearms tensed, and a flicker of danger sparked in his gray eyes. "You will come with me to the Spirit Well."

"I would like that." For once, she wasn't lying.

Tiergan's face relaxed, and he clapped his hands. "Everyone, begone. I wish to have a private discussion with my wife."

CHAPTER 23
MAREN

Every time he said that word, her stomach rolled over and she had to fight the urge to vomit. Tiergan's subjects and servants filed out of the room, and Maren studied their faces so she'd remember who was who. Oh. The woman that had been on the end of the couch had stood in the great hall when Tiergan had first dragged her here swathed in shadows. She'd been on the arm of a nobleman with a sallow complexion and a fine tunic that was two sizes too small.

Maren's lips parted... That woman was another man's wife and Tiergan had her here, in his rooms. Disgusting. As soon as the head servant shut the doors and left them alone, she whirled on Tiergan. "Are you—"

Waving a hand at the doors, Tiergan snorted. "I don't have to force women to share my bed. I do, however, force some of them to have drinks with me and converse. It serves to remind their husbands of what I could do even though I refuse to lower myself."

Well, that was good at least. But still... It had to be horrible to be forced to remain near Tiergan.

"How about we make a deal? I will be pleasant during this little trip to the well if you promise not to force any women to attend to you in your chambers and if you stop mistreating your servants."

Tiergan poured himself a drink, blood red wine flowing into a tall pewter goblet. "You have no power here, Awenydd. Not yet anyway. I will do exactly as I see fit, and you won't say a word about it, or there will be consequences."

"I will happily head right down to the dungeon in exchange for the ladies and the servants."

"What do I get out of that?" He still had his back to her, one of his hands resting on the side table, long fingers steepled on the dark wood.

"I will be the absolute picture of a fine queen during our trip to the well. I assume you will bring a few admirers to ooh and ah over your work there."

She hoped he would so they could serve as a possible distraction while she spoke to the spirits. Maybe they had come up with a plan for Cynnwrf. Plus, she was painfully desperate to hear news of Kynan and the whole crew if the spirits had somehow managed that. She couldn't even delve into that longing and cold, stark fear fully, or she'd crumble. She had to keep those feelings shoved deep inside her heart for now.

Tiergan finished his drink, set down the goblet, then threw his hands wide. Shadows shot from his fingertips, and in the time it took for her to fist her hands and brace for shadow travel, she felt her body and soul hurtling through the intangible corridor of magic. When she opened her eyes, they were at the well. A fog overhead glittered with sunny yellow as if the sun hovered just behind the luminous puffs of white. A spot of scorched earth encircled Tiergan. The tall grasses looked as if they had been burned, their ends shriveled. A patch of moss had lost the blue and green of its fellows and turned a sickly ashen hue.

"What is that?"

He didn't look at her but instead adjusted Cynnwrf at his belt and smoothed his hair. "A mark from the shadow magic. Sometimes when shadow lords use larger workings with their magic, the ground shows the toll the realm paid for the power. Mostly the effects are unseen, the energy drawn from the air, the vigor of nearby plants, and the banked strength inside the stone of my castle, for instance."

Kynan had told her about the price of using shadow magic, but she'd never seen it appear so clearly. "Does this mean the realms are struggling still?"

"It does, but it's nothing serious." He removed a dagger from his belt and twisted it in the day's watery light.

"You'll give your blood to the Between now?" She had to act as if she didn't know he'd already done it once. "What do you do to prepare yourself for this?" She knew the answer was nothing, but perhaps her prompting would get him to show respect and therefore help the spirits further this time.

"I suppose...I take on the air of a servant instead of a king." He glanced at her and then back at his dagger. His voice was oddly quiet. Was he trying to impress her in a new way?

She had no clue what to say to that. Everything in her head sounded like an insult. So she held her tongue and wiped any sarcasm from her features.

Tiergan closed his eyes as if to focus. "Enter with me."

Panic gripped her throat. "I need my wand to enter the Between." Her wand warmed her leg as if it knew she had mentioned it. But she had to mention it— avoiding the topic would surely have made him suspicious.

"Not beside the master of Cynnwrf, you don't." He spoke with his eyes closed and waved a hand, sending shadows to encase her once more. Before the sight of the living world disappeared, the Spirit Well's shimmering depths flashed brightly.

The Between's chill air brushed over her face and neck, and she squinted, willing her vision to clear so she could see the spirits. Their ghostly bodies took shape— well, as much as they ever did—and she smiled, surprisingly touched by their kind waves of welcome and grins.

They crowded around her, their excited voices converging, a thousand different accents and languages.

A human spirit wearing a tunic that went all the way to his toes bowed. He had a pale sword at his belt and a shield slung over one shoulder. He smiled and traded a knowing look with a woman dressed in a similarly long tunic.

"We have news, Awenydd," the spirit warrior said.

Maren turned to look for Tiergan. He stood in the distance, the billowing mist of the Between occasionally blocking him from view as he squeezed his hand into a fist. He would be finished soon. It couldn't take long to drop some blood here and whisper a few words, especially considering he didn't fully respect the spirits. He'd probably rush the job.

"Tell me quickly. I don't have much time."

A slim elf girl of maybe ten or eleven years pushed past the warriors. "Water sprites visited us at the well!"

"What is a water sprite?"

The girl chewed the end of her braid, looking like she was suddenly nervous about her assertive behavior. Maren took a knee so she could be eye level with her. "Don't be afraid to speak up."

Smiling, the girl glanced over her shoulder at a man who had the same wide-set eyes. Her father, maybe? It was lovely to think that they had been reunited despite an early death.

"They are beings of water that can move between the sea and our well and the streams and rivers," the girl said.

The warrior bent over to join the conversation. "High King Kynan sails the Dark Sea in search of the crystal."

"He's alive?"

"Yes, and well. And the crew remains healthy and whole."

Maren exhaled roughly and fought the urge to hug the warrior and the girl. Unshed tears burned her eyes. "This is the best news. Have they found anything?"

"Not yet."

She stood and gave the girl and the warrior a smile. "Thank you for delivering that message. I am honored to speak with you."

All the spirits bowed their heads to her. It pleased her that none paid Tiergan even the slightest bit of attention, but it worried her as well. "Is Tiergan's blood helping you this time?"

Some of them turned to look at Tiergan, who was walking toward Maren wearing a scowl. "It does help, but we prefer King Kynan because his shadow heart is true and his soul is stronger."

The spirits she'd spoken to earlier—when Ceri, Mags, and Neddy had been at her side—had said something quite similar.

The girl raised her chin, and spots of red rose into her cheeks. "I miss seeing the High King. He is so handsome and kind."

"And humble to boot," the warrior woman said, and everyone murmured agreement.

A shiver ran over Maren and she wrapped her arms around herself. "I miss him terribly. If I get my way, he will be back. Does anyone know a way I can take Cynnwrf from Tiergan? And can you tell the water sprites to let him know I'm endeavoring to do so?"

The warrior chewed her lip and tapped a finger on her ghostly axe. "Did you ask the dragon goddess?"

"Yes, she just said to try to claim it, but I don't even know how to start."

The hushed voices of the spirits speaking in every language carried across the space. Perhaps she could somehow hide Cynnwrf here in the Between. But nothing here was of flesh or mineral. This was only her spirit here; her corporeal self, her body, remained in the Underworld. Did Cynnwrf have a spirit of sorts? It certainly wasn't a basic sword. Would its magic somehow function as a spirit?

"Looking for me?" a raspy female voice said into her ear.

She knew that voice. Her face split into a cheek-stretching grin as the spirits looked on and Tiergan approached. "Goddess Nix."

"I'm going to keep a low profile." Nix wasn't visible at all.

"Does Cynnwrf have a spirit, and if so, do you think I could steal the sword and store its spirit here to hide it from Tiergan?"

Nix made a humming, thinking sort of sound that traveled around Maren's head as if the goddess were flying in a circle above her. "Claim the sword with your Bonded blood, with the aid of your connection to its master, Tiergan." Nix said the name like a curse, and Maren was glad they were of the same mind. "Then use your Awenydd magic and your wand to split the sword from its magic. Use your witch's will to push the magic into the Between, to this place of ethereal space. We will watch over it, and the sword will be made like a simple length of metal to Tiergan. He will be able to wield it as any soldier uses a blade, but it will be useless beyond that. You can meld the sword and its magic again once Kynan is in possession and ready to lay his claim once more."

"It sounds too easy."

"It won't be. It will be the trickiest bit of magic anyone has tried in ages. I wish you luck. I must go."

A wave of soft warmth came from above Maren and soaked into her head and heart, and she knew the feeling was from Nix.

"Thank you," she whispered.

Tiergan sheathed his dagger and extended his arms. Shadows pulled Maren roughly from the Between, their chill fingers like icicles that scratched her skin as the Underworld appeared before her once again.

"What did you say to them? What did they discuss with you?" A jealous light glimmered in Tiergan's eyes as he loomed over her. She had the overwhelming urge to knee him in the stones so hard that they came out his nose.

Someday, she silently promised herself. *Someday soon.*

"Nothing aside from the usual concerns of the spirits. They are glad you fed them with your shadow lord blood."

"You're being too polite. I trust you not."

She smiled with all her teeth and braced herself for shadow travel once more.

The ship ground to a terrible halt, and Kynan grabbed Hafwen before she could fall over the side and into the churning sea water.

"We're hung up on wreckage, Captain!" a crewman shouted to Werian and Kynan.

"Get the poles!" Sweating more than Kynan thought fae ever did, Werian was already moving toward the lengths of wood made for shifting the ship when oars and wind wouldn't do. He had one in the water and braced against the broken hull of a ship that had partially collapsed onto another sunken craft.

Kynan, Hafwen, and all those with the strength to do so joined in. With six poles, they pushed together in time with Rhianne's shouts. Dorin, back in half-dragon and half-elf form, wheeled out of the sky where the cluster of cursed dragons flew.

He was red-faced, his eyes wide with alarm. Brielle raised her hand toward him and shouted his name, tears flowing down her face.

"I can't escape the pull!" Dorin veered backward, shifted into his full dragon form, then disappeared behind a larger one of the magnificent creatures.

Brielle let out a shout of pain and whirled to face Rhianne. "Please! Try something! Anything!"

Kynan took up the rhythmic chanting to keep the crew working in unison to dislodge the ship as Rhianne gave him a nod, unsheathed her wand, and threw a line of bright citrine in Dorin's direction. Aury sent a blast of water at the wreck in time with the crew's work, and the ship listed roughly.

"Are we free?" Hafwen asked as sea water crashed over the ship's side and drenched her.

"Not yet!" Axe in hand, Filip leapt from the ship to the wreck. He moved quickly as he searched for a spot to break down.

"There!" Kynan pointed to a window that had eaten one of their ship's planks, ripping it clean away from the hull.

Rhianne's glittering citrine spell charged toward the dragons, hit the cursed area, and blinked away. She stumbled. Werian caught her in his arms as she lost consciousness.

The ship groaned. Filip rained down strikes on the jagged plank. Aury shoved a wave at the wreck once more, the water high above their ship and shaped like a giant's fist. The scents of sea and sage—a magical perfume that seemed to surround water spells—filled the air as Kynan gripped the pole and kept on applying pressure.

There was a crack, a loud snap, and then the ship was moving away from the wreckage.

"Huzzah!" the crew shouted as one.

Filip launched himself back on to the deck.

Pointing to the sky with her mage staff, Aury drove a column of water toward the thunder of dragons. When the sea water touched the cone of their flight pattern, lightning branched across the sky, and the world rumbled.

Hafwen had her wand out too and was casting a jade and lapis colored net of light toward Dorin. Aury blasted the space around the dragons again, the water sizzling as if the very air there was as hot as the fire spewed by its dragon prisoners. The bright-scaled creatures, Dorin too if Kynan wasn't mistaken, veered away from Aury's striking spot, and Hafwen's net slipped inside the chaos. She jerked and fell to one knee, still holding her wand aloft. Kynan gripped her arm and helped her stand again. He stood beside her as she grimaced and the net disappeared into the cursed area.

"I have him!" Hafwen glanced at Werian, who still held the sleeping Rhianne.

Why had Rhianne fallen? Had going against this strange phenomenon drained her energy somehow? "Pull back if you think it is going to drain you," he said, his hearts aching. "We'll find another way."

"I can do this. Don't use your kingly command voice on me right now." She almost grinned even as the perspiration on her face rolled to her neck.

A black spot shot from Aury's watery break in the

cursed area. The streak of darkness spiraled around the outside of the flying dragons.

A sense of information, or a message, passed through Kynan's mind.

All at once. All magic.

"Ivar." Eyes burning, Kynan stared at the black spot and finally noticed the curve of smaller wyvern wings and the whip of his tail. He was alive. It really was him.

"Is it him? Are you certain?" Hafwen asked.

Relief flowed into Kynan's blood and unspooled the tight anxiety that had been crushing his chest. "Ivar is there, and he says to hit the curse with all we've got."

"But what about Dorin?"

"Ivar doesn't want to hurt any of the dragons. They're his distant kin. We need to trust him."

Aury looked to Brielle, then Aury spun her staff, and water launched away from the sea's surface to join the jet she'd already formed.

Hafwen redoubled her efforts, her cheeks flushed and her spell almost too bright to look at directly.

Werian's hands glittered as he healed Rhianne. She came to and quickly retrieved her wand to join the magical force. Her wand shot a beam of watery light at the thunder of dragons, and Kynan loosed a flurry of shadow arrows in the same direction.

The magic tugged at his shadow heart as he willed the arrows into the cursed region. Snarling and roaring sounded. The dragons flew erratically.

Dorin appeared in the midst of them, breathing dragonfire.

Kynan forced as much of himself into the fray as he

had, leaving nothing back and forcing worries for the future to the very dark recesses of his mind. They had to survive here and had to break through if they were even going to reach the next proposed spot of the crystal. Plus, Dorin and Ivar were in need. He could no more ignore Ivar's mentally transferred pain and fear than he could the imminent danger to one of Maren's chosen kin, Dorin.

The various spells converged.

The world went dark.

Kynan tried to see, but the darkness was complete. "Hafwen?"

There was no sound. No deck beneath his feet. No sea spray in the air. If he died here, Maren would be lost just as his first mate.

No. He refused to die now. "Ivar! I need you!"

The black of this new world remained, silent and heavy as a winter cloak.

"Ivar..." Kynan was lightheaded, and he was falling... Falling...

An ear-splitting shriek stopped his fall and moved the darkness away like a roughly drawn curtain.

Ivar and Dorin flew toward the ship with a bevy of massive dragons behind them.

Hafwen was kneeling beside Kynan...oh, he was on the decking. He must have lost consciousness during the spellwork.

"Do they come to attack?" Hafwen asked.

He sought Ivar's mind through the familiar bond and found it, animal and quick. Ivar seemed to be communicating a need for rest, a sense of frantic exhaustion.

"I understand that," he thought back to Ivar, saying the words aloud just to reassure himself that he was alive and not imagining this entire scenario.

Ivar flew, a shard of obsidian leading the roaring, flame-spitting creatures that were not so different from him. Dorin soared to his right, but all Kynan could focus on was the fact that Ivar was not dead. He was truly alive, and Kynan was overcome with gratitude, so much so that thinking was a challenge. He couldn't wait to have Ivar back on board, but what were they going to do with all of those dragons? There wasn't room enough for one, let alone the entire group. If even one of the large dragons attempted to land here, it would sink the ship.

"Aury, can you create an ice plateau of sorts for them to rest on? If not, I'm afraid they're going to drown us. Accidentally but definitely."

"I think so." She pointed her staff, and the water beneath the dragons began to stir.

"Anyone else have ideas? Ivar says they are exhausted and aren't thinking clearly. It's the remnants of the curse bungling their minds."

What could he do with his shadow magic?

Filip put a hand on his shoulder. "Perhaps you could help them fly to land." He jerked his chin in the direction of the distant blue-gray cliffs of Tiergan's lands. "Our witch ladies can feed them energy, Aury can provide a few places for rest along the way as needed, and you can urge them in the proper direction with your shadows."

"Great idea." Kynan exhaled and gave Filip a nod of thanks. It was refreshing to have so many seasoned warriors who were accustomed to magic along on a mission.

The witches took aim at the dragons while Kynan communicated that this was not an attack but that the spells would help them reach shore.

"All friends. Not foes," Kynan whispered, hoping Ivar would be able to confer this information to the horde of scaled monsters hurtling toward them at an alarming speed.

The relief of knowing Ivar was soon to be safely back on board gave Kynan strength as he summoned a swathe of curling ebony shadows, the warmth of the power pooling in his palms and along his fingertips. Magic surged, familiar and pleasant, in his shadow heart and pulsed through the powerful blood running through his veins. He imagined every dragon's snout, visualizing the overlap of smooth scales like Ivar's, then worked a loop of magic through their nostrils as he'd seen cattle farmers do with metal rings and difficult-to-maneuver bulls.

The first of the dragons reached them.

The creature's talons latched onto the main mast, and a roar shredded Kynan's ears. The ship dipped harshly to port, and water gushed over the side.

Hafwen stared up at the dragon, then eyed the rest that were flying this way. "They're incredibly old. I can't imagine they'll live long. I can feel their age in my wand hand, in my shadow heart."

"Very much alive at this moment though." Running to starboard to avoid the dragon's lashing tail, Kynan ignored the crew's panicked shouts. Though he doubted the dragon wished to harm them, the beast was a danger all the same, and he wasn't about to let anything hurt those working toward saving Maren. Back braced on the ship's side, he poured more of his energy into his shadow magic.

The ship tipped further.

Everyone went silent as the dragon leaned farther and a small crack snaked down the mast.

They were going over.

Kynan's shadows obeyed his imaginings and slipped through the air to the dragon on board and then across the expanse of sea and sky until small clouds of darkness hung at every dragon's head. Using the connection between him and the shadow magic, he urged the dragons eastward to Tiergan's kingdom.

The dragon on the main mast roared again, then took off.

The ship bobbed harshly, and two crewmen fell overboard. As the rest worked to retrieve them, Dorin and Ivar peeled away from the ensorcelled dragons, Dorin shifting into his half-dragon, half-elf form. The ensorcelled dragons—all seven of them—turned toward the coast as Kynan's magic urged.

Ivar wheeled down and landed on his outstretched arm. Kynan's face split into a smile, and he struggled to keep his focus on the dragons.

"It is so good to see you again, my friend."

Ivar hopped to Kynan's shoulder, bumped his cool reptilian muzzle against Kynan's cheek, and clicked his forked tongue as the dragons disappeared in the distance.

Ancient kin, Ivar communicated. *Will turn to dust at landfall.*

"Should I not be guiding them that way?" Kynan said aloud to Ivar.

Wish to rest. Tired.

So this was the right choice. He continued urging the dragons he could no longer see with his eyes. Their energy still pulled on his magic, so he continued guiding them until their essences faded from his senses. Then he let his hands fall to his sides.

"Huzzah for King Kynan!" the crew shouted.

"Huzzah for the witches!"

"Huzzah for the water mage and her vicious elven prince!"

Leaning heavily on the side of the ship, Kynan stroked Ivar's talons and tried to catch his breath. "What kind of witch cast such a powerful and evil curse?" He spoke this time in the common tongue and looked about the group of Upperworlders, wondering if they knew.

Rhianne glanced at Hafwen, and both witches shrugged. "Perhaps a dragon once wronged her?" Rhianne's eyebrows lifted toward her mussed brown hair.

Hafwen cocked her head to one side. "Or they were

the cause of the wreck, and the curse was the witch's last gasp of revenge before the sea took her?"

"I guess we'll never know," Rhianne said.

"High King!" a crewman shouted from the prow. "We've reached the approximate coordinates of another potential location of the crystal."

A wave of hope flooded his senses, and he wondered what Maren had been experiencing during the last few days.

Back at the castle, Tiergan watched Maren like a hawk. Night and day she had not one, not two, but at least four guards hounding her steps. And the second dream she'd shared with Kynan kept rising into her thoughts. She didn't want to think about him now. It was too distracting. Too infuriating that he was so far away. But the memory of the dream resurfaced again and again in pieces that made her cheeks flush hotly and her heart hammer against her ribs.

And it hadn't been an ordinary dream. She actually shared that magical dream space with Kynan. His hands had slid down her sides and cupped her bottom. He had drawn her against him and whispered his love into her ear. She swallowed, her body melting at the memory. They had kissed and spoken of their feelings through touch. She should have shaken herself out of the dreaminess and talked to him about Tiergan and what was to come, but in that space, she simply couldn't think straight.

"Nix, if you're listening, I have a guess that's your doing. It wouldn't be so terrible if we have the minds for strategy while we are together. It would be nice to survive this." She could imagine the dragon goddess grinning impishly.

Currently, she was bathing and checking the healing cut on her knee. This was the only place the guards didn't follow. Bethan remained, but even she could tell Maren wanted space and had kindly given it to her. The elderly maid sat in the bedchamber, a call away for whatever Maren might need.

The woven mat beside the copper tub hid her wand. Beneath its fuzzy knots, the magical weapon lay in the linen sheath Ceri had made. Though it was a huge risk to keep it instead of returning it to Tiergan's hideous desk, the wand's presence was a massive comfort.

Tonight, no matter what, she was using her wand and her magic to slip into Tiergan's chambers while he slept. Before sunup, she was determined to split Cynnwrf from its magic and turn Tiergan into just another shadow lord instead of the master of an earth magic sword. She would even the playing field and pray with all of her heart and soul that Kynan, Brielle, Aury, and the rest would arrive while the sword remained without magic. The real question was, could she manage to take over here using her power and the power of Nix once the sword was subdued? Her mind whirled with possible outcomes and consequences.

She lay back and lowered herself under the warm, rose-scented bathwater.

"We will tell your lord," a voice said.

Maren jolted upright, splashing water over the edge.

"Are you all right?" Bethan's voice leaked through the closed door between the rooms.

"Just fine," Maren said breathily. What was that? Had she imagined that, or had it been real? Was it a spirit? But they couldn't travel here...

The water settled. The room was empty of anyone but her. Maren shook her head at herself. She was losing her mind. Lowering herself back under the water, she tried to clear her head for a moment of all thoughts and just be still as she held her breath.

"Your spirits gave us the message about the mighty sword of the ancients!" A chorus of bell-like voices filled Maren's ears, and she opened her eyes under the water to see the shape of three small humanlike figures made of water. She jumped, sloshing the water. Blinking, she sat up. Her breath rippled the surface. The figures rose along with her, and they leaned to one side, appearing to watch for Bethan perhaps.

The one in the front pointed excitedly to the water.

They wanted her to go under again? Perhaps they could only speak to her under water.

She did so and immediately the water sprites—because that had to be what they were—began speaking again, talking over one another in their small, high-pitched voices. Their lip movement didn't match the words, as if perhaps some magic of theirs was changing their language into something she could understand.

"We came through the sea, the river, the groundwater, and into the kitchens in the buckets... So many buckets..." Their voices broke apart become unintelligible chattering, then they spoke as one again. "Your folk are headed into the stramash of vicious fanged beasts."

Fanged beasts? Maren gripped the sides of the tub as they went on.

"That is not their only challenge because it seems that they haven't yet found the Calon y Dderwen." Their accents were completely foreign, their syllables lengthened and the vowels drawn into rounder sounds.

She held up her hands in a motion that said slow down, and they nodded.

"Sorry, Awenydd."

Heart pounding, she moved her fingers to indicate they should go on, but they seemed to have decided to go quiet. "Can you tell King Kynan to find the Blind Pig, a tavern in the castle town? Allies wait there to help us." Bubbles tickled her lips.

"We will." The water sprites morphed into bubbles and popped out of existence.

Maren climbed out of the tub slowly, trying not to make too much noise so Bethan would remain in the other room. She wanted to dry herself, slip on her shift, and hide the wand in the thigh sheath before Bethan appeared. It was never fun struggling to put on clothing when damp, but she managed it all right before the maid opened the door.

"Why are you so against taking my help, my lady?"

She looked genuinely hurt, her eyes wrinkled deeply at the sides and her thin lips tilted into a frown.

"I'm simply not used to the idea. I am sorry if I offend you."

Bethan waved a dismissive hand and left the bathing chamber. "At least I can get you into a proper dress for this afternoon's dining."

Maren missed the old-style dresses she used to wear —simple long lengths of fabric with one low-slung belt. Newer ones involved skirts separate from a stiff bodice and sleeves that were oftentimes tied on at the shoulders. It was ridiculous.

The afternoon dining was even more so, but in a much darker fashion.

Maren sat on Tiergan's right side while nobles in every shape and size flattered him.

One man with a twitch in his eye raised his cup. "The way you handled the council is commendable. We haven't seen such strength in ages, High King."

Strength? More like murder. Maren swallowed, her tongue tasting bitter.

Two noble ladies stood at Tiergan's sides, their mouths pinched with fear. Tiergan preened and ran a hand down one of the ladies' arms. She hadn't stopped looking at the nobleman to Maren's left, and her color was high.

For the millionth time, she longed with every fiber of her being to end his life immediately.

"Oh, don't call me High King quite yet," Tiergan said to the flatterer. "We haven't had the ceremony." He chuckled, and the rest of the room followed suit, laughing like there was some joke here.

Maren gripped her skirts and willed the night to arrive. Tonight, she would steal Cynnwrf and somehow, impossibly, keep herself from lopping Tiergan's head off while he slept. He would look so very good headless and still at her feet.

The main thing right now was to get through this dinner without Tiergan asking her to perform inane magic for the room's entertainment. If he sent someone to fetch her wand and it was found missing—because it was currently stashed under her clothing—her plan would be ruined before it had begun. What would he do if he figured it out? Throw her in the dungeon again? Definitely. Find an innocent soul to torture on her behalf? Most likely.

Thankfully, no one had breathed a word about the missing children. The ones from town were safely in the wilds past the boundary or very near to it, and the nobles' children were with Neddy and Mags.

Not a one of the nobles had given her a furtive look despite the fact that they each had received a note from the rebels telling them their children were safe. It spoke volumes that they were just as happy to have their offspring away from court as she was. There would be help here for the rebels when they sought to overtake the gate guards and move to secure the castle.

The nobles weren't even looking at Maren, acting as though they could see right through her. But someone would talk at some point. That was a given. People talked, and there was nothing one could do to stop that completely.

She wished there had been word from Mags, Neddy, or Ceri on the matter. How far had the group traveled? Were they beyond Tiergan's reach yet? Or at least beyond an easy reach?

There were so many terrible possibilities up in the air that she didn't have the energy to fret over them all. The path right in front of her had to remain the focus, and right now, that was keeping Tiergan from knowing the wand wasn't where he'd hidden it. She had to offer a pleasant distraction before this meal grew dull and he demanded magical entertainment.

Maren stood. "How about some dancing?"

Every mouth hung open, and they were forced to look at her now, though none gave away what they had to know she had engineered with the rebels.

"I've had enough of pouting, and I'd rather dance if I'm to be stuck here." She grabbed her skirts and headed toward Tiergan. "I might as well have some fun."

A light entered Tiergan's eyes, a shimmer his gaze hadn't held since the night he'd shadowed his way into her chamber at Kynan's castle, back when she'd believed he was the good fellow in this debacle. What a fool she had been...

He pushed away from the table and the two ladies, then took Maren's hand. "Dancing!" Gesturing to the lute and flute players in the corner, he smiled widely. "Of course."

It was fascinating how he seemed truly pleased with

this idea. Maren pushed her rage and disgust to the very back of her mind and set her hand on his shoulder as he laced an arm around her waist. The music began, lilting and set in a minor key that echoed the dark feel of the moment.

He pulled her close. She schooled her features, but she refused to outright smile. That was too much, going too far.

"Can I expect more of this compliant nature?" Tiergan's voice was soft. "Or is there some trickery afoot?"

"I'm finished with tricks. I am here for the people. Our people."

A grin flickered across his lips.

"I'm here to keep the balance, and I find no reason to fight you." The lie was easily told, a product of Maren's rough life on the docks in Wylfenden.

"I don't believe you."

"Of course you don't. Doesn't matter."

He inclined his head and kept on dancing, his feet sure and his grip a little too tight.

The lute player went through a staccato section of the tune, high notes piercing the great hall as Tiergan spun Maren in a tight circle. She allowed his fingers to dig into her side, knowing that tonight while he slept she would steal the one high card he had to play in this terrible game. She would even the odds, then tip them in Kynan's and her favor.

"I am loath to ruin this precious moment..." Tiergan's breath dusted over her face, and she fought the urge to claw his eyes out. "But I must tell you that there is a sad bunch of folk who deem themselves rebels."

She forced herself to keep breathing regularly. He was fishing for information. "I know nothing of rebels." Had she answered too quickly? "What would be the point of rebelling? The Bond hasn't yet healed the realms so that I could leave without destroying everyone and everything."

"Good. I thought perhaps you were the type to fight anyway, to argue in the face of logic. I suppose we are destined to have a grand fight in...about a decade or so?" He chuckled, so pleased with his awful self.

"Oh, yes. I've already scheduled it in my diary."

He laughed loudly, throwing back his head, his pointed ears showing through his mussed golden hair.

Bones of the gods, he was completely disgusting.

Once he'd regained his composure, he gazed down at her. "Do I have the spirits to thank for this newfound wisdom of yours? I feel as though they must have told you something of note during our last visit to the Spirit Well."

That could have been the reason. She'd take up this route he'd started. "Yes. They informed me of the extent of the deep damage the poison did to the realms and that our Bond remains delicate, necessary, and of the utmost importance."

Drawing her closer, he set his lips very close to her ear, and she fought a shudder. "I am open to deepening that Bond at any time you desire."

Her stomach rolled. "The spirits are not overly enamored with you, my lord," she said tightly. She had to keep this lie believable with a dollop of truth sprinkled with her genuine hatred for him. Only then would he accept her supposed change of heart.

"They certainly admire you, Awenydd, and so I will bring you with me each time I visit. Would that be a pleasant accommodation for you, my queen?"

"I have another request."

"Do tell. Since we find ourselves in this delightful meadow of compromise, I am your servant."

She rolled her eyes. It couldn't be helped. He chuckled as if delighted by her idiosyncrasies, and she balled her fist at his back.

"My request is that you show the spirits more respect. It's in your best interest because if your offerings of poppies and energy go further, the realms will recover more quickly, and your subjects' farms will yield more fruit at harvest. Thus, you will gain more from them in taxes. You can't milk a dry goat, as the saying goes."

His eyebrow flicked upward, and the side of his mouth lifted in a look that wasn't pleasure, but perhaps interest. She wasn't sure. "You are a clever thing, aren't you? Why do you believe I gather hoards of coin and jewels? Do you think I enjoy oppressing people?"

"I do, actually. It's pretty clear you love the feel of power for power's sake." Maybe she had gone too far... She should steer the conversation back to safer ground.

"Peace results from complete control. Only when a ruler has his kingdom fully in hand do folk like these rebels," he said, twisting his lips, "decide to give up their plotting and go back to their work in their fields and shops. The people must be desperate to accept my goodwill. That is how peace is shaped and formed. First, it is an unpleasant task, but shortly after, the kingdom blooms lush, and all that needs to be done is to tend it."

Complete control. From the looks of the way he ran his court, that wasn't going to be good for anyone but him. "Where did you glean that fantastic information?"

"I have studied the scrolls, works of the kings of old."

"You don't mean the..." She stopped herself, heart hammering wildly. She'd almost said the mad king, the king who had tossed the Calon y Dderwen into the Dark Sea. If she'd brought him up, she'd have set Tiergan's mind to thinking of where Kynan was right now and what he was up to. "...the kings who ruled at the start of the worlds?"

"Ah, no. There isn't enough written about them that is translated. Sad thing, too, because I quite enjoy delving into ancient history."

It was so strange that he was chatting her up like he hadn't been starving her to force her to submit to his demands. What a nightmare he was.

He continued on. "Kynan should have done as I have."

Hearing Kynan's name in his mouth made her blood boil.

"He didn't rule in full," Tiergan said. "The rebels surely had their start under his reign. They didn't gather a network in the handful of days I've been wielding Cynnwrf. Surely even you can see that. Developing a network of spies takes time. No, this mysterious group festered under Kynan's weak hand. He was too easily swayed by the council and too open to suggestion. That isn't true leadership."

Her mind blurred, and she struggled to keep her composure. She longed to disagree and shout about how his kingdom here had likely been wanting to rid themselves of him for as long as he'd been a lesser king here. This rebellion had nothing to do with fighting Kynan. She knew that from the way Ceri said Tiergan's name.

He stared into her eyes. "Do not trifle with me, Lady Wife. I have ways to keep you obedient, ideas you can't even imagine. I don't want to stoop to the level of my forebears if I don't have to, but I will not lose sleep over it if you force my hand. Believe me."

She did. Not trusting herself to say another word, she took his hand and urged him back into the stately dance the other nobles were enjoying—or pretending to —around them.

Night couldn't come quickly enough.

The sea was a slab of obsidian, and its calmness did nothing to ease Kynan's discomfort. That surface might hide another beast like the afanc or another curse that lulled one into thinking all was well until suddenly death was unleashed.

Ivar perched on the compass box near the helm, idly shaking out his wings and surveying the water with slitted eyes. The wyvern communicated a confidence he had in Kynan, which was a kindness that Kynan thanked him for in their special, silent way. He imagined them at the hearth at home, in the study, with all back to usual life. Ivar raised his head and let out a small growl filled with longing while he communicated his wish to be with the lads again.

"Soon, I hope," Kynan said both in his head and aloud, as if speaking it would make it true.

Hafwen was standing over her map, one hand on the sketches and the other shielding her good eye. "Here! Just here." She looked at Kynan and gave him a nod.

It was time once again to dive in search for the Calon y Dderwen.

As planned, the same group traveled within the cage of Kynan's shadows. Werian and Rhianne, Filip and Aury. Weariness tugged at his shadow heart. He had used far more shadow magic in these several days than he was used to. He wouldn't be able to keep up this group underwater mission for long. An hour perhaps. Maybe less.

Did the land and sea understand why he was pulling so much energy from it and pouring it through himself to work his shadow spells? Did the land, sea, and air understand the desperation in his hearts?

Under the water, shadows shifting around him, he spotted a flickering light in the distance. He looked to Rhianne, and she nodded, indicating that she had produced her searching spell again and the magic had picked up whatever she desired or focused on. She'd tried to explain the spell to him after the first time she'd used it, but he didn't completely comprehend.

Taking a deep breath of the magicked air inside his shadow cage, he pushed onward and forced his thoughts to remain logical and stoic, shoving emotion to the deepest parts of his mind so he could think clearly.

The light intensified and glowed a bright rose color with streaks of blue like the poppies at home. Swimming forward, he examined the light. It didn't appear to have a solid form—this was something made of magic. A cage of sorts made of whitened dead coral surrounded the light.

Aury glanced at Kynan, then raised her staff. Her

mouth moved, and bubbles filled with the words of a spell slipped through the shadow bars of her cocoon. Water peeled away from the coral and rock in a foamy column before bending back on itself to strike the coral.

"Don't destroy it. Careful!" His words were muffled by the water and the magic. There was no way she could hear him.

Coral and rock exploded from the blast of her magic, and the light flared brightly, its rose and emerald beams piercing the dark water. The light floated away from its shattered nest of coral then rushed into the dark water.

Kynan gathered the group and moved them into a single line, then he led them past two large boulders covered in sickly yellow growth and toward the light's path.

The light guided them into a tunnel. Sweat broke out along Kynan's brow, though the odd mix of magicked air and salty mist wiped it away quickly.

How long could he hold them in breathable cages? What if they became stuck in this place?

Pushing onward, he turned a corner and eased the others along behind him. The light flickered and dimmed as the tunnel twisted once more.

Behind Filip, Rhianne had her wand out and was motioning to Kynan. Perhaps she wanted to use her finding spell or whatever magic it was she had up her sleeve. He nodded. They needed any help they could get.

She drew her wand up and down, fast like a whip's lash, and her mouth moved, forming bubbles that gathered outside her shadow enclosure. Through the black lengths of his magic, her eyes narrowed, her focus on the light in front of them.

A shiver of cold traveled over his body and through the shadows thrown over the others. Whatever spell she was casting lanced his magic and cut through his energy. He gritted his teeth. He would not fail. But if they were going to continue on through a possible labyrinth of tunnels and chambers, he had to let them know he was running low on energy. Stopping the group with a mental tug on his magic and a fisting of his shadowed fingers, he turned to face them. His movements, though he was encased in air magic, felt affected by the water. He was oddly buoyant in his cocoon of air.

Motioning to his chest, he lowered his head to indicate he wasn't feeling his strongest. He hated having such limitations.

Werian raised his eyebrows and gestured at himself. Perhaps the fae prince was offering healing and energy.

Rhianne sheathed her wand, and the distant rosy light dimmed as her spellwork faded away. So her spell had been increasing their ability to see the light. Smart. Perhaps she could give Kynan some power if Werian grew too fatigued as well, just as she had done for Dorin during the run-in with the dragons.

In the near darkness, with only the pale pink glow of the light, Werian reached through the shadows of his life-giving cage. Tiny bubbles gathered along his fingers, and a fish began nosing his wrist, apparently deciding whether or not Werian was edible. Werian jerked his hand and successfully scared off the fish. He broke through the shadows around Kynan, with Kynan's magical help of easing the flow of power in that one place, and the fae put his hand on Kynan's shoulder. Immediately, warm fae healing magic flowed into his shoulder and through his body. His magic surged, a feeling like waking up shunting through him, and his fatigue faded away.

Kynan gave the fae prince a grateful smile. The fae often acted like a fool with his inappropriate jests, but Kynan found no fault in the way he proved himself during hardships.

Werian retreated to his shadow cage. Filip put a fist in the air, the shorn sides of his head and his Balaur-style braids showing in glimpses through the lengths of black magic. Kynan supposed Filip's gesture meant to carry on, so as Rhianne reworked her brightening spell, he drew them farther into the tunnel.

The space opened up. The mysterious light cast long shadows on a massive cavern. Peaks of stone like great fangs bordered a dark passageway on the far side of the underwater chamber. The light blinked from that place, bright then dimmer again. Inconsistent at best, this strange illumination certainly fit the description Hafwen had read about in the scrolls.

Pulling the party into the passageway, Kynan increased the speed of the chase. It was a tight space here, the light bright on what appeared to be hand-carved walls. Markings along the right side seemed intentional and reminded him of the cave paintings he'd stumbled upon in the highland moors near a cluster of unmapped waterfalls.

He reached out to touch the carvings, the water cold on his fingers but nothing he couldn't handle. Each carving had gathered some type of growth, perhaps an algae of sorts. The inscriptions, or art—he wasn't sure— had been crafted with a sharp tool. This one showed a sunburst. No, it was the head of an animal. Yes, and these next two showed more of the same animal. Was it a lion? No, perhaps not.

The light flickered wildly and was horribly difficult to see as its occasional flares scarred his vision with dots. His magic shuddered, and he tensed and took a deep breath.

A faint mental nudge came from Ivar. He wanted to know how Kynan was feeling and when he would return.

Kynan aimed a sliver of his focus to Ivar. *Holding steady. All is well.*

Then the light went out.

All was darkness. He could still feel the weight of the others on his magic, so everyone was well enough...

A glowing amber and amethyst light sprang to life at the end of Rhianne's wand, and she pointed to herself and then to the continuing tunnel. Maybe she wished to lead with the light.

Kynan eased her shadow cage in front of Werian's, then he spread his fingers and pushed her web of magic with additional shadows. It was trickier to steer her and drag the others, but it wasn't unmanageable. Ignoring the rest of the carvings in order to focus on his shadows, he followed Rhianne farther in.

The water pressed against his magic like a cold hand trying to crush the cages. He took a shuddering breath, then drew Rhianne back a bit so they were as close to side by side as he could arrange them in this tight spot. He set a hand on his chest and shut his eyes, shaking his head.

He couldn't hold on much longer, and that fact boiled his blood. Weakness was not an option when Maren needed him. Imagining Tiergan, he allowed rage to rouse him. Someday, he would stand at Maren's back and help her rip Tiergan to shreds.

Rhianne blew out a breath that released large bubbles beyond her cage as she looked back at Werian, Aury, and Filip. She waved a hand at Aury. Kynan pointed to Aury's staff and spread his hands wide, careful not to untangle his magic. Maybe if she could move the group, he could save what was left of his energy to keep them breathing and safe from the pressure of these deep waters.

Aury spun her staff, and a wave of rippling water distorted the light from Rhianne's wand, and then they were moving without his help. It was a relief. He could keep this up for a while longer. Maren was completely worth the risk, as were his people who were undoubtedly suffering under Tiergan's thumb.

The tunnel opened up again, this time into an incredible expanse of smooth stone, waving stalks of seaweed that somehow lived with no sunlight at all, and a ceiling covered in carvings.

The light appeared again, and it blinked repeatedly, rose red and sparkling, from the floor of the cavern.

Aury drew them nearer. Rhianne doused her magical light.

Strange pale blue stones piled on rock shelves lined the walls of the underwater chamber, and Kynan nicked one as they moved closer to the light. His water-chilled fingers curled around the stone. Unless he was mistaken, this was a raw sapphire. There were so many, a veritable hoard.

He stared at the light, studying the shapes around it. Smooth rock formations housed the light, and what looked like fins reached—

Kynan drew back against the wall of his magic, and for a moment his shadows faltered. Sweating, he pushed his energy into them again as he stared...

At a sleeping dragon.

A thrill went through him from the crown of his head to the tips of his toes. Never before had he seen or heard of a sea dragon. The creature could end him with very little effort seeing as his magic was close to being depleted, but he couldn't help but admire the fierce beauty of the dragon.

Aury slowed their descent and moved them in a semi-circle around the creature. Filip had drawn his axe, though Kynan wasn't sure what he planned to do with it.

The dragon's scales were gray like stone, and the light came from the crystalline spike at the very top of his large head. The crystal was green, the dark hue of the sacred oak's leaves, but the light inside remained the color of summer roses. Sides slowly heaving in and out, the dragon appeared to be asleep and somehow breathing underwater. There were slits along its sinuous neck...

A sea dragon, here in the Underworld. It was such an amazing wonder. A cacophony of questions hit his mind, a combination of his own wonderings as well as

Ivar's, who must have received a bit of Kynan's thoughts accidentally.

The key question was clear.

Was the spike on this sea dragon's head the Calon y Dderwen? Perhaps the mad king hadn't physically thrown the crystal into the Dark Sea. That could have been a disambiguation or some such thing from translations and tellings over time. Maybe the dragon had fought with the mad king, and the mad king had used magic to drive the creature away to this dark, deep place.

The follow up to that being—if that was the famed crystal, how in the name of every god and goddess were they supposed to use it at the taproot of the Sacred Oak to balance the realms? It was attached to a dragon.

He glanced at Filip and Aury, who had moved closer still. Both scowled, and he was fairly certain they were cursing their luck. Going on intuition—it worked for Maren, so perhaps it would for him—he stole a portion of shadow from his cage and formed it into a small sphere of protected air. Setting it against his lips, he spoke a question.

"I propose Rhianne attempt to keep the dragon asleep with some fine magic of hers while I get close to investigate whether or not my magic responds to the dragon's spike. It should be obvious if this is the Calon y Dderwen." An artifact like this would surely react to his power. "Raise your hand if you agree."

Keeping an eye on the sleeping sea dragon, he pushed the sphere toward each individual until all had held the sphere to their ear to listen. They raised their hands, the action only partially in view due to his shadow magic and the darkness of the cavern.

Rhianne spun more of the magical red woolen yarn she had used on the ship from the end of her wand. The length of it hovered above the dragon's eyes, not quite touching, then the wool knotted in three places, and the ends waved in the current. The dragon grew more still, and its breathing slowed. The crystalline spike on its head flickered and glowed as if it were alive and possessed its own will. The spike was attached to the dragon in the same manner as Ivar's smaller variety of crystalline spikes. All dragons and wyverns had them running from the head, down the back, to the tail. Brutally cutting the crystalline spike couldn't be a good idea. He didn't need to be a witch to feel the wrongness of that in his gut.

Holding his breath, he extended a tendril of shadow magic toward the crystal spike. If this was somehow the crystal from the legends, it was one of the most powerful sources of magic in the realms. His shadow tendril curled around the crystal, then disappeared.

He dared to move closer to the sleeping dragon.

The magic hadn't dissipated, but it had split into a multitude of threads that pointed at the crystal as if his power were studying this find. He urged his magic to coalesce around the crystal, pushing at it. His entire body ached with fatigue, but he shoved back, his muscles tensing along his back, arms, and legs. Giving up was never an option.

The pieces of shadow touched the crystal's peak, and emerald forks of lightning spread over the sleeping dragon's body and down its tail. Kynan jerked backward. The light washed over the hoard of sapphires and the stone and sand floor.

The energy left in Kynan slipped away. His shadow heart beat like a bee trapped in a palm, then slowed dramatically. Cursing silently, he waved a quick hand to the others and pointed overhead. They seemed to know he was struggling, their eyes wide with alarm and their mouths set with concern.

Using her water magic, Aury rushed them back the way they'd come. Every second of it was an agony as his magic attempted to go out like a snuffed candle.

CHAPTER 29
KYNAN

Kynan woke to see Hafwen kneeling beside him, grinding herbs with a small mortar and pestle. Werian sat on Kynan's other side, his hands set on Kynan's arm and magic flowing from his touch. Rhianne stood over Kynan's bare feet, casting a multicolored spell of smoke and thread. She had called up the colors of the four elements: white for air, blue for water, red for fire, and a deep green for earth. The green reminded him of the crystal on the water dragon's head. His thoughts were as tangled as one of Rhianne's magical knots...

The next time he woke, he found himself on a cot on deck beside a stack of crates and a coil of thick rope. Daylight streamed through tattered clouds as he stood and dusted himself off. Luckily, he felt strong once more, his hearts thudding regularly and his blood still hot with his need to see his fated mate to safety.

Hafwen stood on the far side of the deck, standing

over her scrolls and chatting with some of the others. He joined them and placed a hand on Hafwen's shoulder.

"I suppose I have some thanks to give out," he said. She turned as everyone regarded him. "I am sorry that my strength failed me so suddenly and quite nearly killed us. I believe that sea dragon had something to do with it."

Hafwen laughed. "I'd say so." She pointed to a line in one of her tattered pieces of parchment. He leaned over to look at the writing, but it was completely illegible.

"I can't read that scribble. Just tell me what it says."

Filip grimaced. "Oh, he's grouchy after he passes out."

Hafwen gave Kynan a wry smile. "He doesn't need a reason to be grouchy."

Kynan glared, but his lips twitched in a half grin. She knew him well.

"It says here," Hafwen said, "that the hallowed stone, which I'm guessing is our Calon y Dderwen, is an artifact one must reason with. Originally, I believed the translation of reason meant locate, as in to understand its location, but perhaps it means we must reason with the crystal. Considering the crystal is attached to a sea dragon, I guess that means we have to return to the sea cave and attempt to communicate with the creature."

Kynan crossed his arms and tapped a finger on his bicep. "How do we reason with a sea dragon? I have learned much during my long life, but that is not something that I have picked up along the way."

Filip grunted and grinned. "Jewel, my familiar, is not easy to reason with. Last time I tried to get her to fly me to a distant camp near the coast, she dumped me on a haystack."

A chuckle came from Aury. "Wish I had been there for that."

Filip pinched her backside, and she smacked him playfully before nibbling his ear. His arm slid around her, and he pulled her against him as he whispered to her. She made a humming, pleased sort of sound. Filip kissed her neck and brushed his fingers over her lower ribs teasingly.

Kynan's thoughts drifted to Maren. He recalled the shine of courage and defiance when she'd told him she'd get the sword from Tiergan. She was a force of nature, sometimes an enigma, and everything about her intoxicated him. His hands ached to run through her hair, to cup her head and bring her lips to his, to shield her with his arms. His shadows were desperate to tear her away from Tiergan's castle and place her on a throne of her own.

He swallowed, pushing the longing to the back of his mind.

Dorin walked to the map table, and Ivar flew from the dragon shifter's shoulder to perch on Kynan's. The feel of his gentle weight was incredibly comforting. And he felt an odd spark of jealousy that Ivar and Dorin had developed some sort of friendship. Silly, he knew, and he certainly wouldn't admit to it.

Filip clapped his brother on the back and eyed

Dorin's large jade-green wings. "Just the man, um, dragon shifter we need to see. Can you tell us how we might reason with a dragon? I am bonded with Jewel, but she has a very simple, straightforward mind. I don't think her thoughts run the same road as yours, Ivar's, or this sea dragon's."

A crew member offered Kynan a mug of watered wine and a strip of dried venison. He thanked the man, drank, then handed the venison to Ivar. His stomach was in knots, and he had no appetite.

Dorin crossed his arms and scowled at the scroll. "Brielle," he called over the deck, eyes searching. "Can you take a look at this scroll with Hafwen?" He glanced at Kynan and Hafwen. "She might be able to uncover more information from this."

Hafwen nodded, looking behind them, presumably for Brielle. "I keep forgetting she knows so much about the old cultures."

Turning, Dorin eyed the crew and scanned the deck. "Where is that woman?"

A splash of water hit the deck as Brielle climbed over the side, wearing only her small clothes and a very strange apparatus over her eyes. She was soaked. Her braid dripped water as she squeezed the end of it. Removing the apparatus, she regarded them with a wide smile and a twinkle of mischief in her eyes. "I just saw something very interesting down there."

"Why were you in the water?" Dorin's voice turned deep and possessive.

"I was investigating. Someone has to keep a close eye on the sea. What if the sea dragon had followed you and you didn't notice until he accidentally tipped the ship over?"

"What was interesting?" Aury's staff was sheathed on her back, and she was sharpening her dagger on a whetstone.

"May I see those?" Kynan pointed to Brielle's apparatus. "I saw you working on this earlier. What are they?"

Brielle took a thick sheet offered by one of the crew. The crewman's gaze skirted to Dorin, then he lowered his eyes like he feared Dorin would roast him for looking at Brielle.

Brielle joined them at the table of scrolls. "Dorin, darling, I am fine. Don't be a wet blanket. This is an adventure! It's my expertise. Kynan, I call them seers." She handed the glass and leather apparatus to him. "They mostly keep the water away from your eyes when you go under." She wrapped the sheet around her more tightly and turned toward Aury. "I saw what I believe is the afanc."

Kynan's gaze shot to Hafwen, who had gone pale.

"I'm almost too afraid to ask," Filip said, "but why do you seem happy about an enormous sea monster? The second of those on today's agenda..."

Brielle grinned, her eyes wild. "I didn't get to see him the first time."

Aury exhaled and paused in her dagger sharpening. "I don't think you understand the words *sea monster*. The afanc is not a sea friend, a nice sea fellow. He is a monster, and monsters eat us."

Hafwen grimaced and nodded.

Taking up a dagger that someone had set near Aury for sharpening, Brielle made a humming sound. "I think the afanc is beautiful."

Rhianne rolled her eyes. "You really do have a thing for the beastly." She winked at Dorin, whose lips bunched and eyebrow lifted.

Brielle chuckled, and Dorin cracked a smile before giving Brielle a burning look.

Kynan returned to staring at the scroll. "Hafwen, will you tell us exactly what you have found and what you're trying to accomplish now?"

"Unfortunately, that one line is all I've been able to find. But I am going through this other writing from the scribe Morgan of the Blue. I'm hoping I'll find one more piece of information. I do wish Costel were here," she said to Filip. "I've heard great things about him."

Filip drew his braids away from his face and tied them with a thin strip of leather. "He has the mind of a giant."

"What motivates a dragon?" Kynan asked the group.

"Riches," Filip said.

"Should we attempt to lure the dragon out of its watery haven by collecting all those raw sapphires I saw?"

Filip looked from the scroll to Kynan, his gray eyes wide. "That's what those stones were?"

"I think so."

Dorin made a noise of disagreement. "I don't know how good of an idea it is to start a plan by stealing from powerfully magical creatures."

"Good point," Rhianne said. "Where is my husband?"

Brielle jerked a thumb toward the spot where she'd come back on board. "He's still down there, keeping an eye out. He can view everything just fine without seers."

Scowling at the scrolls, Dorin spoke again, his voice low. "This sea dragon surely has a way of defending himself or a process for attacking in the water. I don't know what that would be."

Kynan leaned on the table and took a breath. He felt much renewed, but still, the stress of knowing what Maren might be suffering was cutting his strength down hour by hour. "When my magic touched the crystalline spike on the sea dragon's head, emerald-colored power like lightning shot across the creature's scales."

Hafwen chewed her lip. "Tell me more. Don't leave anything out."

"There isn't much more to say. A flare of what looked like deep green lightning washed over the dragon. The crystal itself was green."

"Green speaks of Earth magic," Hafwen said. "But he's a sea dragon."

Aury pounded a fist on the table. "Why is this all so baffling?"

Filip wrapped his hand around her fist and looked at her with soft eyes. "We will figure it out."

She smiled, and her body relaxed as she leaned into him, making Kynan's hearts crack. He wanted to comfort Maren that way. She was all alone at Tiergan's castle. He could imagine how isolated she felt...

He blew out a breath. "Care to share your thoughts, Hafwen?"

"Separating the spike from the dragon would be cruel and barbaric."

Dorin and Filip said, "Aye."

Hafwen nodded. "Such an act isn't in line with balancing the realms. Surely. We aim for the ultimate peace. A balance can't possibly be gained by committing a vicious crime against a creature that lives outside of the troubles caused by the rest of us high beasts."

"Agreed," Kynan said.

Hafwen's golden eye shifted in time with her good eye. "Where else have we seen a dragon in a strange form?"

Kynan rubbed his chilly hands together. "Maren's spirit dragon, the goddess Nix." He recalled the dragon goddess' pale blue fire.

Aury's mouth dropped open. "That's it!"

"What's it?" Brielle glanced at Aury then eyed Kynan and Hafwen.

"Goddess Nix possesses the power of air and fire. Would you agree?" Aury looked around the table and everyone nodded. "And the sea dragon is half earth and half water. Those two dragons make up the entirety of the elements."

Hafwen leaned back on a barrel marked with three Xs and blew out a slow whistle. "Maybe..."

What did that mean? "Maybe what?"

Hafwen tapped her chin. "Maybe they can form the balance we need to free Maren from her Bond with Tiergan."

Kynan grabbed for one of the scrolls, desperate to understand. "But that would mean the story of the crystal was incorrect."

Filip scratched at the shaved sides of his head, shifting the braids knotted on top. "Nix is a spirit though. How could a spirit dragon and one that resides only underwater somehow join?"

Murmurs spread through the group. Perhaps they were completely wrong about the entire situation and all the translations. The spike might not even be the crystal of the stories. But the way the crystal's power felt when it touched his magic... He truly believed it was the legendary Calon y Dderwen.

Kynan rubbed his chin and looked at Dorin. "If we could communicate with the sea dragon, perhaps we could find out?"

"I'll return with you to the sea dragon. We can give chatting a try." Filip studied his brother's wings. "Can you swim with those things?"

Dorin shuffled them, and his eyebrow flicked upward. "I think they might work well actually."

If anyone had the ability to communicate with the sea dragon, it was these two. "I am recovered and can work my shadows for you."

Filip nodded. "I say we swim as much as we can without it. Use your work sparingly."

"Agreed." Kynan took another swig of watered wine, the fruity taste pleasant on his tongue. "I don't care to snuff out so dramatically this time."

"Grab hold of something!" Werian's shout came from the far side of the ship where he was climbing aboard. "The afanc has at last graced us with his mighty presence in full."

Ice frosted Kynan's body as he looked to Hafwen. "Can you distract the monster?"

"I'll try." She glanced at Rhianne and Aury, and the three women began casting spells.

Kynan drew up his shadows. The water gathered and foamed where the afanc swam just under the surface of the sea. Magic heated Kynan's shadow heart, and a net of darkness slipped from the tips of his fingers. He threw it at the wave.

The wave grew long white teeth.

A dark eye showed in the water as the ship listed hard. A tail armored with rough scales the color of rot rose from the water and stole the air from Kynan's lungs.

The tail dashed back down and sent a massive crest toward the ship before disappearing under the surface.

Water crashed over the deck. Kynan gripped the ship's side with one hand and worked shadows with the other, the weight of the magical connection heavy in his chest. The warmth in his shadow heart increased even as the cold seawater pooled at his calves and shouts went up from the crew and the Upperworlders, commands and calls for help overlapping in two languages. His shadows searched the water for the creature's tail.

Hafwen and Aury created an illusion just beyond the ship, a chaotic storm of choppy water, flashing yellow light, and sounds like another sea animal was keening. The afanc's head appeared and swiveled toward the illusion, and Rhianne wisely held back her wand's fire as they all watched to see if the afanc would take the bait. And so what if it did? Could they escape it? Hurt it?

"What happens if it reaches your illusion?" Kynan shouted over the crash of water against the ship, the snap of sails, and the shouts of the crew and Werian. "I can snare it possibly, and then Rhianne could burn it to death?"

"Try it!" Hafwen raised her wand higher as Rhianne shouted a spell, her words swallowed by the din.

Tail swerving a path, the afanc swam toward the illusion, drawn by Hafwen's alluring light and the keening. The beast was most likely hoping for an easy meal, a fine feast before it set to the task of destroying the ship that dared to sail its waters.

The afanc's gnarled head emerged from the sea, and Kynan flung his shadow net around the animal. His magic surged as the beast rose up, opened its maw, and thrashed down. Pain lanced Kynan's chest as the creature, slowed by the net, spun and swam toward the ship. Sweat poured down Kynan's face.

"Now, Rhianne! I can't hold it for long!"

She extended her wand, and flames roared from the end and flew across the sparkling sea toward the afanc. The magical fire erupted over the beast's hide but didn't seem to catch. The afanc railed against the shadows though, fighting to be free. Kynan held him, only five hundred yards or so from the ship, which rocked violently in the waves caused by the afanc's struggle. The smell of burned flesh soured the air and seared

Kynan's nose. His magic dulled, the warmth in his chest fading.

"No."

If Kynan faltered, they'd all die here and now. The afanc would take out the ship even if Rhianne's fire was licking across its scales...

Maren waited until Bethan had been gone from her chamber for over an hour before she drew her wand and called up the dragon goddess.

The blue fire crackled from the wand's tip and gathered in a cloud of flashing light over Maren's head. Goddess Nix's tail grew visible, outlined in lightning white, then the spirit fire spread and formed smooth scales, hand-sized spikes along a sinuous spine, four taloned feet, a long neck, and finally the dragon's majestic snout and deep-set eyes.

"Lovely to see you again, Awenydd."

"Do you know what I'm going to ask?"

Nix's mouth lifted into what might have been a smile, and her sharp teeth gleamed white in the lantern-lit room. "I do, but tell me, how do you plan to get the sword from Tiergan?"

"Classic robbery."

Nix barked a laugh and flew a quick circle around

the ceiling, lighting up the wooden beams and making the dew on the windows glitter. "He should be sound asleep at this late hour, yes? If not, I can most likely help with that."

"I thought you could only affect spirit and shadow?"

"Through his dreams. They are a matter of spirit," Nix said.

Maren nodded, recalling the dreams with Kynan. "Thank you for joining Kynan and me inside our dreams. It has helped me keep from falling apart."

Nix smiled and flicked her tail. "It's my pleasure. Now, what do you want to do first?"

"I have to get past the guards," Maren said. "They aren't rebel plants."

"Two of them?" Nix asked.

"Yes, thankfully. Sometimes, Tiergan sets four at my doors. How did you know there are only two?"

Nix grinned, flashing her dragon teeth. "I can hear the beating of their shadow hearts."

Nodding, Maren felt good about this. She had support in the form of a goddess. This wasn't as crazy a plan as it had seemed. "I'm going to try a spell on them to muddle their minds... Wait. If you can hear their shadow hearts, can you do something to them to make them sleep or worse?"

Nix's light darkened. "You're reluctant to kill them."

"It's not the same as a battle. It doesn't feel the same anyway."

Making a pensive humming sound, Nix stretched her wings, and the tip of her right one passed eerily through the wall and into the bath chamber. Maren walked quickly into the chamber, and, yes, the wing was visible above the cabinet of bathing sheets and squares of lavender soap. She hurried back and jerked a thumb at the other chamber.

"That's so odd. Can you feel the wall at all? Never mind. What about their hearts?"

"First, you need to breathe, little thief," Nix said. "Your head is on backwards."

"I..." Maren chuckled. It must have been a slang phrase from the age of goddesses. She did as ordered, because who argued with dragon goddesses? Not this woman. "Could you slow their shadow hearts? What would that do to them?"

"I have never tried." The dragon goddess' gaze shifted toward the door. "But I'll give it a go. I'll return shortly."

Maren started to stop her, but Nix was already gone, only her tail visible as she flew through the front wall of the chamber and into the corridor. Thumps and a rattling sounded outside the doors, and Maren threw one open to see both guards on the ground, eyes closed.

"Are they dead?" Bodies wouldn't be easy to hide. This wasn't good.

"I don't think so. I don't see their spirits or feel any difference in the strength of their shadow hearts."

Maren swallowed. "Are you still doing something to them?" After tucking her wand into her belt—the spirit fire still crackling from its tip and connecting to Nix—she grabbed one of the guards under the arms and began dragging him into her chambers.

"Yes, I have hold of their shadow hearts," Nix said.

"My magic is chained around them, but I can keep that in place while we move onward."

"Fair enough." Once the second guard was hidden in her chambers alongside his pal, Maren started down the corridor toward Tiergan's chamber. "Don't try that madness on Tiergan. If you kill him…"

"We all die, yes, I know."

"There will be two more guards at his door to practice on."

"I assumed as much."

At Tiergan's door, Nix did her little trick again, and the guards were down before they could call out. No one could see Nix, it seemed. The guards wouldn't have been staring at her if they had glimpsed a spirit dragon flying in the rafters. She swung open the right-side door as quickly as she could without slamming it against the inside wall.

Would she be able to cast a spell to help her grab Cynnwrf while she kept Nix here in the Underworld realm? She had performed layered spells, of course—lifting her own weight and drawing herself toward a rock ledge while climbing that cliff not so long ago when she'd gone to help Brielle. But layered spells inherently worked as one. Keeping Nix here in the Underworld realm while also trying to tug the sword to her and keep its dangerous magic at bay were two distinctly different actions. She might very well fail at both. But she truly didn't want to let go of Nix. First, because the goddess' presence was comforting. She was so casual and calm about everything. She helped Maren keep a cool head. Second, because Nix was keeping

Tiergan engaged in his dreams. Third, because she wanted to immediately hand off Cynnwrf's spirit to Nix for storage in the Between. The less time she had touching that legendary magical weapon, the better. Earth was not her element. She knew that like she knew her own name.

The floorboards creaked under her bare feet, and she froze.

Tiergan's massive bed stood beyond this first lounging chamber with its couch and plethora of fantastically soft-looking tasseled pillows. She could see a face and arms and guessed it was him. No one slept with him.

This is too easy, Nix said into Maren's mind.

Maren jumped, and her hand hit a crockery pitcher on a side table. The pitcher wobbled loudly, and she lunged to catch it before it hit the floor. Her temples pounded and her hands shook as she held still, listening to see if Tiergan had awoken.

He snorted once and rolled over, his bed linens shushing across the form of his bent legs. Moonlight from a row of high-set windows colored his sleeping face in the same shades as a spirit. Most people looked more innocent in sleep. Not Tiergan. His mouth was turned down at the edges, and his eyebrows drew together like he was dreaming about something that displeased him. The sense of evil poured from his presence and hit Maren in a wave.

Nasty beast, isn't he? Nix said.

Very.

As she crept toward Tiergan's bed—with Nix

hovering over her head and casting a haze of light—an imagining of Kynan slipped into her mind. What was he doing at this exact moment? Was he still alive? Her heart shuddered. She could almost feel the brush of his thumb along her jaw. She missed him terribly. Shoving that emotion down, she focused on the task at hand.

Tiergan's weapons belt lay beside him like a sleeping lover. She took one careful, quiet breath, then pointed her wand at the sword.

Magic curled around her heart, then shot down her wand arm and toward the sheathed weapon. Nix flickered above her, then went invisible. She was gone.

Wait! Maren shouted in her mind at Nix even though a stupid shout wouldn't do a thing. She just had to let go of Nix and focus on the sword. She really didn't want to touch it. There were tales everywhere in the Underworld about how the sword meted out justice on those who tried and failed to claim the sword. Kynan had told her them as they had ridden toward their battle with Tiergan.

Her magic sparked and tickled her fingertips. The sword slid from its sheath. A couple of inches of its black and glittering blade showed in the dim.

Her heart seized, magic shooting back at her in a hit like a punch to the chest.

Her spell faded to nothing.

She swore silently and raised her wand again.

Tiergan hadn't moved.

She worked the spell again, pulling the sword toward her with a sticky-feeling spell that had no words, only the sensation of longing. The sword shifted toward her in spurts of erratic movement, and the cross of the hilt caught on the duvet cover. The next movement had the duvet tugged from Tiergan's bare stomach and his hip. The waist of his small clothes showed above the rumpled linens, and he murmured in his sleep.

Maren's heart drummed a frantic rhythm against her spine like it was trying to escape out the back of her body. She drew the sword closer...

The sword rose up and hovered in front of her face, her spell holding it there, her desire to keep it from Tiergan pounding in her heart, wand hand, and head. She eased the sword onto the ground.

Now, how to separate the spirit of the sword from its physical presence. She'd been thinking about how to accomplish the deed. Spirits felt cool and straightforward, unlike living people. Tuning in to the sword's presence, she attempted to sense the spirit.

Was she a lunatic? Probably.

But this weapon had such a glorious history—it would have to after being so long in the world, wielded by rulers in legendary battles—surely such a life, if one could call it that, would leave a mark on the spirit of the sword.

Closing her eyes, she imagined the sword swinging through the air at some dark enemy. In her mind, she saw the weapon's sharp edge cutting a trench in the ground and toppling the spiked wooden walls of an ancient fortress. Stones glittering with gems rolled from a rune set into the moss by the sword's tip.

A scent like green wood touched her nose, and she opened her eyes to see the sword's earth power glowing brightly in shades of jade and emerald all along its razor sharp edges and over the hilt and pommel. She pointed her wand and drew the power toward her.

A breeze blew over her cheeks, and the scent of spring rain and wet earth blended with the green wood scent. Her arm shook with the effort of holding the sword's spirit separate from the blade. Dots danced before her eyes. She stumbled backward, catching herself with her free hand and staring at the earth magic spirit as if keeping a good eye on it would hold it steady.

Envisioning the Between, she summoned Nix.

Goddess Nix, the sword's spirit is ready for you.

Tiergan would wake at any moment. Her body trembled, and the spell began to fall apart.

Nix, hurry…

The dragon goddess blazed to life, lighting the room. Panic burst through Maren before she recalled that Tiergan would only see the goddess if she or Nix willed it so. Breathing and fighting to keep her wits, she linked a wavering line of blue spirit fire from Nix to the spirit of the sword.

To the Between, please, she said silently.

Don't mind if I do, Nix said into her mind.

Maren jumped as the dragon and Cynnwrf's spirit blinked into nothingness. She stood on shaking legs and slipped her wand into the thigh sheath under her skirts.

"Wife." Tiergan's steely voice froze her in place.

She shrugged and looked down at the sword. "I was considering trying to claim it, but..." It was only a weapon now, not a spark of magic anywhere inside it. How long before he realized that? Could she get away before that? Should she use her wand?

He was out of bed in a flash, and his hand clamped down on her arm. Pain spread from his tight hold, and he winced like perhaps he felt it too through their Bond, even though small hurts hadn't seemed to affect either of them in their time as man and wife.

He spun her and glared into her eyes. "Be very careful how you answer now... What are you doing in my rooms?"

He didn't realize she had her wand. He knew nothing right now. But then he bent to retrieve Cynnwrf. The moment his hand gripped the hilt, his eyes narrowed.

Twisting to look into her face, he spoke very quietly. "What did you do, witch?"

No use denying it. "I emasculated your fancy toy, Husband."

He threw back his head, roared like a wild animal, and tossed her to the floor. Her elbow hit the wooden floorboards, and she hissed as heat snaked through her arm. He stormed over to the doors and called for the guards.

A smile grew boldly over Maren's mouth, and she stood slowly. "What's your plan now? I don't know if you noticed, but all the children and innocents have been escorted beyond your reach." He went very still. "You can't hurt me too badly because of our Bond.

You…" She drew her wand and whipped it in a broad circle to call up Nix.

Nix shimmered into view. Her spiked tail lashed across the entry chamber, just behind Tiergan's head. She regarded Maren with glittering spirit fire eyes. "I was hoping you'd include me in this next step."

Maren laughed and willed Nix to be visible to Tiergan and the two guards that burst into the room beside him. All three of them gasped at her sudden appearance, and Tiergan rocked back on his heels.

"How did you get that?" His eyes shot arrows at her wand, and his shadows rushed from his hands toward her.

"Never you mind, darling."

She snapped her wand's spirit fire at Tiergan's unspooling shadows. The fire turned the shadows to ash. Tiergan's magic flitted away on a cold draft of air as he snarled and rushed at her while his guards cowered under Nix's fiery talons. The dragon goddess grinned, showing long, vicious teeth, and the guards took off down the corridor, leaving their master to his fate.

Maren pointed her wand directly at Tiergan's feet and wrapped them in sparkling light. Ankles bound, he dropped like a tumbled stone and hit his head sharply on the floor. A subtle pulse of pain echoed through Maren's temple in the exact spot where he'd hit the ground. She lashed him up fully in ropes of spirit fire and secured his arms to his side.

His face twisted into a grimace and his eyes shot bolts of hatred. "I will see you dead."

"Perhaps, but then you'll die too. Just after, I'd

imagine. So for now, the both of us will have to be content with this situation. Soon, High King Kynan will arrive, and we will set everything to rights. It's just a matter of time." A sliver of hesitation cut her words.

Tiergan grinned cruelly. "You don't even believe your own sad lies. Kynan will be dead soon, his body floating in the Dark Sea or decomposing inside the belly of the afanc."

What was an afanc?

A laugh crawled from his mouth as if he could read her mind even though she knew he couldn't. She set her jaw and wrapped a thread of spirit fire around his head to clamp his mouth shut. His shadow magic exploded from his bound hands and his head, but the pale blue fire from her wand destroyed it as soon as it appeared.

"Stop fighting it." She walked closer, then set a foot on his throat as fire sparked bright blue and white around her. The magic felt like warm touches of a gentle hand on her flesh, but she could tell they were painful to Tiergan as he bared his elven incisors. Victory rode through her veins like fine wine. Her head and heart were pleasantly light, and she felt stronger than any shadow lord or experienced warrior. "I have won. You should do your best to persuade me to keep you alive once you are no longer necessary for balancing the realm and no longer Bound to me." She looked toward the corridor. "Guards! It would be wise for you to come when your queen calls."

The two guards from earlier scrambled into the chamber, their gazes going from Nix to Tiergan to her and back to Nix again.

"Eh, lads, focus on me. I need you to find Ceri and bring her to the great hall." No need for a banner signal to hold outside the window as they had planned. She had control of Tiergan and the castle already.

"But...didn't you hear the commotion, my lady? The rebels have stormed the castle grounds. Many lay dead, but the rebels have taken the hall, and we are in their hands now."

So Ceri and the rest had managed to break in by force. They hadn't waited on her signal. Good. She'd missed so much being trapped at Tiergan's beck and call. Ceri must have been plotting and planning this for a long time. A sad smile stretched Maren's cheeks, and she nodded gravely at Nix.

Nix made a humming noise. "I think it's high time you had this." A circle of spirit fire materialized in front of Maren. "Take it up, Awenydd, and become the Fire Queen you were meant to be."

Maren reached a tentative hand out toward the crown. Did it have a power of sorts to it? What would it do once she placed it on her head? Well, only one way to find out.

She grasped the crown and set it on her tangled mess of hair. A cool tingling traveled from the crown down her body, and her heart surged, feeling stronger. The crown had restored her health and... She looked around and an ache surged in her chest. "I feel...like..."

"Like you are more connected to your new home, the Underworld."

"Exactly." A smile stretched her lips. She breathed in, slow and steady, feeling more like herself than ever in her life. She flicked her wand, and Nix became even more solid, the tiny scratches in her scales from long-ago battles and the lashes at the edges of her dark eyes showing. "You're truly a glorious creature," she said to Nix.

Nix's mouth lifted on one side, displaying wildly sharp dragon teeth. "Thank you. And you, you look like a true queen now." She bowed, her spirit form floating low to the ground and her light making Tiergan's eyes shut tight against the brightness—light that didn't bother Maren. "You are the most powerful of all living queens, my friend, and I am glad to serve you."

Maren didn't know what she felt at that moment. Hope, yes, but she was anxious about the rebels and what they might expect. And who had lost their lives for this?

The spirit fire bonds on Tiergan were strong. Their presence buzzed in her wand hand and between her eyebrows so she was certain they would hold even when she walked away. The magic required wasn't nearly as taxing as all of that sword spirit business had been. A smile stretched her lips. Leaving Tiergan to his struggling on the floor, she left and Nix accompanied her down the corridor and into the hall, where a great shout went up.

"All hail the Awenydd!"

The ground shook, and the flickering torches along the walls abruptly went out, smoke rising into the stunned silence.

A crack crawled up Maren's wand. Nix disappeared.

Kynan couldn't die. Not yet. Not now. They were so close. Victory was a scent on the wind, a cup just out of reach, a silhouette on the horizon.

The afanc reared, rising from the water then crashing back down and sending another wave over the deck. Kynan pushed a thick cloud of shadow from his hands toward the creature, urging the dark swirls at lightning speed over the raucous surface. Ivar rose and followed, his cry loud despite the noise of sea and beast and elf. Kynan tasted blood on his tongue, and a tickling warmth touched his upper lip. His nose was bleeding. The magic must have injured him more than he'd realized.

He curled his fingers into talons like Ivar's, and his shadows took on the shape to latch onto the afanc's head. One shadow talon pierced the beast's eye, and the afanc let out a deep wail that shook the ship and made the sails shiver. Ivar tucked his wings and dove.

"Ivar!"

The wyvern's slim black form shot at the afanc's exposed throat. With one move, the afanc would be down in the water again and Ivar would be smashed into the saltwater, crushed and doomed to drown.

Kynan desperately threw two more sets of talons at the afanc as the witches threw fire and whatever else they could—wind and hissed spells that he didn't comprehend. Ivar hit the afanc's throat, and he dug in with tooth and talon. The beast rolled, and Ivar went with him. Waves careened over their bodies. Kynan's shadows gripped the smoking tail of the afanc, and, as he jerked his hands to the right, the magic secured the tail and pulled it farther from the water. The afanc rolled again, and Ivar was there, still attached to its throat with blood pouring in great gushes around him.

The beast wailed, this time without the power it previously had, and Ivar released his hold and rose into the air, flapping wildly, quite obviously exhausted. With one last roar, the smoking and bleeding afanc dropped below the dark waves, and the sea's surface calmed.

A great cheer exploded from the crew, and Kynan dropped to his knees as blood dripped from his nose.

They had survived.

As the crew dashed here and there, making repairs and tending to the wounded. Kynan shook himself, took a heaving breath, and dragged himself to his hammock to sleep or perhaps to pass out—either one was fine.

He woke several times to Hafwen shoving magical tonics down his throat. His power slowly recovered as he dreamed and drifted in and out of consciousness.

The morning light pushed his eyelids open, and there was Ivar, sitting on his chest and staring him in the face. The wyvern nudged his cheek, so Kynan ran a hand over his tucked wing.

"Yes, I'm alive. I see that you made it through as well. I'm quite glad, my old friend. Now, let's get up. I have an idea."

He climbed out of his hammock and set his booted feet on the boards as Ivar hopped to his shoulder and made a clicking sound of approval. The round window near the corridor shifted as dizziness temporarily turned Kynan's head in circles. He put a hand on the post holding up one end of his hammock and drew a deep breath while Ivar covered Kynan's head with one wing in a show of concern. The dizziness disappeared, and Kynan hurried from the sleeping quarters and up the stairs to the main deck.

Hafwen stood on the leeward side of the ship with Brielle, Dorin, Filip, and Aury. Werian and Rhianne were at the helm with two of the crew.

Kynan rushed to Hafwen. "What about water sprites? Could they communicate with the sea dragon and let the creature know who we are and ask how we are meant to proceed?"

Hafwen studied his face with the quick eye of a healer at her work. "How are you feeling, my king?"

He waved her question off. "What about the sprites? Could they relay such a layered communication? Do you know if they can speak with the sea dragon? They are all magical sea beasts."

"We have been attempting telepathy with the sea dragon." Dorin jerked his chin to indicate Filip.

"No response thus far," Filip said.

"It's a good idea, the water sprites." Hafwen pulled a green bottle from her pocket, uncorked it, and handed it to him.

Not bothering to argue, he drank the bitter tonic down.

Dorin crossed his arms and looked into the distance. "I would guess they could do that. They're powerful beings and seemed fine with delivering a message to the Spirit Well." He looked at Hafwen. "Isn't that right?"

"It's definitely worth a try." She unsheathed her wand and set to calling them up.

Ivar shifted his talons on Kynan's shoulder.

Kynan shut his eyes briefly and prayed to the god of air, Arcturus. *Please let this work. Maren needs us.* He could only imagine the horrors she'd been through with Tiergan already.

The water sprites arrived at Hafwen's beckoning. Daylight sparkled over their liquid gowns and shimmered through their iridescent wings of water as they hovered before her. She drew the same circle with her wand as she had done before, the spell that turned their chime-like voices into words.

"We have spoken to the Awenydd and the spirits as you requested. She will attempt to take Cynnwrf from King Tiergan. Why do you call us once more?"

A shiver went through Kynan, and he longed to shadow himself to Maren's side and obliterate Tiergan and every threat that dared to endanger her. Only in this desperate situation would she risk her life...

"You have been wonderful helpers," Hafwen said. "We are incredibly impressed with your magical skills."

The sprites turned their small heads and watched Kynan, Ivar, and the others with wide eyes of water. The effect was unsettling. "Thank you for your high regard," they said in unison.

Kynan bowed, and the other royals mimicked his move. "Would you be willing to aid us in communicating with the ancient sea dragon that rests below?"

Hafwen glanced from her magical circle to the sprites, probably wondering as he was if it would function properly for him even though he hadn't cast that magic.

The sprites turned away and gathered into a tight circle.

Filip set a hand on Hafwen's arm and leaned closer. His gaze flicked from the spites to Hafwen's golden eye. "What are they doing?"

She shrugged. "I know some but not all about these creatures."

Gaze darting to Aury then to the sprites, Filip studied the magical beings. "Hope it's not what they do before an attack."

Dorin's mouth tucked up at one side. "Afraid of the wee water babies, are you, brother?"

Filip pursed his lips, considering, then nodded.

The sprites whirled around then flew toward where Aury stood silent and menacing. "Magelord of the

Waters, we will do this favor for you because we are distant kin through the sea goddess Lilia. We will continue to help also in the name of the Awenydd who has saved us all."

Aury blinked but recovered quickly and bowed her head in respect. "Thank you very much."

They faced Kynan then, flying so near that he could smell the sea salt in them and hear the bubbling of their fluttering wings. "We honor you, true mate to the Awenydd and friend to Gold Eye."

He bowed deeply and remained there until the sound of them faded. Rising, he watched them fly back to Hafwen.

"Please tell the sea dragon that we are here for the Awenydd," Hafwen said. "We request that the dragon use her earth and sea power to restore the Sacred Oak in full to secure the realms."

"We will speak to her, but she is ancient and may not rise to speak back." The sprites didn't wait for a response but dashed into the waves, gone before another word could be uttered.

"Captain!" a crewman shouted at Werian and met him at the helm. "There's a leak in the hull!"

A leak.

In the middle of the Dark Sea.

Werian and Rhianne began shouting orders the second the words were out of the man's mouth. Crew ran here and there, a knot of them heading belowdecks, their faces taut with fear. Ivar flapped his wings, one brushing roughly across Kynan's cheek.

"Easy, lad. Keep your head," he whispered to the wyvern before following the crew down the steps. "How bad is it?" he asked them.

The crewmen rushed down the tight corridor to where the bilge pump worked. Two men were there already, one with a bucket and the other swearing and doing something with a tin of a foul-scented substance.

"It's not nearly enough," the man said, and then he cursed the tin again.

The men whom Kynan had followed all had buckets. They lined up quickly and began hauling water, passing buckets as more crew members filled the corridor and manned the stairs. Buckets of seawater were traded from elf to elf then presumably dumped over the side above.

Werian leapt quickly down the steps and hurried over, another large tin in his hands. "Start at the top. Secure the rest of the area around the crack with this." He looked over his shoulder as Filip and Dorin appeared with two hammers, a box of nails, and several lengths of wood.

They set to work, and Kynan joined the line of those hauling buckets.

The water continued to rush into the pump room at an alarming rate. "What if this doesn't work? What do we try next?"

Werian lifted another piece of wood and handed it to Dorin, whose wings were tucked tighter than Kynan had ever seen as the dragon shifter tried not to take up too much space in the small area. "If this doesn't work, we are on the skiffs as quickly as we decide it's a doomed effort. Perhaps Aury can get us to the shore before any magic consumes us or the afanc's big brother hunts us down."

Kynan swallowed. The water raged into the room, and soon the men working in the area were trading fearful looks.

"Captain!" the one with the second tin of what might have been pitch called out.

Werian glanced his way, and his shoulders fell. He turned to face the others. "To the skiffs!"

Like the trained men they were, the crewmen headed to the upper decks in an orderly but quick fashion. Kynan let them all pass until it was just him and the other royals, then he trailed Werian back onto the sunlit deck.

"Crew, you know your positions," Werian said. "Get boats one and five down now."

Aury nodded at Werian. "I'll steer us toward shore. Kynan, I assume you are low on energy still?"

He was. He felt as hollow as a year-old gourd. Ivar hopped to his other shoulder. "Sadly, yes. But I will try to help. Do we have boats for all?" he asked Werian quietly.

"Yes. But that's assuming—"

A chorus of shouts and a smack of wood on water interrupted his warning. They raced to starboard to see one of the boats hanging sideways and its inhabitants, including the ship's cook and Filip, swimming in the water below.

"The ropes don't break and damage the boats," Werian finished. He pursed his lips.

"I can fly," Dorin said.

"That far?" Kynan didn't see how it was possible.

"I can do it."

Brielle, Aury, and Rhianne went down in one of the skiffs, taking a few of the crew with them.

The crew loaded the rest of the boats and made room for Filip and his sea-soaked group on another one. The skiffs rode dangerously low in the water. Kynan sat on one of the skiff's board benches beside Hafwen, Ivar on his shoulder. The large ship they'd evacuated groaned and listed.

"Watch out!" Rhianne called from her skiff, just a little way off. She pointed.

The main mast snapped like a tree in a storm and crashed onto the decking. With a great popping sound and a sucking noise, the ship began to disappear under the waves.

"Aury!" Werian called out.

Aury stood, swaying a bit in the skiff, and thrust her staff into the air. The water around each of the skiffs bubbled and foamed, and soon the small boats were slipping over the sea and away from the sinking ship.

The ship gurgled like a dying man, and the waves rolled over the prow. The entire craft was gone.

And they had not a handful of food stuffs and no drinking water, wine, or rum.

The witches had their wands out now, though they remained seated in Aury's skiff. They spun some sort of sky-hued spell that increased the speed of the skiffs, helping Aury's magic work to a greater degree.

"That's enough!" Rhianne sheathed her wand. "Far enough for safety."

They couldn't head for shore yet as they were waiting on the sprites and their message from the deep.

And so they sat on the skiffs, everyone painfully silent; no doubt they shared his fears for their safety. Who knew what else the Dark Sea held? Anything could come up and swallow them whole right now.

Werian stood, sturdy despite the skiff's movements under him. "All right. That's enough fretting. You are worse than my great-grandmother."

A few members of the crew chuckled, and Ivar flew away from his perch on Kynan's shoulder and began circling just above the skiff.

Rubbing his hands together, Werian said, "How about we remain here until sunset, then send off most of the skiffs for shore. Do you agree?" He glanced at Kynan and the other royals in turn. Ah. He wanted to make sure there were some survivors in this. Those that waited for the message would be risking their lives with very little chance of ever going ashore again.

"I have two water gourds," a crewman said, raising one for demonstration.

Brielle pointed a thumb at the satchel she had strapped to her back. "I brought a jug of watered wine as well."

Ivar was a slash of dark in the afternoon light.

Kynan glanced his way then eyed the skiffs. "So we won't die of thirst. I agreed with your plan, Prince Werian, but it is key for our quest that those of us who remain do make it through this event, or all was for naught."

"Of course." Werian looked at Aury. "Perhaps you can remain?"

Aury sheathed her staff on her back, tightening the straps and blowing a lock of silver hair out of her face. "Will do."

"I'll stay here as well," Filip said.

A few of the crew volunteered to remain, but Kynan didn't see the point and told them they were to leave. "Werian, I assume you are staying."

"Couldn't pry me off this adventure with a dagger." He grinned, showing his slightly longer fae incisors.

A smile tugged at Kynan's lips. "Rhianne? What is your wish?"

"I'll go." She and Werian traded a heavy look. "The crew need a witch on board."

"And Brielle and I will see the crew to shore as best we can," Dorin said.

"Good." Kynan caught Hafwen's attention with a lift of his hand. "What do you want to do?"

"I've been thinking about it. I want to stay. I'm the one who can call up the sprites, and who knows how this scenario will wash out?"

Kynan nodded and gave her a friendly smile. She was a jewel of a friend.

Hafwen returned the smile but raised an eyebrow. "Remind me to ask for a position in the council upon return. If we live through the rest of our adventure."

He chuckled. "You know I've wanted you on the council for ages."

A fizzing sounded from the water behind them near the place where the ship had gone down. With a glistening spray of water, the sprites returned, and with them, the ancient sea dragon of the Dark Sea.

What was happening? Heart racing and sick to her stomach, Maren ran a finger over the crack in her wand, then looked up to see Ceri hurrying toward her. The room filled with the sound of worried murmuring, and it was such a stark contrast to the cheers that had first greeted Maren.

"What's wrong?" Ceri asked.

"My wand." She held it up, and Ceri paled at the sight of the terrible crack down the middle. Maren's stomach rolled, and she gritted her teeth.

Ceri studied Maren's face as if she was looking for wounds. "Did you hurt Tiergan? Kill him?"

She shut her eyes and tried to breathe through the panic stabbing at her chest. "I'm not an idiot. That would end the balance and throw us all right back where we started with the spreading poison." Opening her eyes, she set a hand on Ceri's shoulder to apologize for her sharp tongue. Ceri was an ally, a friend now.

Ceri set her large hand over Maren's. "Let's go outside and take a look at the damage."

"Good plan." Maren turned from Ceri and addressed the fellows at the doors and scattered about the room. "Guards, I command you to care for anyone who needs assistance."

They glanced at one another, but they weren't fools and could see she was in charge now. Quickly, they began helping people to stand and moving some to more comfortable spots near the sides of the hall.

Ceri pointed at four elves in blood-stained aprons. "My group there will work on the most injured first."

Maren nodded. "As she says. Aid them as you can, and we will also see to the fallen defenders of the castle." Ceri's head whipped toward Maren, and the guards' mouths dropped open. "We are one people now. The rebellion has succeeded. The castle is mine, and I am your queen now. I will care for all of my subjects."

"King Tiergan never would have done that," one guard said.

"I plan to be very, very different from him." Maren started out the door with Ceri, pushing down her fear. She tried the spell to summon Nix, but only a paltry spark jumped from her wand. "Is my crown still visible?"

"Oh, yes. Looks very bright. Your magic can't all be broken, then, aye?"

"I hope you're right."

The courtyard outside the keep—the place that had once housed fruiting trees and bloom-dotted shrubbery —looked as though a great leech had sucked the life from every green thing in the place. "Bones of the gods..." It was horrifying. "Why is it so bad this quickly? What did I do?" She spun to face Ceri, who was staring at the door they'd come through. Maren turned.

"Because you are an upstart little fool who is enamored with herself to the degree that you are blind to your true calling and your place in the world."

"Tiergan."

Her magical ties must have broken when whatever happened...happened.

"I can see you remain confused at what has transpired." A bevy of very large fellows appeared at Tiergan's sides. These were no nervous guards. These had to be mercenaries, specially trained, elite warriors. She'd never seen them before, but perhaps they'd been hiding in the shadows all along. "Allow me to educate you, Wife."

Maren gritted her teeth as her skin crawled. "I am not your wife. Stop pretending and so will I."

"Is that truly what you want?"

She spat at him.

His lip curled, but he seemed to force a smile, then he whispered something to two of the giant men. They rushed forward and grabbed her, taking her broken wand.

She growled, frustration turning her blood to fire as she struggled against their meaty paws to no avail. Why hadn't she raged at him with whatever she had left? Surely she could have done something.

· · ·

Tiergan threw her into the dungeon. No food. Only meager amounts of water. The world turned cold again, the poison and its damaging effects rising up fast, as if it had been waiting for an opportunity and simply biding its time until the inevitable happened and the Bond between her and Tiergan broke.

He sat outside her cell most days, nights—she had no idea what time it was anymore. He had swathed the one window in shadows, and he lit no torches.

Leaning against her cell bars, he breathed heavily. He smelled like wine and pungent herbs. The man was truly out of his mind now.

"My sad little pet. We will all die now. I prefer it, really. It never could have worked out. I don't know why I thought it would," he said over and over again. "If you simply agreed to return Cynnwrf, we could perhaps repair the realms again, but I don't know. I don't think I even want to."

The realms had fallen into cold again because of the way she'd bound Tiergan and worked against him. She knew it like she knew her own name.

"You wish to die?" Coughing, she looked up at him from where she sat on the filthy floor. The last time he'd visited she had argued with him, railing, venting her rage.

He repeated the same nihilistic phrases over and over, drunk as a skunk and out of his mind.

She could only imagine the horror of what might be happening outside the dungeon. Were the spirits growing hungry again? Were they rising and taking energy, killing all those she'd tried to save?

She'd bungled the whole thing. She was an idiot.

Had she been an idiot, an optimistic fool for hoping she could come out of this with the realms whole and healthy and her wrapped in Kynan's arms? Because that was what she had been aiming for. And she had never even been close to achieving that goal.

For all she knew, Kynan was seriously injured and stuck in the middle of a cursed sea.

No, she wouldn't give up. Not yet.

MORE TIME PASSED.

Her legs would no longer support her. Thirst was the only fire she possessed now. Hunger was its toothed companion, tearing at her insides with a strength she certainly didn't have. Had she ever been powerful? It all seemed a dream now. An imagined scenario.

Closing her eyes, she tried very hard to keep hoping...

CHAPTER 35

KYNAN

A shiver rolled over Kynan's body.

The dragon lifted herself partially from the water, head looming over the skiffs and dropping water from her long snout and her slightly exposed teeth.

Kynan fought the urge to put a hand to his sword and pushed his magic back down into his shadow heart. This was no time to start out aggressive.

The dragon's spikes cracked the light and shot beams in every direction. The earth magic crystal at the top of her head swirled with glittering emerald and sage hues, power evident.

The scent of the creature's magic overwhelmed the smell of the sea. It was akin to crushed sage, like Aury's magic, which had to be the water power the dragon held. The earth magic had more of a mineral type of scent, like turned dirt or fresh logs just before they caught fire in the hearth.

Everyone but Dorin had frozen and seemed

incapable of speech. Granted, the dragon was still rising from the water, massive beast that she was. Her huge jade-and-steel toned wings appeared to work as fins. A wave bumped the skiffs roughly, and Kynan gripped the side at the same time that he caught Hafwen's arm to keep her from falling in. She didn't even look at Kynan because now the dragon was flapping its mighty wings. Water sprayed everywhere, and the sprites' chime-like voices rose in what appeared to be celebration. The dragon lifted herself fully from the water until she hovered above the gathering with her mighty spiked tail whipping about and narrowly missing Werian's horns.

Dorin left his skiff and flew up to the dragon's eye level. Impressive bravery there. "Greetings, fair and powerful dragon of the Dark Sea."

Would the dragon understand?

The creature lifted her head. The tension was palpable. Kynan knew they all had to be worrying about the same thing—that the dragon was about to snap forward and take Dorin's head in one bite.

But Dorin held his position, his much smaller wings working to keep him there.

The sea dragon tilted her head and gazed at him, then she faced Kynan and stared. Kynan's hearts raced, but he stood slowly in the skiff and nodded his head in respect.

A series of musical tones flowed from the dragon's mouth as her throat moved, and soon the sounds became words.

"To the true mate of the Awenydd, I offer my service."

He took a quick breath and didn't bother to fight a smile. Her words were strongly accented, and the rhythm was quite different from the way others spoke the shadow elf tongue. "Thank you very much. What would you like for me to call you?"

"Athielia is my name."

"Greetings, Athielia."

Everyone murmured her name and bowed their heads as Kynan's mind scrambled to come up with a plan.

"We believe you and your power could be a match to the power of the dragon goddess Nix. With your earth and water and her air and fire, you might somehow come together at the Spirit Well and fully heal the Sacred Oak's roots." Kynan looked to Dorin.

Dorin nodded. "We don't know how to go about this or if the idea about your elemental magic is even accurate. Will you tell us what you know?"

The sea dragon flew in a tight circle above their heads. Her scales shone like the glacier water that flowed from the highlands. "I will think on this."

She plunged into the sea, the sprites following. The wake of her exit threw the skiffs into a rocky rhythm, and several members of the crew nearly pitched overboard.

Werian took up an oar and set it against the back like a rudder. "I say we start for shore. Athielia says she will speak to us, and I have no doubt she can find us when she's ready."

"Agreed," Kynan said.

They set off for shore, Aury and the witches doing

what they could to help the boats along at a quick clip. After a full day on the skiffs, Kynan's strength was restored, and he added his shadows to their spellwork so they could pull back and rest a bit. Dorin occasionally took flight to scout the waters in front of them, the stars casting a net of blade-sharp light along their course.

Once his turn magically driving the skiffs was through, he fell into a deep sleep that probably had something to do with Hafwen and that look she'd given him an hour back.

Kynan dreamed of Maren once more.

Her hands alighted on his sides, her fingers like feathers brushing up to his bare chest. His entire body burned with need for her. The longing to claim her, to make her his once and for all was nearly unbearable. His breath stuck in his throat as he stared into her eyes. Her look showed both wisdom earned in difficulty and the tentative love she held for him. But he could tell she was afraid.

"Of what, my wild one?" he whispered into her soft neck.

She inhaled, her breath stirring his hair and making him grip her waist more tightly. "That you are not here."

"You should wake," she said, her voice odd and disjointed.

The world trembled, and she disappeared, replaced by Hafwen's one concerned eye and one golden orb. "Wake up, my king. The dragon is speaking to you."

Kynan gasped and rose to a seated position.

Apparently, he'd slumped onto Hafwen's lap during his dreaming. "Apologies, my friend."

A half smile graced her lips. "Look up now, my king. It's time to embrace your fate."

The sea dragon swam toward Filip's skiff and sniffed him. She clicked her forked tongue. "You are the dragon kin's brother?"

"Yes, Lady Athielia." Filip's eyes were wide, and his hand, though not on his hilt, was at his side and ready to move if need be.

"Why does the dragon blood sleep in your veins and not his?"

"I don't know. It is perhaps because he spent more time with the dragons in the mountains growing up than he did with his elven family."

The sea dragon uttered a noise that might have been a chuckle, then she slipped just beneath the surface and swam toward Kynan's boat.

"You are awake now, Shadow King and Awenydd's mate?"

"I...I am. Apologies for missing your arrival."

"All is well. You dream of her. I can scent her in your thoughts."

How? "She is always in my thoughts and on my hearts."

"As she should be." Athielia suddenly lifted herself farther out of the water, exposing her wings. They looked as though they dripped silver in the star-strewn water, sloughing off the misty scales. "I will travel to the Spirit Well, but the Awenydd must call up my counterpart. For this to work, the goddess must be asked. She must agree willingly. I have not met her, nor do I have the capability to do so unless the Awenydd is present. I can go to the Spirit Well by way of the waters deep beneath the Underworld. Once I am there, it is up to you and your mate to bring the goddess and seal our powers."

"Will you...lose your freedom in this act? I know nothing."

"I will lose my power and my life. I am willing."

"You are?" Hafwen covered her mouth as soon as the question was out, as if she'd surprised herself.

"I have lived too long. The mad king had his witch curse me and send me to the depths to wait in a suspended existence. He believed I was the cause of the trouble he had in controlling the folk of his lands. Of course, I was not, and once he set that curse upon me, the Source demanded a Binding between an Awenydd and a shadow lord."

"I worry that Tiergan is on his way to ruin just as the mad king once was," Kynan said, more to himself than anyone else.

Athielia nodded her head, water dripping from her snout. "Hmm. Indeed. But as for me, you need not worry on my behalf. I have been waiting for my fate. I hope this is my glorious end." She whirled to face Dorin, who bowed quickly. The man was a kingly sort, Kynan thought approvingly. "Dragon kin."

"Yes, my lady Athielia," Dorin answered.

"Can you hear this?" She eyed him silently, and he shook his head. "Hmm." The water splashed, and she moved faster than Kynan could follow, and suddenly Dorin was bleeding across the forehead.

Brielle stood up, nearly toppling in, and shouted, "Leave him alone!"

Athielia grinned and cooed. "Peace, mother of dragons and elves. I am only creating a bond so that we may speak through our thoughts. It will be useful as I travel one way and you the other."

Scowling, Brielle remained quiet as Rhianne murmured something to her. Kynan supposed Brielle would be the mother of dragons and elves seeing as she carried the child of an elven dragon shifter. He had to shake his head. These kin of Maren's were anything but boring, that was certain.

"I hear you, Lady Athielia," Dorin said, wiping a drop of blood from his cheek. He didn't seem perturbed at all that he'd been cut.

Filip ran a hand over his warrior braids. "You can hear her words in your head?" It made sense he'd be interested considering he could communicate in such a way with his familiar, Jewel. But to hear actual words...

"Aye." Dorin turned to the sea dragon. "I hear every word as if you are speaking into my ear."

"That's more than I can do with Jewel."

"And more than I can do with Ivar," Kynan added.

Athielia swam forward and circled the boat holding Aury, Rhianne, and Brielle. "Good. We will need specifics."

"How can you speak the common language?" Brielle asked.

"I know all languages. I was there at the birthing of

the realms. All tongues stem from the core language." Athielia raised one wing from the water, then rolled before swimming closer to Kynan. "How do you plan to defeat the pretender to the throne when he has Cynnwrf in hand? The waters and their guardians, the sprites, have told me much. It takes time to receive information, but it does come."

"To be honest, I don't know. But I have faith the Awenydd will find a way."

"Her power is great."

"Indeed."

"I will meet you at the Spirit Well. I will be there before you, I'm sure, and I will wait." With one last survey of the group, Athielia dropped beneath the surface.

A thrill ran through Kynan's blood. "It is time for us to storm Tiergan's castle and help the Awenydd rise."

Maren drew a rune in the dirt of the cell floor. Tracing over and over again, she forgot what it actually meant. A circle, a staff, and a jagged line like a feather. Why had she been drawing it? She couldn't see it in the dark, but she felt the shape of it in the cold grime. A shiver rocked her bones, and she curled in on herself, the rune fully forgotten.

Her stomach gnawed itself. Pulse pounding in her temples, she tried to open her mouth but stopped when the movement cracked her dry lips and shot pain through her raw flesh. Touching her mouth, she felt deep cuts that were barely bleeding. She'd had them long enough for them to mostly seal over. What did that tell her? She couldn't think. Nothing. It told her nothing.

Shifting her head against the grit of the cell floor, she looked toward the two buckets in the corner. Did one hold water? Thirst rose in her like a panicked snake, rearing and lashing and sinking its fangs into her throat. She dragged herself across the floor, too weak to rise. Her fingers curled around the bucket, and she tipped it to look. The scent of drinkable water hit her nose. She sat up, took the bucket in both hands, and drank it down.

She had to get out of here. Soon.

CHAPTER 37
TIERGAN

Scratching the back of his neck, Tiergan paced a circle in his rooms. "I'm going to watch it all die. That witch will crumble into nothing." A jittery laugh bubbled from his lips. "I'll crumble too."

He stopped and stared at his shaking hands. Another laugh echoed through his room. Turning, he glanced over his shoulder, but no one was there, so he resumed his pacing. "They will all pay for rising up against me."

A smile cracked his lips, and he felt warm blood run down his chin. A buzz traveled over his skin, and he scratched at his neck again before rubbing his forearms and his chest.

They were all going to die.

Throwing his head back, he laughed again, savoring the echo of his voice. "It doesn't matter!"

Patience had never been Kynan's strongest attribute. Perhaps he should have worked on that at some point during his long life. He gritted his teeth and bit off the urgent demands the darker part of him wished to shout at the crewmen currently docking the skiffs. They were doing a good job. They didn't deserve his ire.

"You're about to explode, aren't you?" Hafwen asked. "I have some bluerran root. I can whip up a paste. It won't taste good, but it'll keep you from decapitating your allies."

Breathing through his nose, he closed his eyes. "I do not need it."

"You do."

"I do not."

Hafwen's grip found his elbow, and he opened his eyes to see her sternest look.

He tilted his head back and took another breath. "Fine. But only a pinch. I need to be sharp."

She nodded and released him so she could dig around in the bag at her belt. By the time they'd walked down the planks and onto the dock, she had a paste smashed into her palm. He accepted it with a humble thank-you and dutifully consumed the bitter stuff.

The trees lining the road were wilted, and the air bit at his cheeks. He paused and eyed the land. "Hafwen."

She stopped and turned. "What is it?"

"Look around. Am I imagining things, or is the land suffering?"

Everyone halted and gathered close as Kynan pointed to trees that should have been lush with growth.

Hafwen, a hand on her hip, cocked her head. "I think we need to hurry to your Lady Queen, King Kynan."

Swallowing panic, he strode forward.

The town nearest the dock was a little place called Niwlog. As they approached the gates, the guards called out, "Who approaches?

Kynan threw his shadows at the guards and the gate. Black tendrils that filtered from his fingertips pinned the men against the stone walls, and dark wisps of magic threw the gate wide open.

Hafwen glanced at him. "Not taking effect yet, hmm?"

He gave her a look. "Perhaps not."

As planned, none but Filip followed them inside. The rest of the royals waited in the cover of the trees beyond a curve in the road. A gurgling fountain greeted them on the main thoroughfare, and the banging of a blacksmith's forge sounded beyond a row of merchants selling leather goods and meat pies.

Kynan, his leathers covered in a homespun cloak given by one of the crew, approached the smith. "We are in need of several horses. Know where I could ask?"

The smith's gaze traveled quickly over Kynan and Filip but paused at Hafwen. Hafwen turned, acting casual, and smiled, the black patch she'd borrowed to hide her golden eye shifting with the movement.

Narrowing his eyes, the smith gestured at a low awning that had been painted a yellowish brown. "Aye. Master Turith, just there, can help you."

They walked away with a thank-you, and Filip came close to Kynan and Hafwen. "I don't think he liked you, Hafwen."

"Likes his ladies with two eyes. Such limitations. His loss." She grinned at Filip.

Kynan gaped at her. "You're enjoying this little mission of ours, aren't you?"

"I'm just happy that we're off that horrible sea."

Filip opened a wattle gate and waved a hand at Hafwen. "Even if we are headed right into a battle to the death and our odds are atrociously bad?"

"I'd rather die in battle than spend one more moment anywhere near that much water."

Nodding, Filip led the way under the yellow awning. "Are you part cat?"

Kynan ducked to follow Hafwen, and a fellow with a distended belly and a set of very bushy eyebrows called for them to halt.

"What's that you need now?" He had the heavy accent of the eastern shore.

Kynan inclined his head and readied to school his own accent so it matched that of Tiergan's lands. "We are in need of eight horses."

"You look fine enough to afford it. Cloak's not fooling anyone, mate."

"One can't be too careful."

"Aye, and that's true enough."

The fellow set them up with the horses, mares all, and after they'd purchased some food and drink, they were on the road to Tiergan's castle.

"Only a matter of hours now, lady of my hearts," he whispered. Maren's fierce eyes flashed through his mind, and the fire-bright connection between them—a bond that would never die no matter what evil their enemies wrought—strengthened his resolve in a way no magic ever could.

RIDING HARD, THEY FINALLY STOPPED AT AN abandoned quarry. Walls of pale rock stretched to the ever-darkening rain clouds, and a pond of clear water lay to the left of the path they'd ridden down. They dismounted, rubbed down and watered the horses, and set to hunting and making a fire. Werian returned with a brace of rabbits, and Dorin ignited the stubborn wood they'd gathered. Filip cleaned the rabbits and portioned out the meat.

Kynan broke the leaves off a slender green branch,

then speared his small meal on the end. The fat crackled and snapped as he turned the rabbit over the fire. His mouth watered even though his stomach was not certain about eating.

The others ate nearby in companionable silence, and they passed around a skin of watered wine as well.

A chiming sounded from the pond. Rhianne drew her wand, but Hafwen stayed her hand, gently lowering the magical weapon.

"It's them," Hafwen said quietly as she walked toward the pond.

Glittering bodies rose from the still circle of water, their fins fluttering until they worked as wings in the air. The firelight turned them shades of bone and citrine. Hafwen unsheathed her wand, most likely preparing to draw her golden circle spell to turn their sounds to words, but the water sprites lifted their tiny hands.

"No need. We know now how to speak to you. We have a message from the Awenydd."

Kynan stood, dropping his last bite to the ground. "What is it?"

"She bids you visit the Blind Pig, a tavern in the castle town." They collectively pointed northeast, where the flickering lights showed in the windows of thatched homes near a dark walled town. Beyond it, Tiergan's keep loomed a pale spirit-blue against the black clouds.

Rain began to fall in sheets.

The sprites spun in the drops, clearly enjoying themselves.

He walked to the very edge of the pond. He could feel everyone's eyes on him. "What is at the tavern?"

"Your allies." And with a peal of chiming sound, they dissolved into the rain and left only a rippling of current in the pond.

Half-timbered and dangerously lopsided, the Blind Pig sat between a chandler's shop and a fabric merchant's stall. The tavern's sign, hung on a swing arm, bumped against its chains as the wind increased along with the cold rain. The rain was too chilly, another sign that the Bond between Maren and Tiergan was failing.

What did he do to her?

The question bucked every other thought in Kynan's mind out of focus. If he had set even one finger on her, if she had even a hair out of place, Kynan would lengthen Tiergan's death. Draw it out. Watch him suffer.

He fisted his hands as his head thumped painfully.

Hafwen swung the tavern's doors open, and he trailed her inside. Three elves sat at a table rolling dice, their mugs pushed out of the way of the game. They took no notice of Kynan and Hafwen. Two farmers with fresh dirt on their trousers traded a story about the rain and their fields. A woman with a severe look stood behind the bar top, a rag slung over one shoulder. She was built like Hafwen—strong arms showing beneath the rolled short sleeves of her tunic.

The whole place reeked of despair, and no one wore anything brighter than a frown.

He walked over a blood stain on the pale wood floorboards. It didn't look old, not that it was easy to tell. Inhaling, he took in the scent of blood and refuse, but no one here appeared injured or laid up. The farmers smelled of manure, but the other scent wasn't that of an animal but of a human.

Hafwen must have noticed the dark atmosphere as well because she cast a wary look his way.

Werian had glamoured Kynan and Hafwen so they could walk around town without being recognized. Not many here would know what Kynan looked like, but they did know his description, and if he'd come in with a woman who had a golden eye, well, for certain they'd be found out. Because of the way the Underworld occasionally hampered the Upperworlders' magic, Werian told Kynan the glamour wouldn't last long. How long, Kynan didn't know.

Wearing a face with a larger nose than he usually had and the normal gray eyes of all shadow elves, Kynan approached the bar with a magically shortened and aged Hafwen at his side.

There was no time for clever ruses or research into code words to reference the rebels, so he simply raised his eyes to the barkeep and said, "We seek those who support the Awenydd, those who would see Tiergan fall."

The barkeep's mouth fell open, but she shut it quickly and waved them into a back room. Once inside the small chamber, she shut the door soundly.

"There is no rebellion. Not anymore," the barkeep said, her gaze going to the door repeatedly as if she was afraid someone might barge in.

"A fae glamoured me, but you should know I am King Kynan, and I'm here to free the Awenydd and set things to right."

The barkeep narrowed her eyes. "A fae? The prince that fought alongside the Awenydd in the battle against Tiergan?"

"That's the one," Hafwen said. "Allow me." She withdrew her wand and traced a star shape in the air between Kynan and the barkeep.

The barkeep jerked back, but there was nowhere to go. She gasped, studying Kynan's face. "Teeth of the goddess, you are him. Those eyes..." Dropping to her knee, she bowed her head. "Apologies, lord king."

He took her arm and lifted her. "My ego needs no stroking. Please tell me what you know."

The elf's name was Ceri, and she had been a healer at the castle until the rebels overtook Tiergan's gate guards and attempted to hold the fortress. All had been well until Maren had been forced to bind Tiergan in spirit fire, damaging the Bond and therefore hurting the realms. Maren's wand had been destroyed, and Ceri had barely escaped when Tiergan had taken Maren to an undisclosed location. Neither Ceri nor any of the spies still within the castle had found Maren. She wasn't in the dungeon Tiergan normally used. He must have placed her in a secret spot only a few of his closest knights knew of.

Next, Ceri told them of the portal that went from Maren's chamber to the Spirit Well. Hafwen asked several questions, but Kynan couldn't focus on that. He was so close—so very close to Maren now.

"Tell me again what she did to Cynnwrf." Kynan paced a circle in the small room as Hafwen and Ceri looked on.

Ceri wrung the rag she'd had on her shoulder and stared at the door. "I don't understand it myself, but she stripped it of its powers."

"How is that even possible?" Kynan whirled to face Hafwen. "Is it possible?"

Hafwen chewed her lip and studied the floor as she thought. "She has the power of the Awenydd... Spirit fire..." She looked up. "I'm sorry. I wish I knew, but I'm lost too."

Kynan stopped his inane pacing and crossed his arms. "If Cynnwrf is truly negated, the playing field, so to speak, is evened. I have to risk it. Risk going in, shadows unfurled."

"But if we're wrong?" Ceri set the rag back on her shoulder.

"Then I die. But the realms are crumbling again anyway. There is no time!" Kynan realized he was shouting and cleared his throat. "What do we do about Maren's wand? She will need it."

Hafwen handed hers to Kynan, her eye fixed on him.

"Take mine. It won't be like having her own, but I believe it will listen to her magic, as it is the only wand born in the Underworld still around today."

After the way she'd spoken of her wand being akin to a limb, this was no small sacrifice. He accepted the weapon with careful fingers and stowed it in his belt, making certain his borrowed cloak covered it fully. Then he took her hand.

"Thank you for this sacrifice, Lady Hafwen."

Ceri's mouth was hanging open. "You're...you're the witch."

Hafwen grinned at Ceri. "Nice to meet you."

Curtseying low, Ceri said, "And you, Lady Witch."

They talked for a few more minutes, Ceri giving details on the castle layout since it had been an age since Kynan had visited. Ceri also gave them information about the portal and who would be helpful inside the keep if they needed assistance.

Kynan breathed in and out slowly, focusing his anger into a rough plan. "The fight will not last long. I will either tear my way in and get her out, or I will go down rather quickly, I'd imagine."

CHAPTER 40
KYNAN

"I can't shift." Dorin stood beside the fire, staring at the flames as if they'd wronged him. The rain had stopped, but only a dragon could have handled starting a fire in this damp weather. "It's the Underworld. This place pulls on my power and slows the magic in my blood. And I think the curse that I tangled with among the dragons over the sea drained me. I can summon dragonfire though. I will take out the first line of guards at the inner bailey."

Kynan drank the last of the watered wine they'd brought, then ate a bite of the rye bread Ceri had given them. "That will be more than enough."

Werian held Rhianne against his chest. "I will shoot down anyone on the walls."

She smiled up at him, a wicked gleam in her eye. "And I will thrust the gates open with a neat little spell I've been working on."

Brielle sat on a fallen log, sharpening her throwing knives. She held one up to the firelight. "I'm eager to try my skills on a shadow lord again." She grinned maniacally, and Kynan was quite glad she was on his side.

Aury and Filip regarded Kynan quietly. Those two seemed to take battles more seriously than the rest. Kynan appreciated that. "We will have your back, Kynan," Filip said as Aury nodded, her mage staff on her back.

Hafwen threw them each a portion of the bread, and they ate quickly before mounting their new horses. "Do you have any ideas on where to look for Maren?" she asked him.

"I don't. I can only assume he would keep her close, so I will start my search on the floor where his chambers are."

With one last check on weapons, they rode toward the keep.

Thunder rolled as Dorin flew away from his horse to soar into the air. The guards called out but were silenced with Dorin's rippling flame. Five more rushed out of the gatehouse and were torched before they could say a word.

Werian rose, still mounted, and unleashed a volley of arrows at the warriors readying their bows on the walls. Tiergan's guards fell like stones to the ground as Rhianne blasted the wooden gates open with a blinding flash of amethyst and gold magic.

Kynan rode through, sword drawn. He cut down an elf running at him with a mace. With another slice, he severed the head of a warrior bearing two short swords.

If they wore Tiergan's livery, they were dead to him.

He summoned his shadows, warm and tingling along his palms and fingertips, sparking magic unfurling from his shadow heart.

Hafwen shrieked as she stabbed a man attempting to pull her from her horse. Kynan threw his sword, and it pierced the attacker's chest and threw him backward.

A rushing sound turned Kynan's head, and he saw Aury waving her mage staff in the air. Her silver hair flew behind her as she rode. Beads of water rose from the wet ground of the inner bailey and crackled as they became shards of ice. She shot them at a line of warriors storming from the keep's main doors.

With a wild shout, Filip leapt from his horse, axe held high. He dispatched the warriors not taken down by Aury's ice, and soon Kynan was off his horse and striding into the open keep doors. A woman ran at him, calling for aid from Tiergan's knights. She brandished a short sword and seemed quite skilled with it, but his shadows yanked her to the ground. Two guards threw down the boxes they'd been holding to rush Kynan. He extended his hands, and shadows encircled their throats. They were dead before they hit the ground.

With Hafwen behind him, watching his back with her sword extended, he found Tiergan's quarters. Tiergan was absent. No one was inside. Kynan stormed through the chambers, searching the bathing room and the lounging area. He kicked over a chair and table, feeling impotent with rage.

"Where is she?" His anger was a fever making him imagine all sorts of horrors. He couldn't get to Maren quickly enough.

Hafwen grabbed his arm tightly and pulled him to a stop. "Wait. I feel something."

"What?" He kept his shadows swirling around them. The sounds of fighting echoed from the corridor.

"Hush." She shut her eyes, and he did as she commanded. Her eyes flashed open, and there was glee in her smile. "A location rune. She has inscribed a location rune. The smart little Upperworlder. Come!" Hafwen took off down the corridor and stopped at a set of winding steps. "Where did Ceri say this leads?"

Kynan pictured the image Ceri had sketched out for them in the back room at the Blind Pig. "The laundry and the servants' quarters."

"Let's go."

He pushed in front of her and thickened the shadows at her back to protect her.

She shoved a hand past his shoulder. "There! I feel the pull of the rune in that direction!"

They ran down more crumbling stairs, through a hallway partially open to an underground tunnel that stank of the sewers, then along a narrow corridor until they found a wider set of steps lit by a torch on the wall. A rumbling sounded from floors far above, and dust floated onto Kynan's head. A row of rusting cells lined the right side of a long chamber with high ceilings. It smelled atrocious.

But all he could think about was Maren. Maren. Maren.

Movement in the dim light caught Kynan's eye. A knight stabbed a short sword toward his stomach. His shadows dashed the blade to the ground, where it clanged against a moldy stone wall. Kynan's magic snaked around the knight's neck and ended him before he fell.

"Kynan?"

His world halted at the rasping sound of her beautiful voice.

Another of Tiergan's minions stepped out of an alcove. The look on his face spoke of the evil in his heart. He was at home here in this terrible place. "I am Maddox, King Tiergan's Facilitator." He placed his hand on his chest as he bowed—a spiteful movement that was clearly only done in hopes of surviving. His fingers were speckled with blood. "High King Kynan," he said silkily.

Kynan's ears rang. "Whose blood is that?"

"It's Maren's blood," Hafwen answered, her glare as hot as coals.

Ears buzzing loudly as rage whipped through him, Kynan flung his shadows and crushed the pathetic excuse for a person into nothing, the beast's screams fading fast into silence.

With three more steps, he saw Maren on the ground, shackled and bleeding from a long cut on her forearm.

His heart caved in.

"Stay back, Hafwen. Cover your face, my heart." He threw his shadows at the bars and ripped them from the stone walls in a shower of rubble. Tendrils of black magic sliced the metal of Maren's shackles. He rushed forward and lifted her gently into his arms. His gaze couldn't study her quickly enough to suit him. "Are you all right? What can I do?"

She leaned her face into his upper chest and whispered. "Just get us out of here."

Hafwen was already running toward the steps.

"Take the right this time," Kynan shouted as he carried Maren, trailing Hafwen. "We are headed to her chambers."

"You know..." A cough cut off Maren's words. "You know the way?"

"I do. I met your friend Ceri."

"She's alive?"

"I'm no Awenydd, so if I spoke to her, yes."

"This isn't the time for you to pick up my kind of sass, Kynan." There was a spark of joy in her teasing.

"As you command, my queen."

Her fingers gripped his tunic, bunching the fabric. "He killed some of the rebels. The rest fled when Tiergan went into a mad rant."

They reached the corridor where her chambers were located. Beyond her door, a balcony overlooked a hall where the tops of dark banners could be seen. Three knights turned away from the balcony and ran at them.

Kynan opened his mouth and roared. Warm shadows poured from his lips, tasting like ash and pomegranates, and they shot at the knights, combining to form a great hand that grabbed all three and tossed them over the balcony. Their screams were music to his ears.

He kicked Maren's chamber doors open, and one fell from its hinges with the force.

Maren pointed at the bed. "Underneath. Trap door." She coughed again and swallowed.

"The portal?"

"Yes. I assume you can't shadow us out of here for some reason."

"Rhianne put a tracking spell on me so they too can find the portal. I can't shadow everyone out of here."

"They're here?"

He set her on the floor, and Hafwen quickly linked her arm around Maren's waist to support her. Maren looped an arm around Hafwen's neck and whispered, "Thank you."

"They are. All of them. That's all that noise. Well, some of it. They're taking care of Tiergan's warriors." Kynan took Hafwen's wand from his belt and handed it to Maren, who looked confused.

Hafwen nodded. "I want you to have it. Maybe later, you can give it back, but for now, we need your magic if we can get it."

The castle rumbled, and the floor shook like the realms were crumbling.

Kynan's shadows shoved the bed against the windows, and the smaller tendrils lifted the boards covering the place Maren had indicated. With some maneuvering, more shadow magic, and a rope ladder each of them dropped through the trap door and to the dark passageway beneath the castle.

Kynan took Maren from Hafwen and helped his love walk toward the glimmering portal. It was beautiful. Like a waterfall set with sparkling gems. Hafwen passed through, and Kynan prepared to help Maren step over the portal's shimmering boundary.

"Ah, the darling couple, here to finish off the destruction they started."

Rage as hot as the Upperworld's sun burned through Kynan's blood as he turned to see Tiergan standing in the passageway.

Kynan spoke to Maren while keeping his gaze on Tiergan. "What are your orders, my queen?"

"Cover my back, darling." She raised Hafwen's wand.

With Kynan beside her and a wand in her hand, Maren felt alive again. Her body trembled with fatigue and hunger, but her blood sizzled with power that tickled her palms and warmed the spot between her eyebrows.

But would Hafwen's wand work for her?

Only one way to find out.

She whispered words of fire and destruction and raised her wand...

Tiergan spread his arms wide. "I will bring us all down!"

A storm of shadows exploded from his body. In a breath, the air was filled with cracked stone and crushed mortar that blasted across her arms and face, tearing at her skin and hair.

A rock the size of a horse fell through the broken ceiling and bumped down the passageway. She ducked. It sailed over her head, and Kynan used his shadows to blast it into small pieces. He shouted something, then the warm rush of his shadows circled her body.

The noise was deafening.

Stones tumbled past, more massive rocks that must have been part of the castle's foundation. Loud banging sounds and ear-splitting shrieks—from both twisting metal and suffering people—tore at Maren's mind.

She struggled to stand inside Kynan's protective shadow shell, only to see Tiergan's bloodied face and mad grin as he pulled down his fortress with shadows. He wasn't even properly protecting himself in the midst of his own storm.

Summoning her magic with Hafwen's wand, she tried to send fire to stop him, to control him somehow, but another block of masonry crashed down just past them, and her magic sputtered and went out. She had to focus. This wand wasn't as easy to use as her own.

Kynan said something she couldn't hear, and then Tiergan let out a shout of pain.

Tiergan's magic went quiet, and the booming fall of rock and stone came to a stop. He stood, one eye swollen shut and shadows slithering around his body.

"This is madness, Tiergan." Kynan's voice was a warning.

If the portal was gone...

Maren spun to see it glowing still—unmoved by Tiergan's mad outburst.

The sky showed overhead. The castle was in total ruins. Smoke leeched from piles of rubble, and elves wept over what had to be numerous deaths.

Tiergan lurched forward a step, blood running from his temple and his nose.

Who had she lost just now? Brielle? All of them?

Kynan glanced at her with fierce eyes as she spoke her words of fire and drew a line of unsteady, crackling spirit magic with Hafwen's wand.

He touched her arm. "You can't kill him yet. I have a plan. But not yet."

She whirled the spirit fire at Tiergan and wrapped him tightly, just as she had done before. The world shook under her feet as he fell, his arms tight against his sides. Kynan looked around, and she noticed the frost spreading over the ground.

She wanted to dance on Tiergan's prostrate form and spit into his face, but the Sacred Oak needed her and whatever plan Kynan had up his sleeve.

"Let's go!" Kynan gestured to the portal.

Using the spirit fire's strength, she dragged Tiergan through the portal with her. The portal's magic was cool against her face, and, closing her eyes, she inhaled deeply as she stepped onto Kynan's homelands. She opened her eyes to see Hafwen, face grave, standing at the edge of the Spirit Well.

As if Kynan shared all of Maren's thoughts—goddess save her, but she wanted to fall into his arms and savor the feel of him—he met her gaze with blazing eyes then ran with her to the edge of the well. They knelt in the frost-cloaked grasses as Tiergan railed on the ground where she'd left him bound by spirit fire.

After a quick glare at Tiergan, Hafwen, beside

Kynan, shifted her weight to her other foot. "Is it too late?"

The water was dark and incredibly still. Too still.

"I don't know," Kynan said, his voice barely a whisper.

The taproot of the Sacred Oak was pure white, and the air...

Maren touched Kynan's hand, the only contact she could handle without losing it. She had to focus, to figure this out. "It is completely dead here, isn't it?"

She glanced at Hafwen, who was staring at the dead moss on the rocks that supported the Sacred Oak where the tree disappeared into the Upperworld. It was difficult to look at. The realms weren't lined up physically, but spiritually, and Maren's eyes couldn't handle the old magic cloaking the area.

Kynan stared into the water. "The Calon y Dderwen is a spike on the head of an ancient sea dragon. She is to meet us here. If you are able, call up the dragon goddess, and together they will somehow Bond to secure the realms, relieving the need for you, the Awenydd, to Bind yourself to anyone."

The roots of the Sacred Oak shivered, and a cracking sounded. A break in the taproot snaked from the water upward.

Kynan made a low warning sound in the back of his throat.

"Where is this dragon? If we wait much longer, there will be nothing to save." Maren looked back at the water, her mind spinning. A sea dragon. Who would have guessed? Exhaling deeply, she released her witch's intuition wide and sought any sign of spirits. Nothing. "We have to do something. Now."

She used her spirit fire to draw Cynnwrf from Tiergan's belt. His eyes flashed with rage, and the fire holding him tight flashed brightly across his bound lips. Using the blue-white magic carefully, she set the sword beside Kynan.

"How did you manage this?" He stared at the lifeless sword.

"I did the opposite of what I'm about to try."

Setting the tip of the wand against the flat of the sword, she visualized its past deeds, the glow of its power, the scent of its magic. She called up Nix, willing her to show herself and speak to them all. The goddess shimmered into being, her scales like opalescent stone and her eyes blazing with spirit fire.

"What can I do to help?" Nix said.

"Can you return Cynnwrf's spirit to me?"

The goddess bowed her head once, and an outline of the legendary sword glittered into being. Maren released Nix, who disappeared. Sweating, heart pounding, Maren touched Hafwen's wand to the lighted silhouette then carefully, delicately drew the sword's life back into its physical form by bringing the spirit to the blade.

Light flashed, blinding her momentarily.

Cynnwrf glowed before Kynan. He gripped the blade and the hilt, and blood pooled around the fingers holding the sword's sharp edges. He spoke in the shadow elf tongue, his voice low and intoxicating. His full lips moved quickly, and his eyes fluttered as the sword shimmered brightly then darkened into its original form.

He stood and lifted the sword, his movements incredibly graceful and sure. Extending a hand over the Spirit Well, he sliced his forearm with Cynnwrf. Blood dripped down through the icy air. The moment the blood hit the dark, still water, the water cleared and shone, and a dragon burst from its depths with a roar.

They fell back as a dragon with scales the color of shadow elf eyes drew itself up and extended jade-and-steel hued wings that brushed frost from the roots and moss around the well. The sea dragon's head sparkled with many spikes as all dragons' heads did, but one crystalline spike at the very top flashed with a bright rosy light. The dragon remained in the well, its body partially submerged.

"I am glad to meet you, Awenydd." The dragon blinked its large eyes at Maren.

She stuttered for a moment, then nodded. "And you as well. You are ready to meet dragon goddess Nix?"

"I am."

The earth just beyond the well cracked open, and the sound of hungry spirits began to rise from the water around the sea dragon.

"Quickly now," the dragon said. "Draw out my spirit and take me to the Between to meet the goddess."

"The Between? But it will kill you."

"I am prepared."

There was no time to argue it. Maren placed the wand's tip on the dragon's head as she had with Cynnwrf. She took in the feel of the dragon's spirit. Deep ocean sounds echoed in her ears. The calm and steady sensation of the tides filled her own soul. The taste of salt touched her tongue. The scents of sun-warmed earth and green wood swirled around her. She drew the spirit from the sea dragon and whispered her intention to enter the Between.

The pleasantly cool mist of the Between brushed her cheeks, and she opened her eyes to see the dragons hovering side by side just above her head. No spirits were present, and her stomach knotted with fear.

"Greetings, dragon of water and earth," Nix said, her wings flapping slowly as she hovered.

"Greetings, goddess of air and fire." The sea dragon's wings worked just as Nix's did, although she had four additional wing-like limbs that extended from her sides —fins, perhaps.

They began flying in a large circle, chasing one another high in the misty reaches of the Between, their blue-white and gray-green scales reflecting the subtle light that glowed here. They flew faster and faster until Maren couldn't tell where one dragon ended and the other began. Their colors combined, and they became one ring of dancing light.

All of Maren's hunger, thirst, and pain faded to nothing. She felt renewed, reborn. As strong as an ox and as light as a feather.

Nix's voice echoed through the mist. "The balance is renewed for all ages. Thank you, Awenydd, for your acts of courage. You are free to follow your heart forevermore."

Magic that smelled of snowy mountains and deep ocean blasted Maren backward, and she blinked, opening her eyes to realize she was back in the Underworld, standing beside Kynan and Hafwen.

Gasping, she reached out for them, and they caught her arms. Her clothes were clean, and the tears they'd suffered in the dungeon were gone. She looked at her fingers and the nails that had been caked in filth. The magic had cleaned her. Taking a deep breath, she realized she felt healthier than she had in ages. Nix and the sea dragon had somehow healed her too.

Kynan pressed a kiss into her hair and murmured, "My powerful heart. My queen. My Awenydd."

Darkness shot between them, and Kynan was thrust backward onto the ground.

"Maren!" Kynan was up before she knew what was happening, one hand of shadow encasing her and

Hafwen and another closing over Tiergan—trying to, at least.

Tiergan was standing and free of her spirit fire bonds. His palms bore spinning cyclones of shadow magic that tangled with Kynan's magic. A spear of pure black pierced Kynan's swirling shadows and went for Kynan's throat.

He choked, then he bared his teeth, eyes turning to rubies and smoke. Shadow wings unfurled from his back, broke away to become wyverns, and hurled themselves at Tiergan. Gasping, Tiergan extended his arms wider, and a whirling mass of darkness cloaked everything.

Maren couldn't see anything. Fear clawed at her chest. She raised her wand and thrust crackling spirit fire in the direction of where Tiergan had been standing when the darkness fell.

"It's no use, Awenydd," Tiergan sneered through the dark. "I have Kynan's throat laced with my power. It is over. It is over for all of us!" His maniacal laugh echoed through her mind and in her ears.

She threw more of her energy into her spirit fire and gritted her teeth as her body trembled with the effort. Her fire cleared a circle of shadow away.

Was Kynan already dead?

Forcing herself to focus, she increased the magic. The shadows blasted away from her stream of dancing light, and she blinked as everything once again became visible.

Cloaked in rippling shadows, Kynan stood strong and held three of Tiergan's shadow spears at bay.

"Do as you see fit, my queen," Kynan said.

Heart surging with fear and love and desperation, Maren drove her spirit fire into Tiergan's chest. He dropped to the ground, but his shadows covered him like armor. He grunted and struggled under the constant stream of spirit fire, spitting what had to be curses in the shadow elf tongue. They had no effect on her.

She walked closer, driving him onto his back and sending her fire through his shield of shadows. "As long as you are alive, you will threaten everyone and everything in the realms. I cannot allow it." With one last push of magic, she burned her way into his dual hearts and turned them both to ash.

Tiergan lay gray-faced and unmoving.

At last, her greatest enemy was dead.

Turning away from his body, she watched as the grasses near the well turned green. Life sprang from the well and across the earth of Kynan's homelands just as it had once before. This time, the change was permanent. Nothing would ruin the balance that gave this change life. Her gaze followed the bloom of lush clusters of blue poppies and bright yellow and green mosses. The Spirit Well was clean, and the surface rippled lightly as the spirits' voices echoed in the warming air.

Kynan walked over slowly, his eyes burning into her. He lifted her chin with a knuckle then kissed her gently, slowly. He pulled away and lowered his head. A lock of black hair fell over one eye. "You have won, Awenydd. You have saved us all."

She could hardly believe it, but the terror of the last

days was over. "Not only me. The sea dragon, goddess Nix, and all of those dear to my heart helped me." The realms were healed. And they were alive.

Ivar flew over the well and landed on Kynan's shoulder. She turned to see where he'd come from, and there they were—her chosen kin stood with bloodstained clothing, tired faces, and loving smiles on the far side of the Sacred Oak's taproot. Her heart sang with relief. They must have found the portal.

"Missed you," Brielle said, giving her a wink.

Tears burned Maren's eyes as she took in each of their faces, reassuring herself they were all alive and well.

Spirits rose from the well and gathered around Kynan and Hafwen. They bowed to Maren as one as she willed them visible to everyone.

One spirit—an elven woman wearing a simple headdress and a billowing, belt-less dress—came forward and touched her hand to her head. "Now begins a time when peace reigns once more. You have balanced the realms in a way that has not been seen in ages."

"Thank you for being by my side when you could. Thank you for holding back your hunger."

A little girl with two very long braids peered from the crowd of spirits. "We didn't think you noticed that!"

Maren had to laugh. "I definitely noticed. My job would have been nearly impossible if you hadn't managed that. I'm only one woman."

The spirits grinned, but the elven woman's face grew serious.

Filip and Dorin whispered something that made Aury chuckle.

Maren's heart was so full.

"With your help, Awenydd, we can send your chosen kin to the Upperworld once more."

"Oh." She felt sick. "Of course." She turned to Brielle, Aury, and the others. "You heard that, right? They can send you home."

"Are you coming?" Aury asked, raising one silvery eyebrow.

She looked to Kynan, and her heart pounded against her ribs. He went to one knee and took her hand gently.

His eyes burned into hers. "The Underworld holds no claim on your freedom now, Awenydd, though you have captured our hearts with your valor."

It was as Nix had said. She could do as she pleased. Did she want to return and leave Kynan, Hafwen, and this dazzling realm? Or did she want to remain here with the only one who had captured her soul and reign with him over the good shadow elves she'd come to love? She thought of Ceri, of Saffir, Eefa, and Devon... She brushed a hand over Kynan's pointed ear and along his strong jaw. The feel of his skin under her palm was like coming home.

The spirit raised a finger. "Do not look so conflicted. You can visit the Upperworld quite easily every Samhain now."

A weight lifted from Maren's chest, and she lunged at Kynan, hugging him fiercely. "You're not getting rid of me that easily."

He laughed and kissed her lips and her cheeks and her forehead, and then she was weeping. She pressed her mouth to his once more, savoring the taste of his tongue and his scent—like incense.

Straightening her clothing, she walked to the other side of the well to say a temporary goodbye.

Brielle tugged her hair gently as Maren squeezed her. "Don't be late on Samhain. I want to throw a true festival for you."

"I won't. I swear it." Maren gave her a smile before moving on to Dorin, whose embrace was quick and rough.

Filip and Aury enclosed her in a hug, laughing. "Don't let him get too comfortable, Maren," Aury said. "Be the queen you are."

Maren gave her hand a squeeze before grasping Werian and Rhianne in another messy tangle of goodbyes.

"Tell Kynan to dress like a water sprite for Samhain," Werian whispered. "Act like we're all doing it, and it'll be the best thing to see his face when he finds out it's a prank."

Maren snorted, and Rhianne shook her head. "This one will never grow up," Rhianne said.

Maren broke away and returned to Kynan and Hafwen. "I will see you soon. Thank you for everything. I adore you all."

The spirit surrounded the Upperworlders, and everyone faded away, some waving hands and others curtseying or bowing as they disappeared.

"Maren." Hafwen's curt tone had Maren spinning to see what she was pointing at.

A wand lay in the blue poppies beside the well. Maren reached down and lifted the length of oak to study it. "What is this for?"

"For you, I'd imagine." Kynan's arms snaked around Maren's middle, and his breath tickled the top of her head. "The Sacred Oak has provided for you. The Source sees your courage and rewards you."

He leaned sideways to watch a glorious smile spread over her lovely lips. She ran a finger over the wand's smooth grain, and tiny blue-white sparks followed in the wake of her touch.

Hafwen stretched out a hand and smiled. "Not to ruin the mood here, but can I have mine back now that you're taken care of?"

Maren laughed—such a joyous sound and balm to Kynan's soul—and she returned the borrowed wand. "Thank you very much for the loan, my friend."

"I'm sure she enjoyed the adventure." Hafwen tucked the wand away and eyed Kynan. "Since the realms are fully healed, is there any chance you can shadow travel now? I'd like to go home and begin rebuilding right away."

"I think that can be arranged." Keeping one hand on Maren, he drew his fingers through the air and used shadows to shift Hafwen back to her manor.

Finally, they were safe, and they were alone.

He pulled Maren into his arms, setting her tightly against his chest. Her soft cheek on his palm, her curving body, and her warm laugh against his neck were the very best gifts the Source could ever have given him. He cradled her face.

"I'm going to kiss you in a very naughty manner now."

"I was hoping you'd say something like that."

Pressing his mouth to hers, he drew his tongue over her bottom lip and tasted the salt and sweet of her. A groan echoed from deep inside him because there were even more pleasures to come. And soon. He longed to possess her, to be one with her, to ensure she was his and his alone.

Her lips opened further, and she took a quick, stuttering breath as her chest rose sharply against his. Heat poured into his blood, and he forced himself to go slowly, to take his time exploring the feel of her waist, the give of her flesh under his thumbs, the shape of her lower back... They had forever. There was no rush, and indeed it would be the greatest delight to draw out this joined discovery until she was begging for more.

CHAPTER 44
MAREN

Shadow elves were very strange about weddings. Surrounded by bustling servants carrying ivy and drinks and trays of fresh bread, Maren stood under an arch of black roses, waiting for Kynan. "Black, huh?"

Saffir's oddly blueish eyes blinked repeatedly, and her cheeks went rosy. "You don't like it?"

"Oh, no, I love it. It's gorgeous. I'm just spewing nonsense. Ignore me."

Eefa finished the black rose crown and set it on Maren's head. "She's nervous, Saffir. Don't take offense."

Well, they were right that Maren was nervous. She was about to wed the Shadow King. Yes, he was simply Kynan to her, but still. It felt...momentous.

Eefa straightened the crown and stood back to admire her work. "To shadow elves, black is the color of passion."

Heat rose in Maren's cheeks even though she wasn't

normally a blushing sort of person. She cracked her knuckles. "Right. Good. Yes."

Saffir giggled. "And you will be crowned three times. Well, you are already crowned in spirit fire as the most powerful Awenydd in history. Now we crown you in love for your mate. Next, we will crown you as Queen of the Underworld." She curtseyed and dragged Eefa away as the music started up. Gentle notes emanated from a bowed lyre played by a tall fellow on the far side of the courtyard. He was soon accompanied by a young elven woman with a reed flute.

Crowned three times. Maren shook her head. It was unbelievable, but she would do everything she could to take care of those who needed her and those who loved her.

The trees along the herb-and-rush-strewn pathway shaded the increasing crowd of onlookers. The gates were swung wide open to allow anyone to attend.

Maren spread a hand down her black velvet dress. The neckline matched the belt—a gold and silver pattern of tiny wyverns and tree roots. The dress fit rather snugly and made her wonder if she should have eased off on meat pies during the last few weeks. She wore a necklace of silver, gold, lapis lazuli, and jade. She was definitely bringing the piece to Samhain for Brielle to study. Eefa had said the gems were originally rune stones from the ancient dragon clans of the Upperworld. The magic in them wasn't strong anymore, but a slight sense of calm flowed from the stones.

Food was already being set on three long tables that crowded the eastern side of the courtyard. She supposed the ceremony—of which she had been told exactly nothing—wouldn't take long. All the better because she was more than ready to have Kynan in a room away from all these eyes.

"That's a cheeky grin if I've ever seen one," Eefa whispered as she passed by with yet another crown of black roses.

"Wait, who is wearing that one?"

"Why, High King Kynan, of course!" She laughed like Maren was being ridiculous.

"Of course," Maren murmured.

The music grew louder and faster, and the crowd turned toward the castle doors. The doors opened, and out walked her true mate.

Her throat went dry at the look of him. Surrounded by tendrils of branch-like shadows, he wore a sweeping black cloak. His hair hung loose over his wide shoulders; it had grown longer in the time she'd been here. The fire in his eyes heated her from head to toe, and she took a quick breath, trying to calm her pounding heart. His long legs were swathed in tight leather trousers, and the short tunic he wore on top spread slightly at the neck to show his collarbones and the first hint of the muscle that spread across his broad chest. Boots as black as the rest of his clothing came to his knees. Cynnwrf was sheathed at his belt. He didn't look ready for a wedding as she'd imagined it. He appeared more than prepared to conquer her.

Heat unspooled inside her, and she gave him a wicked grin.

She truly loved this elven king, even if they had started out on the wrong foot.

He joined her under the arch and took a knee. Eefa handed Maren the second crown of black roses, and Maren set it on his head amidst his usual crown, the magic and metal acting as supports for the roses. Standing, he took her hands in his.

He didn't look silly with the additional crown. The opposite, in fact. He was a god adorned in lush beauty, a feast for her gaze.

"I claim Lady Maren the Awenydd as my mate." He placed her hands over his hearts, then dropped his hands to his sides.

Easy enough. She took his hands and set them over her human heart. "I claim High King Kynan as my mate."

The burn of his fingers on her bare skin was enough to send her heart into a full gallop.

The crowd cheered. "Our king and queen!"

Kynan smiled then, his eyes softening. "I'm going to pick you up now unless you have a problem with that."

A nervous chuckle left her. "Go ahead, King Kynan."

He scooped her up as the crowd roared approval.

Soon they were back in the castle and falling onto Kynan's wide bed. He quickly shucked off his boots, sword, cloak, and belt. She pulled his tunic over his head and ran her hands down the chiseled perfection of his chest and flat stomach. Not only was he the one who had come for her despite the odds, despite the fact that doing so might destroy the realms and everyone in it, but he was also the most beautiful creature she'd ever seen in her life.

His shadows rolled her over gently, and with deft fingers, he unlaced her gown. With him behind her, she felt as though she'd surrendered herself, but she trusted him. She was fine with it, though her stomach was absolutely packed with butterflies. Every slide of his fingers against her dress was an exquisite torture even with the fabric between them.

He slipped a palm under her stomach and turned her over to face him. While using both hands and shadows to draw her dress off her shoulders, he dragged his lips across her throat. A sound like a quiet growl rumbled in his chest. The vibrations echoed through her and her body clenched with pleasure. The touch of his shadow magic warmed her skin. He sat up, his weight on one elbow as his shadows caressed her torso, then down her body, all the way to her toes. Ruby light glowed in his black eyes as he kept his gaze locked on her face. Heat poured through her body, gathering low. Her heart beat hard at her pulse points and her lips parted.

His tongue brushed her ear and she gasped. "I aim to make you shout my name by morning, Fire Queen."

She leaned away and grinned before grabbing him carefully in a very delicate place. "I have a similar goal, Shadow King."

His eyes shuttered closed, and his breath caught. He was all hers.

"I live to serve you, Lady Maren, my heart, my lady of the mists."

When he opened his eyes, they were lit bright as red-hot coals, and his answering smile was sharp as a sword. His shadows slid beneath her and dragged her dress from her body so all she wore was a thin shift. Nostrils flaring once, he edged closer and brushed his mouth over the exposed skin above her chest. Chills scattered over her body as his lips slid lower. He bit the neckline of her shift and pulled it lower. She tangled her hands in his hair, spilling several black petals from his crown. As he pressed himself against her, he lifted one petal and drew it over her chest very slowly like he appreciated every curve, every turn…

Her back arched, her body responding to him unlike it had to anyone she'd met before. His shadows shoved her shift roughly over her knees. He grinned wickedly, sharp white teeth showing as his hands followed in the shadows' wake and his palms flattened against the backs of her thighs.

He kissed her lower stomach through the shift's linen wrinkles, the dampness of his breath making the fabric stick to her skin. Fingers digging into her slightly, he pulled her near and closed his mouth on her hip, which sent lightning strikes of pleasure through her center. Melting into the mattress, she dug her fingers into his shoulders as his lips, shadows, and hands made their way back up her body. His teeth grazed her neck, and she bucked her hips, longing for him to get closer.

Locking his body to hers, his weight on her an aphrodisiac, he moaned her name.

"Not quite a shout, but we'll get there," she

whispered into his ear before biting the pointed tip gently.

An animal sound tore from the back of his throat, and suddenly he was moving over her with increased fervor—kissing and touching and claiming her with a gentle ferocity. She was alight with sensation, feeling everything at once—shadows sparking across the back of her knees and along her hips, one of his hands cupping her head and the other gripping the back of her thigh as he looked into her eyes.

"You are mine, Maren. Say it."

"What will you give me?"

His hips answered for him, and she couldn't fight the cry of delight that came from her lips.

"I am yours, Shadow King, and you are mine." She crushed herself against him, then flipped him to his back, his shadows helping her along. Straddling him, she rocked her body against his, the feel of him exquisite. She pressed a kiss to his full lips.

"I am indeed yours," he said against her mouth, "and may your fire consume my soul entirely."

"Did you imagine this when you first stole me away?"

His shadows lifted her, not gently at all, and pinned her against the cool stone wall of his chamber. Her toes brushed the pillows on the bed. He stood and stepped onto the pillows. His body pushed against hers and she savored every single point of contact. Into her neck, he whispered hotly, "No, my witch queen. You have possessed my elven heart, my shadow heart, my soul, and my body in ways I could never have dreamed."

"Then take your queen and prove that you are worth all the trouble." She grinned and reached out to pinch his chest.

Growling, he gripped her leg and pulled it higher over his hipbone, then he spun with her, and cocooned in shadows, he brought them both down onto the bed. He fit her so perfectly; they seemed designed for one another. She supposed they were, being fated and all.

He planted soft kisses over her cheeks and throat. "My queen, you unmake and remake me with every sigh." His tongue slid over the corner of her mouth, and his scent enveloped her.

The coverlet bunched in her hands, and pleasure rolled down her body. She bit back a moan.

He lifted his head and looked at her through black lashes. "That's cheating."

"Never said...I would play fair," she panted out.

With a grin that could melt ice, he drew his fingertips down her sides. She shuddered with delight. They moved together as one, joy blooming bright between them.

Wand in hand, Maren walked side by side with Kynan between two groups of nobles dressed in velvets of emerald green, ruby, and ocean blue. The crowd bowed low as Maren and Kynan passed on their way to the dais in the great hall at Calon Dywyll. Hafwen stood at the right side of the three steps leading to the platform where two thrones sat, tall and ornately carved. Wearing a long, straight dress of pure white, Hafwen held a pillow as dark as Kynan's shadows. On the pillow, Maren's third crown—a gold and sapphire coronet—reflected the glow of the wall sconces.

Kynan rubbed a thumb over her knuckles in a way that reminded her of last night. Heat pooled low in her body. "Show them your power, my queen," he purred into her ear. "Let them know they are protected by another fierce ruler who loves them as deeply as I do."

She did love them. Lifting her wand high, she flicked it toward the ceiling. Blue-white spirit fire sparked to life over the heads of the court. The nobles straightened to watch her loop the fiery magic into a circle that mimicked the appearance of the ouroboros created by the goddess Nix and the sea dragon Athielia. Her magic glimmered in the eyes of the shadow elves as they cheered for her.

"Our Fire Queen has saved us!"

"Long live the Fire Queen!"

Many held up their hands in the rebels' bird symbol and shouted, "We fly free! Thank you, Queen Maren!"

Ceri had told her how the bird came to be the rebel symbol. A boy born into a common family had developed shadow magic that showed in the shape of a bird's wings, with odd little white specks of magic along their edges. Tiergan had killed the boy, ranting about twisted magic, but Ceri said Tiergan was only afraid that the boy would somehow cause him trouble in the future. Seems he may have been the boy's father, which was doubly tragic. Maren shook the sadness away for the time being and smiled at the rebel courtiers, the spies that had helped her succeed.

She sheathed her wand and continued on, her velvet dress dragging across the mosaic tiles of the floor. Eefa and Saffir had used gold thread to embroider tiny wyverns and swords shaped like Cynnwrf all along the hem and down the shoulders and bell-like sleeves. It was astounding how quickly they could sew. She didn't think she'd ever grow used to how skilled shadow elves were.

When they reached the dais, the courtiers went silent in a way humans could never achieve. With one gentle hand, Kynan swept Maren's loose waves over her shoulder so that his coat of arms showed where Eefa had stitched it in more gold thread. A gleam of possessiveness flickered through his onyx and ruby eyes, and the corner of his lips lifted in a wicked grin.

Normally, she would have given him a sharp word to restrain his desire to show the world she was his mate. It was such an elven notion, so beastly and primal. But right now, she savored the ferocious glint to his eye and the way he angled himself to display to the crowd in no uncertain terms that no one was to touch her ever unless he willed it.

She leaned close. "Enjoy showing off, darling. Later, I'll be the one in charge."

A chuckle rumbled in his broad chest, and his grin widened. "I look forward to it."

He spun to face the court, his hand wrapped around hers. "Let us thank our queen for her sacrifices, for her courage, for her love of our realm."

The court erupted in glad shouting, Hafwen joining in. Ceri stood at the set of double side doors beside Bethan, who had begged for mercy and been quickly forgiven. Neddy and Mags spoke in the corner, their smiles aimed at Maren.

Kynan held up his free hand until they quieted. "And let us show the Awenydd that her power here is absolute in the same way that her heart has been steadfast in its commitment to our kingdoms."

Maren's chest warmed, and she smiled at the room full of her people. Her people. She belonged here where two doors promised a friend for every adventure and challenge, where the folk wore courage like a second skin, where she was not the Deadspeaker, but the Awenydd—Keeper of the Well, Great Seer of the Spirits, and Beloved Lady Queen to the most powerful shadow lord in the realms.

Eyes shining, Kynan took the crown and placed it on Maren's head. Everyone knelt, Kynan included. He looked up at her much like he had at the well when he had asked if she wanted to stay with him.

"We honor you, Awenydd, Queen Maren." He bowed his head, and the court repeated his phrase.

Maren bent, careful not to let the crown slip, and took his hand. She urged him to stand, and he did. She turned to face the court. "I thank you for helping me find my purpose. This is my home now, and I will never forsake you."

A final great cheer went up, the echo shaking the hanging chandelier of thick candles and the vases of blue poppies set into the walls. Kynan took her in his arms and kissed her.

Later, in the privacy of their curtained bed, Maren shoved Kynan onto the mattress, and his shadowy crown flared. A dangerous grin cocked his mouth to one side, and wisps of dark tendrils uncurled from his hands to wrap her wrists.

"You are unlike anyone I've ever known," he said quietly. "Kind and fierce. Honest and a little bit dangerous."

She huffed a laugh as he pulled her on top of him,

and his shadows drew her dress and shift down over her shoulders to her waist.

"You're an uptight brute, but I love you anyway," she teased.

He scowled, then flashed his sharp incisors as his gaze slid over her body. "Your beauty takes my breath."

Each touch of his warm magic tickled her skin and sent shivers down her legs and across her back. He watched her so very closely, and his lips parted slightly at her every gasp. His large hands gripped her waist, his thumbs drawing tantalizingly slow circles on her flesh.

"You are truly a goddess," he breathed, his eyes onyx black and ruby red, smoldering like hot coals.

She tugged his tunic over his head, then set to work on his belt. He'd already removed his weapons. "Let's enjoy your godlike status as well, please."

His bare chest rose and fell with quick breaths, the planes of his muscled body scarred from battles. She traced a wide scar along the ridiculously divine layout of his abdomen, and he shivered under her touch. Smiling, she leaned down and kissed that scar and several more she found along his sides and over his hipbone. His snug trousers couldn't hide the way his body was responding to her. She pulled them free and tossed them to the floor. A sliver of candlelight fell through the bed curtains to illuminate Kynan's tousled hair, one wickedly gleaming eye, and the shift of his chest as he sucked a breath and watched her study him.

"A shadow god indeed." She couldn't tear her eyes from the beauty of this male form. He was splendidly built from head to toe. Swallowing, she lowered herself onto him.

A quiet growl echoed from him, sending tremors through her body. He rolled her to her back. Her thighs opened wide, and she locked her gaze on his.

"Mine," she said breathily.

"Completely," he said as he moved in a rush of motion that made her head spin delightfully. "Eternally." His body crushed hers, and she bit her lip as sensations built stronger and stronger, heat flooding every inch of her. "With all of my power and my pain, I will see you treated as the greatest queen in the history of the world." He thrust forward with every word.

She delighted in each caress, the pleasurable pressure, and all the kisses he set on her shoulder, neck, and chest.

"Don't hold back, my king."

"Are you certain?" His gaze licked her bare stomach then lingered over her throat and face. The color in his cheeks darkened, and his hair fell over his forehead.

He kissed her, drawing his tongue over hers, each taste a wild treasure that sent lightning through her veins.

"Very," she whispered. She arched her back under his grip as he increased their pace.

Waves of rapture crashed over her as he claimed her again, his raspy voice whispering her name over and over. "Maren, lady of my hearts. Maren, Maren, Maren."

Afterward, he sheltered her in his powerful arms, shadows dancing around them and the barest hint of candlelight washing through the curtains. Her happiness was so complete that she could almost see it sparking in the air as she fell asleep beside her king.

Every morning when the pink sky announced the day, Maren rode out with Kynan to race through the rolling woodlands. They laughed and teased one another, their love growing deeper year by year. They ruled with humor and justice, never forgetting Tiergan's once isolated kingdom. Emissaries from all over the Underworld visited their court for advice and rulings, and great feasts were held in the hall to form new bonds between those who had been enemies.

But when Samhain arrived, Maren and Kynan always left the dark beauty of their home to dance under the wide arms of the Upperworld's Sacred Oak with those their hearts would never forget.

Readers,

Thank you so much for visiting this world I created. Your support means everything to me. If you would like to read a prequel to the first book in this duology, just join my newsletter at https://www. alishaklapheke.com/free-prequel-1 and I'll send it to you for free. You can unsubscribe at any time. If not, maybe leave me a review. Reviews are very important for my career as well as for readers like you.

· · ·

ASIDE FROM *STOLEN BY THE SHADOW KING* AND *RISE OF the Fire Queen,* there are four other books written in this world that feature Maren's chosen kin and how they all met. Start with *Enchanting the Elven Mage.*

THANK YOU AGAIN FOR BEING ABSOLUTELY AMAZING.
Keep dreaming. Keep reading.

LOVE,
Alisha

ACKNOWLEDGMENTS

Thanks to Emily, Rachel, Ali, Megan, Kelly, Andra, Ashley, Amanda, Heather, Liz, Carol, and all of my Typo Hunters, Dragon Denners, and Uncommon Crew for helping me create this story.

Thank you to my family and friends for putting up with my crazy schedule. Turtles reign. Fairy mushrooms are the best. Shield wall!

Thank you to all of my amazing readers!